What read
Sons of Zeruiah: Th

"*As a pastor I know the Biblical story, but* Sons of Zeruiah *gave it LIFE. Three characteristics define a historical novel: an enjoyable read, historical accuracy, and a true picture of the characters. The* Sons of Zeruiah *exhibits all three.* **It is a well written and enjoyable book.** *Meyer clearly portrays the lives of David, his nephews and the principles that guided David to become a great leader and a man after God's own heart.* **Great read!**"

- Rev, David Matthews

"**Enjoyed the book tremendously!** *The author brought the characters alive but left enough unwritten to let your imagination go farther…*"

"*I'm normally not a fan of historical fiction…***I was legitimately surprised at how much I ended up enjoying this book.** *I would highly recommend it for readers interested in antiquity, war stories, Biblical history, or historical fiction.*"

"*Somewhere in that grey area between Fiction and Non-Fiction lies this very interesting and mostly unexplored field of 'Plausible Fiction' …***Cleverly woven within the tapestry of Biblical truth, we get a clear picture of how it probably happened.** *Unlike a Hollywood version of a Bible story, which is usually tainted with a disdain for all things holy, we get an honest picture of the human perspective, but with an underlying reverence for a deep faith in a living God.*"

* * *

*"**Gritty and action packed**…not your grammy's bedtime Bible story!"*

*"**Sons of Zeruiah is full of what everybody wants in a war story…Not for the faint of heart…** The battles are full of feasible tactics, keen descriptions of martial prowess, and all the gore you can possibly feast your imaginative eyes on. But this isn't a romp of gore and hulking men, or at least that's not all there is to it…SoZ manages to paint a world that is full of characters whom you want to root for, not because they're labled 'the hero,' but because **everybody can understand the desire for revenge, for belonging, for family, and redemption.**"*

*"…since I was introduced to Star Wars and Bruce Lee as a kid, I would always wonder...if I was impressed by a martial artist or Jedi taking out ten opponents at once, how much more epic could stories from the Bible of warriors facing whole armies be, if done properly? **Thanks to this author, I now have my answer.**"*

*"…**impossible to stop reading**…The camaraderie, the emotion, facing challenges, learning from their mistakes, and so much more. **I can't recommend this book enough!**"*

*"…**I was immediately drawn in**…You feel like you are there in the story and don't want it to end."*

*"I usually avoid reading religious books because the author's tone always sounds fake…This book did not have that feel at all. **It was action packed and left me on the edge of the seat.** I was emotionally invested in the characters and (slight*

spoiler) may have cried a bit…"

"This is a book that will have a lasting impression on its reader. **You will not be able to stop once you open it***…very well researched…A good read…"*

"… breathes life into the ancient world through rich detail. The battles are fierce, and **my attention was captured throughout the book.** *My only regret was that the book ended…"*

*"**A wonderful read! It was packed with action, suspense, hatred, love and battle scenes.** This book makes Bible stories come to life…I couldn't put the book down so I read it in one day."*

-reviews from Amazon.com

Sons of Zeruiah
The Mighty Men of David

Brian Lee Meyer

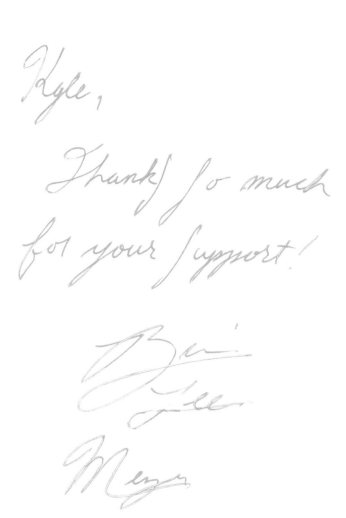

Kyle,

Thanks so much
for your support!

Ben
Zell
Meyer

ISBN-13:9780692137970

For Nanny, who introduced me to the wonder of reading.

Prologue

I decided I would commit murder.

I was in agony for months. All my life I cared for two people above all others, Mishael, my closest friend since childhood, and Dinah, my cousin, with whom I was in love beyond reason. I confessed my love for Dinah to no one.

No one but Mishael.

For years I hoarded coins like a miser for her dowry. At night I lay in bed imagining the sound of her laugh and her dark, mischievous eyes. I was obsessed.

I remember the day when my share of the tithes was pressed into my hand, and I finally had enough coin to offer a decent dowry. At last I could ask my uncle for her hand.

At last she would be mine.

I ran to share my good news with Mishael. But he had his own news to share. He had asked for Dinah's hand himself; they were to be married within the year.

My anger boiled up inside me. Before I knew it, Mishael's mouth was bleeding. I do not even remember striking him, but I must have. My knuckles felt like they had been smashed with a mallet.

There was no anger on his face at being struck, only

misery. I ran away, hot tears streaming down my face, not of sadness, but white hot rage. My heart was a smith's forge, the bellows stoking it to burn away all pity.

I am a Levite. I keep the door of Solomon's Temple. I am an usher to the pious and a guide to tourists.

"Wait just a moment, sir. Please, gentlemen, mind your sacrifices, don't let them soil the porch. Very good, right this way, sir. The priest will see you now, sir. Gentlemen, please don't touch the carvings. Yes sir, they're solid gold, not gilded."

I wake up hearing myself say these things in half-sleep.

On the day of Mishael's betrayal, I tore my robe, collapsed into the hearth, and rubbed the ashes on my face and hair. I then went to the temple and fell prostrate before the altar. I asked Yahweh to kill Mishael and avenge me of my enemy. I told my father, a scribe named Anah, of my recent calamity and my prayer for retribution. He only clucked at me.

"Son, do you honestly expect God to answer a prayer like that?" he asked.

Ever practical, my father offered to arrange a marriage with a number of young women from good families among his connections. I demurred. How could I think of another woman when I had just lost the love of a hundred lifetimes?

I believed him, that God would not answer my

prayer. Though I would have never blasphemed aloud, I considered God no more of a friend to me than Mishael now. I knew that if I were to find justice in the land of the living, I would have to see to it myself.

For several days I stood on the porch of Solomon's Temple performing my duties woodenly, speaking without conscious thought.

"Right this way, gentlemen. Sir, please mind your goat; that's cedar it's chewing on. The priest will be with you shortly, sir."

I had been in awe when I first assumed my duties. The columns, the graven pomegranates, the golden cherubim, and carved palm trees struck me dumb. The air was perfumed with incense, and the sweet melody of psalms gave it an otherworldly atmosphere. It was a palace for God, and I had the privilege of seeing it every day.

But when you see something every day, it eventually loses its power to impress you. The monotony of my work wore away my sense of wonder, and the glamour of the temple lost its shine. I became annoyed at the gawkers staring up at the wonders of the Temple.

So what? *I thought.* It's just a carving. You can buy a replica of it in the market.

But I was stuck. As a Levite, I could own neither land nor business. I was born into this vocation and would live with and live off the temple until I died.

Ten days after Mishael's revelation, I was walking up the Temple Mount to perform my duties. It was raining, not hard, but still miserable. I was slogging through the mud when I had my epiphany.

I could run away.

I would kill Mishael, take Dinah, and together we could run to the city of refuge in Hebron and begin a new life together where no one knew who I was or what I had done.

No more would I sweep dung off of Solomon's porch and shuffle commoners around the finery of the temple. I could learn a trade or purchase some land and start a farm. I still had my savings. It was not much, but we could make a start.

Best of all, I could make Mishael pay for what he had done to me.

It never left my mind. Even as I performed my sacred duties, I was consumed with thoughts of murder. As I watched the rain fall, I debated should I stab Mishael's heart, or should I slit his throat? Did I need a special kind of knife? I knew nothing of violence. Generations of excusing Levites from serving in the army had bred martial knowledge out of us. But mania had me in its grasp. No matter the cost, I would find a way to kill my enemy.

A bent old man appeared, his long beard dripping with rain. The hand that held his staff had a prominent, pink stump where his finger had once been. He came to the porch and waited patiently for me to open the door and let him in. He knew what to expect, and I did not bother giving him instructions. He came to the Temple every day to pray for as long as I had served there, even in the rain. No one was in the queue in front of him, so I ushered him in without a word. He thanked me politely, as he always did, and left me standing on the porch alone.

Still damp, I began to feel a chill in the cool of the early spring morning. I stepped inside to warm myself. My father arrived, and we greeted each other. But for the old man, we were alone.

My father looked at the old man. "I see Abishai is already here."

"Who?" I asked. "The old man?"

"That old man," my father whispered. "Is Abishai, son of Zeruiah, nephew of King David."

"The Abishai?" I asked.

Could it really be Abishai the mighty man of David's host, the assassin, Abishai the avenger? *He had been right under my nose every day, and I never knew it.*

"The same," he answered, pleased with my reaction. My father delighted himself in knowing important people.

I could not believe my good fortune. I needed to kill a man and had not the faintest idea of how to begin, and here was a man who had snuffed out more lives than probably any man living. If anyone understood my need for vengeance, it would be him. I could take him as my mentor. With him to advise me, nothing could spare Mishael from my ultimate and perfect revenge.

"I know you've been unhappy, son," my father said. "Why don't you talk to Abishai? He's a man of God these days. Perhaps he can give you some guidance. Here."

He put a gold coin in my hand. "Give him this, and ask him to give you his blessing."

Surely this was a sign from God that my vendetta was just and that He was on my side after all. My own father was urging me to seek assistance from the old murderer. I bounced on the balls of my feet and drummed my fingers as I waited. I must have stood at the door for hours. How much could one man have to say to God? Had he fallen asleep?

At last Abishai wobbled up into a standing position and regarded the altar for a moment, his eyes glassy with regret, as if the sacred item brought up a painful memory. He tore his eyes away and shuffled toward the door.

"Abishai?" I began but then hesitated.

He blinked. "Yes?"

How do you ask a man to teach you to kill? I took a deep breath and handed him my father's coin.

"Will you pray a blessing upon me?"

He smiled and his eyes twinkled as they regarded me, as if he was amused that someone would ask for his blessing.

"What kind of blessing did you have in mind?" he asked.

I felt my face flush.

"I don't know," I stammered. "I just thought a man...like you would know what to do in my situation."

He raised his eyebrows in interest. "Oh! It's a situation is it?"

He put a grandfatherly hand on my shoulder.

"Let's talk about this 'situation' over a cup of wine," he suggested. "My cottage is across the road. You can tell me all about it there."

I followed him out of the temple.

Abishai had been generous calling his home a cottage. It was a mere shack. There was hardly any furniture, just a cot, a small table, and a couple of cushions. Still the place was clean and comfortable in a rugged, practical way. Coming in out of the rain, he seated me on a cushion and fetched the wine.

I poured out the whole story for my host. He never interrupted with a question, he just listened and nodded. I could not stop talking. All the hatred and bitterness I had stoppered up flowed out, until I even confessed my desire to kill Mishael and run away with Dinah.

He did not so much as raise his eyebrows but nodded with empathy, as if killing your closest friend was the most natural response in the world. I asked him if he would tell me how to kill Mishael, how to prolong his suffering and my gratification, and how to get away with it without being stoned as a murderer. He did not answer right away but stood, walked over to the door, and stooped to pick up something I had not noticed when I entered.

It was a spear. Its shaft had been snapped in half and had been leaning in two pieces beside the door. He placed it in my hands and resumed his seat on the cushion next to me. The wood was smooth, polished not by deliberate sanding of an armorer, but by years of handling, though it was beginning to rot. Even with my limited knowledge, I could see it was old-fashioned, a relic from another time, before iron weapons dominated the warrior's kit. The bronze warhead of the spear had a light patina the color of algae, but it was still wickedly sharp.

"What is this?" I asked.

He laughed. "I know Levites are men of peace, but I thought you would at least recognize a spear."

"I know it's a spear, but how am I supposed to use it? It's broken."

"The story of that spear," said he. "Begins in a brothel many years ago, when I was only four years of age."

"A brothel?"

What did the king's cousin, now a holy man, have to tell about a whorehouse?

"The story of the spear is my story," he said, pouring more wine into my cup. "If you will indulge an old soldier, I will tell it to you."

His gaze flicked from the cup to my face, and I saw that all mirth had fled from his eyes.

"And from my tale, I promise, you will learn

everything you need to know of killing and of revenge."

1

I am the only one of my brothers who could remembers
the brothel, and that only faintly. I was born there but
remember little of the place. It exists in my mind as a
dim impression of grime and unease. I could not find
the place now, even if I had the desire.

I remember well, however, the day we left. That day
my mother took a customer into her chamber. I heard a
scream and a loud smack. She emerged from her room
with a red weal around her eye, her mouth bleeding.

Her burly customer had an evil scowl. Even as a
child, I could tell the man was soused. He terrified me.
To a four-year-old boy he seemed monstrous.

The man lunged at my mother and caught her
around the throat. I flung myself at him, swinging my
pathetic, tiny fists at his thighs. He let go of my mother
and swatted me away with the back of his hand. I flew
back sprawling in a corner. The man kicked me in my
belly. I could not breathe, it was the worst pain I had
ever felt.

When I caught my breath, I sobbed miserably. Tears and snot streamed down my face. I had soiled myself. I felt ashamed and helpless. The man raised his leg as if to stomp me like a rat.

While the man was distracted with me, my mother grabbed a piece of fire wood. She brought it down on the man's pate with all her strength, and he dropped to the floor. A friend of my mother's rushed in to see what happened.

I don't remember all of what was said, or even the name of the woman. I only remember my mother saying, "If we don't leave now, it will never stop." Then she looked down and placed her hands on either side of her belly, already beginning to swell. I could not understand then, but now I can see it was my brother she feared for. The two of them hugged, and my mother and I fled the brothel.

My mother and I travelled for a night and a day. She carried me more than half the way. Thinking back, a pregnant woman carrying a four-year-old that far, I do not know how she did it. We journeyed to Bethlehem, where my mother was treated like a leper. My mother was born and raised there, but if anyone recognized her, they pretended not to.

She led me to her father's house. As you know, my grandfather was Jesse, a well respected man of Judah. The meeting was awkward. I shall never forget my mother hanging her head in humiliation, the raw, red weal transfigured into a violet bruise, nor my grandfather's disapproving look as he appraised his daughter and me, his grandson. That was when I first realized what it means to be a bastard, to have judgement passed on me before someone took the time to know me. I learned that lesson from my own grandfather.

Not wanting to lodge us with the family, but equally unwilling to send us away, he made a place for us to live among the servants. The only children who played with me were the children of slaves. We began to carve out a niche in Jesse's manor. It was not much of a life, but at four I hardly knew that. It was better than the whorehouse.

My brother, Joab, was born not long after we arrived. When other babies were born among the servants, it was an occasion of joy. People congratulated them, and the parents would smile and proudly display their infant. Not so for us. Though I do not doubt she loved him as much as other parents, Joab was a source of shame to my mother.

When a stranger saw the baby, he would congratulate my mother who thanked him stiffly. But at the first inquiry of who the boy's father was, the room would grow quiet. Someone would whisper in the stranger's ear, and he would look uncomfortable. I was young but I understood. Joab was a bastard like me, and no cause of pride for anyone.

In time a servant named Shua asked to marry my mother, and my grandfather consented with relief.

Though he would have been beneath my mother's station when she was younger, Jesse was glad to make an arrangement that helped him avoid embarrassing questions. Shua tended my grandfather's sheep, replacing my uncle who had gone on to grander things. He never liked me or Joab, but I did not care. My mother was content, and that was a big improvement.

After that, my second brother was born, and for the first time in my life my mother was truly happy. This time everyone did congratulate her, and she gratefully basked in the blessing God had given her.

She named him Asahel, "made by God," which fit him well; he was the prettiest baby I ever saw. His hair was fine, the color of chestnuts with a pale streak running through it. His fingers and toes were chubby, and he would kick in his crib when excited, which was often. Joab and I were crazy for him.

As I reached adolescence, my step-father decided I could take over for him tending Jesse's sheep, freeing him for more domestic duties which would allow him to spend more time with my mother. Joab accompanied me, making me both shepherd and babysitter. Shua took me out one day, showed me what I must do and where I must go, then left me and Joab alone. Everything else I had to figure out myself.

Being a shepherd is a tough, hard-bitten job. At one time every Hebrew was a shepherd. Even Father

Abraham himself and the great law-giver Moses tended their flocks themselves. But centuries of living with the Egyptians, who disdained shepherds, had rubbed off on our culture. We as a people developed a distaste for the profession, but not for the wool, meat, and milk that sheep produce.

Shepherds are roughnecks–slaves, bastards, and the poorest of the poor working class. A shepherd must push the broad rumps of his sheep from pasture to pasture, and then into the rugged wilderness itself to find food. In the winter, the sheep live in the shepherd's own cottage, which is usually little more than a tent or shack.

They do not own their flocks. They do not wear the wool, nor eat the meat and cheese their flock produces. If their master is unusually generous , they might be rewarded with a kid on feast days.

Yet there is a solemn pride and affection whenever a shepherd speaks of "his" sheep. Like a military commander, he knows every sheep and goat intimately, and works tirelessly to meet their needs. Special care is given to the lambs. Too weak to keep up, new lambs are swaddled under the shepherds' tunics. He is more attentive than their own mothers.

A shepherd is carved from stone, lean and gaunt. Shepherds have eyes like hawks and skin like well-worn leather. They must always be on the lookout for wolves, bears, jackals, and lions, not to mention two-legged predators. When threatened, a shepherd places himself between his flock and danger with no regard for his personal safety.

But if his master decides to hold a feast or entertain a guest, he will not hesitate to slit the throat of the lamb he had recently been cuddling in his sleep to keep warm. What is more, he will do it with a stone face and dry eye.

Despised and distrusted by society, shepherds are clannish, hard, and possessed by the dark sense of humor known only to slaves, soldiers, and other bitterly miserable professions.

I was well suited for the work but also shaped by it. I did not know it at the time, but God was using those dirty, brown sheep to teach me. He was shaping me, making me suitable for an even harder, bloodier trade.

When Asahel grew old enough, he desired to accompany Joab and me on a drive outside of our grandfather's manor. We had exhausted the forage on our grandfather's land and were about to drive the flock into the wilderness. Worrying that we rough boys would be a bad influence on his son (justly so), Shua refused. Asahel whined and wheedled, but in the end, had to ply our mother before his father would consent.

It was hard work, and we were on our feet as the sun rose until long after it had set. While I did not know it then, it was one of the best times of our lives. My brothers and I lived like half naked savages camping out under the stars.

We left our grandfather's land provided with corn, barley, and hard cheeses, and supplemented this with fish from the streams and wild fowl and hares brought down by our slings. Free from our mother's futile attempts to somehow make us respectable, we could swear and fight freely.

Here is one story I remember to give you an idea of what it was like.

Joab was bored and told us as much. I was distracted counting the flock, and suggested he go hunting. He reminded me that the snares we laid out had already caught two hares that morning.

"How about a race?" suggested Asahel.

"So you can embarrass me again?" said Joab with a wry grin.

Asahel was lithe and fast. He could outrun and out-leap any boy in Bethlehem. The pale streak in his hair remained, giving him a rakish appearance that belied his natural speed and agility.

Joab's chin was already manifesting a black fuzz, hinting at the dark, swarthy man he was to become. Unlike Asahel and me, he was shorter and stockier. Even as a child, he looked like a bear.

"Why don't we play giant slayer?" he suggested. It was his favorite game.

The story of our uncle, David, the hero of the nation, captivated us. Every shepherd boy wanted to be him. He went from tending sheep to a courtier in the palace and the boon companion of the crown prince.

Every bastard, orphan, and cripple loved that story. Like every shepherd boy, we hunted and fished, fought with our staves, and gambled away the few coins we had. But recreating that battle was our favorite pastime.

"You always make me play Goliath," I groaned, even though I knew we would end up doing whatever Joab said as always.

"You're the biggest and strongest," Joab answered, hoping flattery would sway me. It worked, I gave in.

"I want to be David this time," said Asahel, bouncing on the balls of his feet. He was always jumping, bouncing, and tumbling around, as if he had more energy than he could expend.

"No!" I said.

"You're not a good enough shot yet," agreed Joab. "How about the giants's armor bearer?"

"Come on, you always get to be David," whined Asahel.

"You can be King Saul," I suggested.

"Who wants to be a king who hides in his tent?" sulked Asahel.

We had to concede, it was a fair point. Before the Battle of Elah, any us would have happily taken that role, in fact fought and argued over that very privilege, but those days were over. Saul had been supplanted.

"How about Abner?" suggested Joab. "Or Jonathan?"

He perked up at this suggestion. The crown prince, David's closest friend, was a mighty war hero himself.

Asahel knew his place in the hierarchy of three brothers. He accepted that this was the best he could hope for.

I found an old, discarded clay pot in a nearby trash heap and put it on my head to represent the Philistine's headdress. I leered, making a face like a monster. My brothers laughed at me. A stick and a woven basket lid made a serviceable spear and shield. Joab picked up his staff and sling and prepared to confront me, the Philistine giant.

"What am I, a dog that you come to me with a stick?" I roared, in what I imagined was a good imitation of the giant's voice.

"You uncircumcised Philistine," began Joab. Asahel giggled at the lewd insult. "You come to me with a sword and shield and spear. But I come to you in the name of Yahweh, whose armies you have defied and who will deliver you into my hand. And I will give your carcass to the birds of the air!"

As he spoke, Joab placed a stone in his sling and began swinging it underarm in a circle. The stone in its leather strap, hardly more than a pebble, began to whistle through the air. Joab released one end of the sling, and the stone hurtled toward my head.

The clay pot shattered, leaving my head untouched and unhurt. It was a stunning display of Joab's marksmanship and my stupidity, which we had performed many times. I pantomimed staggering in bewilderment and fell backward.

"No," interjected Asahel. "You have to fall forward. He landed on his face."

"Asahel's right," said Joab. "That's how it happened."

I rolled my eyes, but what could I do? They were right. I flopped onto my stomach. Joab sauntered over to me, the fallen seventeen-year-old giant, pulled the imaginary sword from my belt, and decapitated his fallen foe.

"Now what does Jonathan do?" asked Asahel, ready to play his part.

Joab shrugged. "Now David and Jonathan become the best of friends."

"But we're already the best of friends," Asahel said.

I narrowed my eyes at him. He never spoke that sweetly unless he wanted something.

"Let me have a turn at being David."

Ah, so that was it. Joab looked at me questioningly.

"I'm not going to be the giant again," I said with arms crossed.

"Fine," said Joab, picking another cracked vessel from the heap and placing it on his own head. Asahel whooped. It was the first time we allowed him to play at being the giant killer.

My brothers recited the speeches again. Asahel insulted the giant with all the vulgarity and color his eleven-year-old imagination could muster, much to our approval. Mother would not have approved of the language we were using, or for that matter, that we were hurling rocks at each other's heads.

But Mother was not there.

Asahel's sling began to hum as he took aim at the pot. His face screwed in concentration, he released the stone. The pot did not shatter, but Joab roared.

The stone had struck him in the forehead.

When he regained equilibrium, Joab glared at Asahel's skinny backside fleeing downhill in a cloud of dust. Furious, Joab started to sprint after him, but there was no way he could catch him with that much of a head start; the boy ran like a roe buck. He loaded a stone in his sling.

"It was an accident, Joab," I said, trying to cool his head.

But Joab paid me no mind. There was no dissuading him when his temper was up. He hurled the rock, a little bigger than the stones we used before, at our brother's fleeing form. The missile struck Asahel in the back of the skull, knocking him to the ground. He lay sprawled, face-first, in the dust.

"You killed him!" I said.

The rage on Joab's face gave way to fear. *Mother is going to be furious.* He jogged down the hill to survey the damage. We frantically tried to fabricate a version of this story our mother would believe that would not get us thrashed, but we came up empty. When he got to him, to our relief, he had started moving again.

"Asahel!" Joab said. "Are you alr-"

Before he could finish, he was tackled, and the two

went down flailing and kicking.

I laughed so hard, I fell onto the grass.

A few years later, the smaller streams dried up in the heat of the summer, and shepherds scrambled to find water for their flocks. We were especially desperate to find water, for our flock had greatly increased thanks to Joab's management.

Joab had a natural talent for making decisions with a clear mind. All three of us worked hard, but what set Joab apart was how quickly he noticed things, like signs of sickness among the animals, or when competition between the rams got out of hand and they needed to be separated, even signs that rough weather was coming so the flock could be moved to shelter. He knew when a ewe was ready to breed. When a pasture was depleted of grazing, he never wandered randomly to the next spot, but had already scouted out the richest pasture.

That is the difference between a decent shepherd and a real professional. Though older, I deferred to him on almost every decision. So, it was Joab who decided to avoid the Gilo River, where most of the other shepherds would be gathered. He reasoned that the water would be fouled by the feet, urine, and feces of tens of thousands of animals. Also whenever multiple herds mingled, animals went missing. Shepherds were not known for their honesty. Besides all that was a bigger problem.

Us.

Even among shepherds, bastards were at the bottom of the social ladder. Whenever we were around a large group of people, there was trouble. We *loved* to fight, and someone was always giving us an excuse. Whenever one of us cracked the skull of one of the local toughs, the others kept their distance. That did not mean that we were well thought of exactly, but it was a kind of respect.

Most recently, a half-dozen strutting cockerels from the village caught Asahel alone. He seemed like an easy target by himself, a gangly boy of sixteen. They shoved him, insulting him and our mother. Asahel lunged at one, and the other five tackled him laughing. Their laughter ceased when Joab and I materialized almost magically. *That* had been a scrape to remember!

Our mirth dried up when one of the villagers brought in one of their banged-up sons with a broken arm to our grandfather's house. Jesse had to pay the physician's bill and gave us a dressing down. After that scolding, we wisely decided to lay low for a while.

It was decided that I, who was slightly more taciturn and the least likely to get into trouble, would push east to the city gate and the nearby well. Asahel would remain on our grandfather's land with a small group of sheep and Rags, our dog, and Joab would push north to a relatively unknown pond. I understood and agreed with the decision, but I did not like going to town any more than my brothers.

It did not take long for trouble to find me when I got

there. I had just pushed the herd to the well and filled the earthen troughs with water, when I saw Asher approaching. Asher was the son of the miller in a town that was known for grain.

In other words, Asher was rich.

Like many rich boys, Asher had grown pudgy and soft, especially when compared to a skinny shepherd. Also typical of rich boys, he had a mob of cronies following him. They were the same boys we had fought before. When his eyes lit on me, they glowed with malice.

Here we go, I thought.

Asher already had everything I did not. Why was that not enough? Why must he and boys like him taunt me and make me even more miserable?

"If it isn't Zeruiah's little gift," he sneered.

I rolled my eyes. I must have heard that one a thousand times. It was an obvious play on my name, which meant "a gift from the father." Why my mother thought it was good name I will never know. The way she named her sons seemed almost cruel. Joab's name meant "God is the father." Could there be two worse names to give illegitimate children? Unless you *wanted* them to be mocked. She might as well have named me Bastard.

Asher grinned unpleasantly, seeing he had struck a nerve. All of Asher's smiles were unpleasant. It seemed like his teeth were too big for his face.

"If I were your mother, I'd return *this* gift to the

merchants. It's covered in fleas and smells like sheep."

His minions laughed at the jest. I ignored them all, refusing to let them get a rise out of me. I was not as smart as Joab, but I was too smart to give these fools the sport they came for. Still Asher would not let up.

"Maybe she could trade it in for something more suited to her. Maybe a few jars of *shekar.*"

I did not want to let them see me cringe. It was no secret that my mother preferred the liquor and drank far more than she should. The boys kept up their snickering, making sure Asher saw them.

"Of course, it's hard to return a gift when you're not even sure who gave it to you. There were, after all, *so many* men."

Asher's voice was like a knife twisting in my bowels. My face felt hot. I silently prayed it did not show on my face. I was glad Joab was not here. The fight would have already started by now.

"Is the old whore in town with you? I have plenty of coin." He allowed himself to laugh at his own wit. "I mean, she's not much to look at, but no one has more *experience.*"

I wheeled to face Asher, my face dispassionate to hide the rage boiling within me.

Asher smirked triumphantly. "Yes, those old whores are the best value for your money. They just come so *cheap.*"

The fire in my chest became a block of ice. I rested my staff on my shoulder nonchalantly. I kept my face a mask and my voice monotone.

"Speaking of old whores, tell your mother I'll cover my feet in my tent over there. I've never laid with a woman so fat and covered with warts. But I'm just a poor shepherd. I don't have plenty of coin and can't be choosey."

The other boys pressed their lips together to stifle their laughter. Asher's face went purple, and his eyes bulged out. He bellowed like an ox and charged.

It was not even difficult. I side-stepped the fool and brought my staff down with a *crack* against his skull. The fat boy plopped face-first into the dust like a skinful of yogurt and did not move. The other boys stared dumbfounded at the miller's son lying still in the road.

I took advantage of the pause and leveled my weapon at them. "Now listen! We all know I can't beat all of you, but I'll let *Sheol* take me before I let any of you walk away without bleeding or breaking. You can walk away now, and that will be the end of it. But you had better decide if this pile of ass dung is worth it before you try anything."

The speech worked. The cowards grabbed their fallen leader and showed their heels, looking over their shoulders with wide eyes.

2

Around that time David became even more famous due to the circumstances surrounding his recent marriage. The king's oldest daughter, Merab, was promised to him, but in the end the king reneged. David accepted this breach without complaint. After all, who was he to marry the king's daughter?

He was promoted to captain over a thousand soldiers, and the king's daughter, the princess Michal, fell in love with him. Still he thought himself beneath asking for the hand of one so high born. The young warrior could not imagine being son-in-law to the king, even after it was once promised to him. Even for one who had climbed so high, it seemed too ambitious.

It was whispered among the servants that Saul would give David his daughter, provided he could pay a very unusual dowry. Knowing that David had little money and no lands, the king would be satisfied to have the dowry paid in Philistine blood, or more accurately *skins*.

Our old foe was creeping ever eastward into the land of Israel, plundering Hebrew villages and taking slaves. Abner, Jonathan, and now David led the king's forces in bold counterstrikes, and Saul wanted to send the invaders a message. He wanted David to kill a hundred of the enemy and bring back their foreskins.

Without hesitation, David marched his men toward Ashdod on a daring raid. When he returned, he laid a basket at the kings feet with not a hundred, but two hundred of the grisly trophies. This time, Saul did not renege, but ceded his daughter's hand to the young hero.

The couple became the talk of the countryside. David loved the princess, and she was smitten with him. While girls sung his name after the battle of Elah, they sighed the name of David after his more recent and romantic exploit. Everyone said that he was the greatest warrior in Israel since Samson himself.

For our part, the rough shepherds made ribald jokes about what the king had wanted the foreskins for in the first place, and what became of the basket and its contents. One creative jester suggested that David had not killed the Philistines at all, but merely "converted" them. We howled with laughter at the idea of two hundred hunched-over "proselytes" waddling around in discomfort.

Well-wishers came to Jesse's door almost daily. His prestige as the father of the young war hero doubled as he was now father-in-law to the king's daughter. He was invited to sit at the gate in a prominent seat.

Gossip circulated about the king as well. It was said that an evil spirit troubled him, a demon which robbed him of his reason. It was said he threw his *chaneeth,* the wicked javelin he carried with him, right at David as he played music on the stringed *kinawr* to soothe his spirit. The needle sharp tip buried itself in the wall. The quivering missile would have impaled David had he not moved out of the way.

This got us thinking. David could have been killed trying to win the dowry for his new bride. It was whispered that this is what the king had in mind all along.

"I don't understand," I said as we were lazing under a sycamore, discussing the latest gossip. "Why would the king want to get his best warrior killed?"

"Jealousy," said Joab. "The king's been jealous of David since Elah. Remember that little ditty about 'Saul slaying thousands, but David *tens* of thousands?' The king wasn't happy about *that.* Besides, he's afraid of him."

"King Saul?" I said frowning. "David would never hurt the king."

Joab shrugged.

"David's going to be the king one day," piped in Asahel. He jumped up, caught a branch, and swung to and fro as he chatted. "The prophet anointed him king, and Saul knows it. He wants the kingdom to go to his son the way they do in the heathen kingdoms."

"That's just a story old Judith tells," I said. The servant was known for telling old wive's tales.

"Jephthah says it's true," said Asahel. "I believe it."

"Sure," said Joab. "They're going to let a shepherd be king, and Rags is going to be his general. Maybe they'll make Stump the high priest of the Tabernacle."

Stump was a wild ass that Asahel had chased down and caught. Joab had broken him to ride, but we mostly used him to carry our packs. Asahel did not appreciate the sarcasm and made a rude gesture at Joab.

"*A brokh!*" I swore. The count was short. "A lamb's missing."

"Are you sure?" asked Joab.

"I can't place the new one that Broken Horn sired by Big Nose."

Joab quickly scanned the hill and confirmed it.

The lamb was gone.

We decided that Asahel would remain with the flock while Joab and I would find the maverick. Rags trotted behind us. The shaggy bitch was useless at tracking, but as it turned out, we did not need her. The predator's tracks were plain.

We followed the tracks for half a mile when we saw the striped hyena. We heard bones cracking as her powerful jaws ripped off a shank. Three cubs were digging their little snouts into the meat to feed beside their mother. Joab grabbed the scruff of Rags's neck to keep her from dashing in and scaring off the hyena. If we let her get away, she would keep coming back to take more lambs; she had three babies to feed.

"Should we get Asahel?" I whispered as I looped a cord around Rags's neck.

Joab shook his head. "We can't let her get away. We can handle her ourselves."

He studied the area, formulating his plan. "I'll sneak around from behind and downhill. You keep her distracted with your sling. I'll finish her off with my staff."

My heart thudded in my chest like a carpenter's hammer. Some said that the bite of a hyena was more powerful than a lion's. My mouth went dry, hearing the *snap* of the lamb's bones in the hyena's jaws.

My hands were so sweaty, I feared I would not be able to grip my sling or staff. Joab, however, seemed to have snow and ice in his veins. If he felt any concern at all, it was that the hyena would escape.

Joab crawled on his belly in a wide circle around the creature and began to close in on her, moving stealthily to different places of concealment. The hyena paused and sniffed the air. I jumped up, sling in one hand and Rags's leash in the other. A larger stone than I was used to was in the pocket of the whirling sling.

I was not hunting a hare this time.

Rags strained against the cord around her neck. I let fly. I aimed for the eye, thinking if I missed it would hit the head. But the larger projectile and having to pull Rags's leash back threw off my aim. The missile struck the hyena in the ribs. She wheeled on me with a snarl.

Joab crept closer.

I loaded another stone in my sling and began swinging. Just as I loosed, Rags yanked at the leash. I thought my shoulder was going to pop out of its socket. The stone flew wild. I swore. I should have left the dog with Asahel.

Now hitting the hyena anywhere on her body felt like a victory. Joab would never let me live this down, no matter that it was Rags's fault. The frustrating thing was that I was actually *good* with a sling.

Joab was almost near enough to finish the hyena with his staff. I kept shooting, keeping her attention away from Joab. Another wild shot caught one of the cubs, who squeaked in alarm and pain. The hyena whirled to find the thing that had attacked her cub, and she almost spotted Joab before he flung himself behind the tall grass.

Rags became difficult to control. I dropped my sling to hold on with both hands, but the cord slipped through them no matter how tightly I squeezed. The rough hemp abraded my palms. When the last inch of cord broke away from my grip, the dog streaked toward the hyena like a comet.

"Rags," screamed Joab, forgetting stealth entirely. "No!"

We knew the dog was no match for a hyena, but both creatures were deaf to us now. Rags snapped at the larger hyena, then darted back. The hyena circled the dog to interpose herself between her and her cubs. Pure instinct drove the beasts, one to protect her cubs, the other to protect her boys.

We sprinted to catch up to the fight. I was swifter, but Joab was much closer. In a few strides he stood over the hyena with his staff overhead, ready to deliver the fatal blow.

But he was too late.

The hyena already had her jaws around the back of Rags's neck. We heard a sickening *crunch* and saw Rags's body grow limp. "No!" Joab screamed, and brought his staff down with all his might behind the head of the hyena, breaking her neck.

I skidded to a stop. Joab was driving the butt of his staff into the skull over and over, turning it to mush. Hot tears were streaming down his cheeks.

Rags was always Asahel's dog, but Joab was taking it hard. I did not even think he liked the dog. He was always kicking her and cursing at her. I still had much to learn about my brother.

"We have to take care of the cubs," I said. I grabbed one of the cubs and twisted its neck, dropping its lifeless carcass in the grass.

"You're right," said Joab.

He grabbed a cub by its hind leg as it squealed in protest. Joab swung the cub and smashed its skull pitilessly against the trunk of an oak.

I felt uncomfortable. Of course we had to kill the hyenas, but the way he was doing it felt wrong. Killing vermin is part of being a shepherd, but this was different. He was not killing hyenas to protect our flock, but to get back for our dog.

This was vengeance.

Shortly after the new moon, Jesse decided to sell a good portion of the flock. Joab and I drove the sheep into town, leaving the remainder with Asahel, who was not happy about being left out. But there was no way around the arrangement. Joab was needed for his haggling skills, and I to keep him out of trouble.

I promised to bring back some dates to soothe his injured feelings. The extravagant promise worked, and Asahel's usual smile was back. Each of us had some coins squirreled away, but the treat would set me back. I could never stand to see him disappointed.

The market was buzzing with the latest news about David. Soldiers were coming to Bethlehem to find him. He was a fugitive from the king. The stories varied wildly, often conflicting with each other. Some said the king flung his javelin at David again. Others insisted that it was David who threw the spear at the king.

"He's hiding out in Naioth. My brother-in-law seen him not a week ago." said one.

"You're wrong," said another. "He's in Nob. I heard the priest gave him bread and a sword. I heard he's on a secret mission, and the kings only *pretending* to chase him."

"Well, I heard he went mad," another sniffed. "Raving and foaming at the mouth, he was. He fled to

Gath, the addle-brain, as if the Philistines will give him a warmer welcome than Saul."

One report had Jonathan helping David escape, but another said the prince shot at David himself with his bow as he tried to get away. One story had Michal, David's bride, running from their chamber in horror after he tried to stab her with a dagger. Someone else claimed she hid a statue in his bed to confuse an assassin sent by King Saul.

As confused and contradictory as the stories were, everyone agreed on one detail. The king claimed that he uncovered a plot to overthrow him and place David on the throne. Joab and I knew it was a lie, but the crowd was sharply divided.

"We have to tell grandfather," said Joab.

I nodded. We sold the sheep quickly to a distracted merchant, not bothering to haggle. After striking hands with Joab, the merchant curled his lip and wiped his hands on the front of his tunic. Joab snarled, but I was used to it. We *were* dirty and smelled of animals. But Joab was always proud.

We hustled back to our grandfather's estate to tell him what we had heard. When we arrived, the house was already in an uproar. Servants laded asses with supplies for a journey. Asahel had brought the rest of the sheep in from the hills, and our mother was with him, leading Stump who carried our meager possessions. My mother looked weathered for her age, the worry on her face making her look all the older. She sighed in relief at the sight of our return.

"What's happening, mother?" I asked.

"Your uncle, David, is in trouble," she answered. "They say he's conspired against the king."

"We know," said Joab. "We heard in the market. How did you hear?"

"David sent a messenger," she answered and pointed to a youth who was nearly as tall as I and well-muscled as Joab. "He was a soldier in your uncle's company."

We looked at the young man with envy. He was about our age. He must have come from a well-connected family to be enlisted in David's thousand.

"We're going to join Uncle David," said Asahel with an excited grin.

Unbelieving, we looked to Mother for confirmation.

"That's right," she said. "It won't be long before the soldiers come to question us. We have to leave. Besides, David needs us."

Again worry lined her weary face.

"He's all alone out there."

"Do you think it's true?" asked Asahel. "Would David betray the king?"

"He would never," said our mother.

"Then the king has betrayed *him,*" said Joab, and a dark look passed over him.

"Best keep that thought to yourself," she cautioned. "Hopefully this will blow over like a storm. Better chance of that if we all behave like good, loyal subjects, at least in earshot of other people."

Our cousin, Amasa, was talking with the messenger. Amasa was the son of our aunt, Abigail, and Jether, an Ishmaelite. Our people were forbidden to breed mules, but there was no law forbidding us from buying them from our neighbors. Jether exploited this loophole, selling mules to the farmers in Bethlehem. He became wealthy enough to buy respect among the Judaeans, Ishmaelite though he was. Our grandfather, Jesse, doted on Amasa in a way he never did on us, even though we lived on his estate. We had little money and no esteem.

Amasa was well dressed and oiled, shining like a cherub compared to ratty shepherds like us. He fingered the handle of a new bronze sword sheathed at his hip. I imagined he fancied himself quite a warrior.

"Oh no," said Joab, rolling his eyes. "I hope that pretty boy isn't coming along with us. He'd better stay on his side of the trail if he knows what's good for him."

To our relief when the caravan left, Jether, Abigail, and Amasa stayed behind .

We were fascinated by David's messenger. Asahel was the first to let his curiosity overcome his shyness. He trotted to the front of the line where the young man was leading.

"Greetings," he said.

The youth reached out and clasped hands with Asahel.

"Benaiah," responded the young man. "Son of

Jehoiada, of Kabzeel."

"I'm Asahel, son of Shua."

"Well met, Asahel. I'm honored to be in your company."

Asahel smiled back. "How long are we going to be traveling?"

"Three or four days, I should think," answered Benaiah. "We're meeting David in Adullum. We'll be going around both the Israelite garrison and the invading Philistines' camps, and I imagine we'll travel slowly with your grandfather."

Benaiah leaned over and spoke low.

"To tell the truth," he confessed. "I'm glad to have someone my age to talk to."

"You should meet my brothers." Asahel waved us forward.

We hung back, pretending not to listen. We exchanged shy glances and trotted forward.

"Brothers," said Asahel, affecting Benaiah's courteous tone. "Meet Benaiah, son of Jehoidah. Benaiah, these are my brothers, Abishai and Joab."

"I'm pleased to meet you both, sons of Shua."

I cringed at having to correct him.

"We're not Shua's sons."

"Abishai and I are the sons of Zeruiah, David's sister," said Joab in a confrontational tone. It was a tacit admission of our illegitimacy; only bastards are called after their mother.

Benaiah bowed.

"I apologize for my mistake. I am at your service, Abishai and Joab."

There was no trace of irony in his voice. If he was embarrassed to associate with bastards, he did not show it. Joab smiled.

"Jehoidah of Kabzeel?" said Joab. "Wasn't he the hero who fought against the Canaanites?"

"The same," said Benaiah grinning.

"What's it like to be the son of a great hero?" asked Joab.

"What's it like to be the nephews of the great giant slayer?" returned Benaiah, refusing to be elevated over his new friends. We laughed. He had won us over completely.

We peppered him with questions. The boy told us about life in the army, caught us up on what had been happening in the palace, and told stories of the exploits of our uncle and other heroes we would soon meet.

Of course David never betrayed Saul, and Jonathan had remained loyal to him and helped him escape. Some of David's soldiers also remained loyal to him, fleeing to his side even though they knew it meant being declared traitors. Among them were three lieutenants who had earned notoriety in David's company, and were known simply as "The Three."

There was Adino, who Benaiah swore killed eight hundred Philistines in a single battle. I'm still not sure if I believe that. More than just a great fighter, Adino managed all of David's intelligence.

Then there was Eleazar (not to be confused with Eli the priest's ne'er-do-well son), who covered himself in glory before joining David's command during a famous battle. The Philistines had put the Israelites to flight, but Eleazar, filled with battle rage, refused to retreat. He stood alone, hacking at the enemy until he looked around and found no one left to fight.

He sank to his knees as he heard the soldiers cheer. He could not let go of his sword; he had to pry the fingers off one by one. The rest of his company, who were too cowardly to fight, cheerfully removed bracelets and earrings off of the slain.

After that he vowed he would only fight for David. David in turn vowed that Eleazar would never be left to fight alone again and that he would stay on the field so long as even one of his soldiers had the will to fight. He later kept that promise, when he and Eleazar, fighting back-to-back, defeated a company of Philistines in Pas-Dammim while the cowardly Israelite soldiers fled.

That kind of talk attracted Shammah, who had the same thing happen to him. His company abandoned him in a field of lentils as the Philistines charged. He littered the field with the bodies of the slain before he realized he was fighting alone. I had an uncle named Shammah also, but he was very different. My elder uncles had hidden in their tents when David answered the giant's challenge.

Adino, Shammah, Eleazar, and many others joined David in Adullam. Saul had not only lost David, but many other champions from his army. Only Abner and Jonathan remained to keep Saul's army intact, and Jonathan refused to hunt down David, whom he knew to be innocent.

Other less prestigious men were also allying themselves to our uncle. Somehow word had gotten through to Israel's underworld of David's location. Cutpurses, manslayers, and brigands had found him, begging him to let them join him. Some claimed that they, like David, were innocent of whatever crime they stood accused. Others flatly confessed they were as guilty as Satan. But all wanted a fresh start, a second chance to redeem their honor.

Traveling with Grandfather's household was not unlike herding sheep. We moved slowly and stopped when we felt like it. Our youth and vigor left us with a surplus of energy at each stop. We wrestled and jousted playfully with staves. Benaiah was impressed with our ability with slings, and we in turn were impressed with his army training.

I was more than a match at fighting staves with Benaiah after years of handling a shepherd's staff. Asahel proposed a foot race with Benaiah, who to his credit, nearly beat him. Used to being the fastest in his regiment, Benaiah was dazzled by his speed. Ever the show off, Asahel performed flips and high jumps, tumbling and capering like an acrobat to the delight of his audience of one.

Joab and Benaiah were a near even match in

wrestling. Benaiah had the benefit of training in the sand pits, but Joab was cunning, and would never fall for the same trick twice. Benaiah was taller and stronger, but Joab learned to use his short, stocky frame to his advantage and matched him toss for toss, pin for pin.

The elders shook their heads at the our antics, but we were oblivious. The trip became a romping, rollicking, good-natured scrap interrupted by long marches. Around the night fires we pestered Benaiah with questions about life in his father's manor on the outskirts of Edom and in the barracks. What kind of food did they have? How much was he allowed to take? Did he really get to sleep under a roof *every night?*

While Benaiah seemed to live the good life to us, our life appeared absolutely idyllic to him. Sleeping under the stars, hunting every day, being able to swear, scratch oneself, and be rude without anyone hassling him sounded fantastic to Benaiah.

On the fifth day we arrived at Adullum, though not the city itself. Benaiah led us into one of the many grottos nearby, and there was David himself. He was taller than I by a head, and his shoulders were half again as broad as Joab's. He was well dressed, and on his back was a mammoth, single-edged sword of iron. I doubted I could swing the sword with both hands. It was four cubits long, counting its unusually long hilt, and had a sweeping curve with a wicked barb near the tip. It was made for a giant; there was only one sword like that in the land.

The sword of Goliath.

Two dozen rough looking men surrounded him. Upon seeing us, he jumped up and embraced his father and brothers. He even greeted me and my brothers by name; I did not think he would remember the three of us. I thought we would find him in poor spirits, but he and his men seemed cheerful. He asked for news from Bethlehem and of the extended family. I could see the worry etched on my grandfather's face begin to ease. He saw now that his boy would be fine.

Gomer, an old servant woman, approached shyly, as if restraining her joy at seeing David. He embraced her, and the two spoke quietly for a spell. I supposed she felt tenderly for him, having watched him grow from boyhood.

"Father," said David as he returned to speak with the family. "I have some connections with the king of Moab. He has made a place for you and our house to stay until the danger is past."

Worry returned to Jesse's face.

"I will not leave you, not when you need me most."

"Father," said David. "I say this with great respect. You are not as young as once you were."

Grandfather did not like hearing that, but David continued.

"You know I would rather have you with me than almost anything. But you would only slow us down. In Mizpeh I would know you were safe, and I can focus on keeping myself safe."

Jesse agreed with a reluctant nod of his bowed, ancient head. My heart sank. *Mizpeh?* I had been sure that today would be the start of a new life for me. No more would I be pushing sheep around Bethlehem. I wanted to be part of David's story and share his adventures. I could tell from my brothers' glum expressions they felt the same way.

Then another messenger returned.

"My lord captain," he addressed David as a military man.

"Abiathar," said David. "What is it?"

The man took a breath with the air of one bringing ill news.

"Ahimilech the priest is dead, he and forty-four of the priests of Nob."

"What?" asked David incredulously.

"Abiathar," said Benaiah. "Your father?"

Abiathar shook his head and tears spilled down his cheeks.

"They were slain at the command of the king. Doeg the Edomite, Saul's servant, informed the king of your visit to Nob and the help the priest granted you there."

David's slumped and leaned against a stalagmite.

"What Hebrew would dare slay a priest of the Most High?"

The room was thick with grief and indignation. Few had met Ahimilech, but he was a *priest*. It was sacrilege of the worst kind.

The young priest answered David, though his question seemed rhetorical. "The soldiers would not kill the priests. Doeg executed them himself."

David's cry of rage reverberated through the cave. It was echoed by cries of anger from the lips of every man there.

"I knew it," he said. "I knew that day, when Doeg was there, that he would tell Saul."

His fist slammed into the rock wall.

He addressed Abiathar. "I have caused the death of your family."

That night, my brothers and I decided to approach our mother together. She was nursing a bottle of wine, the only spirits she could find in the cave. We told her we did not want to go to Mizpeh. We wanted to stay with our uncle and be part of his company. There was no future for us in Moab any more than Bethlehem we were sure. But David was destined for greatness, and we desired to follow his star for glory.

She regarded us as thoughtfully as her drunken state allowed.

"I knew a day like this would come," she said. "Three different fathers begat three different sons. At least I think it was three different fathers."

"*Chara,* mother," said Joab. "Do you have to talk like that?"

"Watch your mouth," she snapped.

She always hoped people would forget we were bastards if we did not talk like bastards.

They never did.

"You all three are part of me. You have my thirst for freedom. But you don't know what it has cost me."

Her eyes gazed past us, out of the cave and across time.

"My father betrothed me to a poor, ugly shadow of a man before I left home. His name was Hananiah, and I hated him. I was plainer and younger than Abigail, and father said it was the best he could do for me."

She scowled. "I felt like a slave being chained to this man, forced to keep his house and bear his children. He was a nobody, but still I was beneath him–a woman always is. I couldn't live like that, so I ran away."

I wondered about this man my mother had nearly married. If she had, would he be my father, or would I have never been born? Maybe a different father would have created a different son, and I would not exist.

Mother leaned forward.

"I traded my honor for freedom. In the end I learned I could never be free without my honor. My sons, *never* surrender your honor. Once it is lost, it cannot be replaced."

"Honor?" spat Joab. "We have no honor. You robbed us of that chance before we were born."

"You're wrong," she said. "Fight at David's side and never retreat. And when you have killed enough men, you will find glory, and no one will ever call you 'bastard' again."

She was interrupted by the sound of the harp, David's *kinawr*. His voice rose to accompany it. Never shall I forget the sound of his voice, and the anger and sarcasm he poured into the words.

"Why boasteth thou thyself in mischief, O mighty man?
the goodness of the Lord endureth continually.
Thy tongue deviseth mischiefs
like a sharp razor, working continually.
Thou lovest evil more than good,
and lying rather than to speak righteousness."

For a moment the music stopped, not because the musician was lost or his emotion overcame him. It was a deliberate pause, negative space that let his words steep in the air. He then strummed the harp angrily. His voice lifted with fury. If one could sing fire and brimstone down, that was what it would have sounded like.

"Thou lovest all devouring words, O thou deceitful
tongue.
God shall likewise destroy thee forever.
He shall take thee away,
and pluck thee out of thy dwelling place,
and root thee out of the land of the living.

"The righteous also shall see, and fear, and shall laugh

at him.
'Lo, this is the man that made not God his strength,
but trusted in the abundance of his riches,
and strengthened himself in his wickedness.'"

The song whipped me into a frenzy. I was ready to kill Doeg myself with my bare hands. I felt like no force on earth could save our enemies from us, so long as we were led by David.

And then the tone of the psalm changed. David was awash in gratitude and peace. The tempo slowed. It was like jumping in a cool stream on a hot day, so startling was the change.

"But I am like a green olive tree in the house of God.
I trust the mercy of God for ever and ever.
I will praise thee forever, because thou hast done it.
And I will wait on thy name, for it is good before thy
saints."

I was confounded by the extremes of the song. I lay thinking about the words all night; I could not reconcile the first part of the psalm with its conclusion. David had taken us on a journey through the wrath of God, and beyond, we found something we did not expect.

Mercy.

3

I thought shepherding was tough, but soldiering is brutal. Hundreds of men had arrived in our camp at Adullum to join David. My uncle knew that if we were to amount to anything in battle, we had to acquire discipline, and tactics would have to be drummed in our thick heads. Only a few of our merry band of outlaws had ever been soldiers. The rest were a motley assortment of low class trades and professions, the dregs of society, hardly more than useless, and that included me and my brothers.

The former soldiers were made sergeants, no matter his previous rank, except for The Three and three other lieutenants. David needed sixty men in the lines to lead nearly six hundred untrained louts. Men who were captains, equals in rank to David, accepted the demotion without complaint. It says a great deal about our leader that they thought it better to be a sergeant for David than a captain for Saul. Pimple-faced footmen who were digging latrines while their betters hardly waited for them to jump out before they relieved themselves, even they suddenly found themselves in a position of responsibility and scrambled like mad to catch up.

My new friend, Benaiah, was made our sergeant. Woe to any soldier that finds himself at the mercy of a new young sergeant! Whatever warm feelings there were between us cooled. We learned to *hate* him. His zeal and eagerness, I was sure, were going to get us killed, not by the enemy, but from sheer exhaustion. He woke us hours before dawn to march through the hills of Adullum. We wolfed down a meager breakfast, dry barley cakes like bricks, and geared up for the march.

We had not yet scavenged any armor, so we borrowed armor from the veterans in shifts. I understood now why David refused Saul's armor at the battle of Elah. When you borrow armor, it hardly ever fits. The amor is made by sewing rectangular brass or copper plates onto a leather jerkin. You hope for something too short because it is lighter, and armor that is too long sits too low on your hips and chafes you as you march. The shields were wood and plated with metal, and the conical helmets were solid brass.

Your neck feels spindly and unable to support your head when you first wear a helmet. Add greaves and gauntlets to your outfit and you become twenty to twenty-five pounds heavier. After that we would carry a pack of everything we might need on campaign: blankets, cook pots, bread, cheese, corn and barley, and two full skins of water. We were loaded down like asses. And *then* we shouldered borrowed spears and shields. I must have carried half my weight in equipment and supplies.

The first day we were told we would march five miles. *What of it?* I thought. I was a shepherd, used to tramping through the hills and staying on my feet all day. I could not have been more wrong. Not a mile into the march and my feet throbbed in pain. Muscles I never knew existed burned around my shins and hips. I felt like the weight of my pack was driving me into the ground like a sledge drives a tent stake. Still Benaiah kept up a sadistic pace. Any man straggling was forced to run around the entire formation before resuming his place in the ranks.

And then the sun rose.

I used to think sunrises were beautiful, but now the riot of color that accompanied the sun's apparition on the horizon was as cheerful to me as seeing the hue of an enemy's banner. The sun did not come to warm and cheer me, it came to torture me with punishing intensity. The skins of water we sipped even as we kept marching. There were no breaks and no rest. The bronze helmet that once merely weighed my head down now baked it.

Other sergeants allowed their compliment to carry their helmets on their packs, but not Benaiah. He would wring every drop of agony out of the march as he could, and it worked. The five miles were excruciating. I learned that walking downhill could be as painful as walking uphill. Our shoulders drooped, and our heads bowed in weariness. Benaiah barked at us to keep our heads up and stay alert.

At last we arrived at the field Benaiah set as our destination. I wanted to collapse, as many of our comrades did, but pride kept my brothers and me on our feet. Benaiah ordered us to set down our burdens but retain our armor and weapons.

Now the real training would begin.

First we learned to form a line, and move within that formation. Advance, hold, cover, uncover, advance, retreat–it was tedious and monotonous, but still a challenge. Heat and fatigue dulled our wits. We misunderstood simple instructions, and basic orders flustered us. Any one who did not respond immediately to a command or coordinate his movements precisely was subject to censure, but we all shared the punishment, which was running in armor. Even Asahel did not enjoy running in thirty pounds of hot bronze after a five-mile march.

After that we paired off and practiced with weapons. We sheathed our spears in cloth so they would bang "harmlessly" off of our armor. Still we saw stars after every blow to the head. Those unfortunate enough to draw a helmet too large or too small would often have it fall or be knocked off. Large helmets also tended to cant to one side and sit on your ear, and any blow would be agony.

A small helmet was just as bad; its edges dug into your skull with every hit. Every man's knuckles were bleeding from being cracked by his partner's shaft, and more than a few were doubled over from a blow to their unprotected testicles. That pain was instructive, and we learned to fight defensively.

I derived small satisfaction from being slightly less awkward with my spear than the former tanner I squared off with. But Joab was a natural. He understood each movement immediately. Benaiah paired him up with some struggling trainees. I was proud of him. Of the three of us, I knew he would rise the highest.

When the sun was high, Benaiah told us to cinch up our packs. It was time to march back, the whole, long way. It was a miracle we did not mutiny and kill him on the spot. Murder was on every man's countenance, yet we shouldered our gear and humped back, swearing and sweating. The cave was the most beautiful place I ever saw when I got back. I gulped down some mush that was served, stretched out, and fell asleep on the spot. It was hours before sunset. I did not even unpack my blanket.

I cannot tell you how long I slept; I only know it was not long enough. I woke to a plethora of aches and bruises. My sandals were covered in dried blood that had oozed from large blisters on my feet. Benaiah woke us again before daybreak and told us to get breakfast.

It was time to go again.

* * *

The thing that struck me most about our little army was how much David loved them, and that love was returned ten-fold. He looked after our needs like a father, even though he was younger than many of the rough men who followed him. He never ate until he had first made sure his men had eaten. When we slept, he often crept through the cave to check on us like a father watching his children sleep. With a clap on the back or an encouraging word he would enflame us to work ourselves to death for him, but a disapproving look could crush us.

One day while the Philistines were camped in the valley of Rephaim, the three lieutenants, Eleazar, Shammah, and Adino, snuck off. The only clue that they left was a brief command to their sergeants to look after the men while they were gone. David was beside himself with worry. For three days he asked everyone if they had come back. Had we seen them or heard from them? No, none of us had seen them since they disappeared in the middle of the night.

When they reappeared, they were dirty and beat up as if from a battle. Adino was limping, and Shammah had a cut above his left eye. They were grinning triumphantly like little boys returning from their first hunt with a scrawny hare to show their father.

"Where were you?" demanded David.

"Bethlehem," answered Eleazar with his tongue in his cheek.

"No one can get to Bethlehem," said David. "The

Philistines have the town cut off."

"Don't we know it!" said Shammah. "We tried to sneak through but had to fight our way through their lines."

"Fighting through wasn't as bad as fighting our way back out," said Adino.

The three of them shared a dark laugh. They had just been on a fine adventure, and for them, this was the climax, the reward for all the peril and hardship they had faced.

"I don't understand," said David. "Why was it so important to go to Bethlehem?"

"Do you remember when you were pining for a drink of water from the well by the gate?" said Eleazar.

Shammah held out a skin. I could hear the water sloshing inside. David took the skin.

"You fought your way to Bethlehem," said David. "Just to get me a drink of water?"

The three men smiled and straightened their shoulders. David was awestruck by their devotion. So was I. I had never seen anyone do anything so reckless, not even for the love of a woman.

"I can't drink this," said David.

The men's smiles faded.

"But we went all that way for it," protested Eleazar.

"And I am grateful," he said. Tears welled in his eyes. "More grateful than I can say. This water is this the most precious gift I have ever been given. I love you all for it. But I am not worthy to drink water that was bought with your blood."

He called Abiathar and poured the water out solemnly as a sacrifice to Yahweh. Then he drew the three men into an embrace. That night David had lambs stuffed with rice and roasted and made a feast for his lieutenants.

Even though David was my uncle, his connection to these men was stronger than any family tie. Blood is thicker than water, especially blood shed on the battlefield. I wanted to prove myself as they had. More than that, I thought that though life had denied me the love of a father for which I yearned, on the battlefield perhaps I could earn a deeper, truer love. I wanted that very much.

My first battle was at Keilah. David received word that the Philistines raided the city for its grain and looted the threshing floors. We from Bethlehem understood the economic blow of a town losing its crop of grain. David thought we should go after them. He reasoned that if the public saw us rescuing the citizens and doing good, they would be less likely to cooperate with Saul in our capture.

His lieutenants hated the idea. They were afraid Saul would roll his army in and crush us. If we marched to Keilah, we would be exposed to the Philistines *and* the armies of Saul. Better to lay low, they reasoned. Saul drove David away, let the king figure out how to deal with the Philistines without him.

David and Abiathar exchanged a look and a nod. David announced he would seek the counsel of Yahweh and pray for His wisdom.

The next day it was decided, we were marching for Keilah. David feared neither the Philistines nor Saul, because God was with him. The men who served with him before accepted this. David had earned their confidence. For myself, I must confess, I was dubious. It did not seem like any way to lead an army.

David's ranks had swelled enough that he needed more line sergeants. Joab and I were chosen to lead squads of ten, Joab because of his natural leadership ability, and me because our band of misfits was desperate. I would have to do.

We asked that Asahel be transferred to one of our squads. At seventeen, he was the youngest in the unit, and Joab and I were not willing to let him out of our sight. We were reassured that our leadership tried to keep brothers together. David made sure that Asahel was in my squad and that Joab's squad would be adjacent to mine. They intended for the three of us to stay together in this battle.

Among the other sergeants chosen were Ahimelech and Uriah, Hittites, and an Ammonite named Zelek. The Hittites had pale skin, an unfamiliar accent, and wore wonderful steel swords on baldrics. It was strange to march at the shoulder of Israel's ancient enemies, but they seemed like decent fellows. I was surprised that they too had come to worship Yahweh. Some of the

Nesiti, as they called themselves, were converted when our ancestors had invaded the land. Zelek, however, was only there because he *hated* Saul.

These men had prior military experience in their nations' armies, which was invaluable to David. As outsiders are wont to do, we sought refuge in each other's companionship. Benaiah, once again a peer to us, rounded out our circle of friends. We forgot our rancor at his hard training now that we had our own soldiers to prepare.

Benaiah was relieved. Being a sergeant had been lonely for him, and he hated the distance he had to keep between us.

"One day," he said. "I will be captain of the hosts for David, as Abner is for Saul. And you three will be my top commanders."

I smiled at his grandiose dreams of the future, but knew they would never come to pass unless I found a way to survive the coming battle. We picked the brains of the Hittite warriors but found them lacking infantry experience. All they ever talked about was the superiority of the cavalry.

"I say thees to you, een *Hatti,*" said Uriah, meaning his homeland. "We no trudge on foot, but *ride* eento battle."

His accent was thick, but intelligible.

"Een the light infantry, we train our horses to respond to the lightest touch. We dart een like lightning, wreak havoc on our enemy, then dash away to safety.

But the *heavy* infantry, ah!"

Here the Hittite rolled his eyes and shook his head.

"We had iron chariots pulled by two, sometimes four horses. We roll through eenfantry lines like juggernauts. The lancers and archers fight secure een those boxes. David, he need horses and chariots. Then he *crush* hees enemies. Saul can no touch heem then."

Benaiah could not resist ribbing the foreigner.

"Well enough. But we handled you heathens on the battlefield just fine without cavalry."

Uriah smiled. "That not because you eenfantry better than our cavalry. That because you God stronger than our gods."

He waved his hand, taking in the column.

"That why I here. Eef you God can save you from our chariots of iron, I no want the gods of Hatti. But now maybe you fight king weeth same God. You God must choose wheech one He help and wheech one He destroy."

"Which do you think God will choose?" I asked, amused with his reasoning.

"Eef eet were me," he answered. "I choose David. He a better man than Saul. But I theenk maybe thees time you God choose man who has chariots."

The soldiers all laughed. Uriah's theology may have been simple, but it was practical. I too chose to fight with my uncle because I was confident he would win, no matter how great the enemy we faced. But now, going to battle against a much greater army, I could only hope I chose wisely.

The march to Keilah was easy after training with Benaiah. Most of us did not have armor to wear or swords to carry and became the "light infantry" by default. Though we were still laden with provisions, we felt light on our feet with only our spears and little of the bronze the heavy infantry carried.

There were three different moods in the column. The young men in the army were energetic and joked and bragged, but there was a nervous edge to their bravado. The older men who had never fought were silent and wistful, perhaps thinking about wives and children at home.

The veterans were relaxed. No change came over them since we left the cave. No matter how hard I tried to imitate their easy manner, I knew I looked more like the boys my age. My movements felt jerky, my smile forced.

Keilah was a gated city to the Southeast. The gates were described to us as thick and heavy, with iron bars, rare and worth a king's ransom, to prevent our entry. It was going to be tough. We were lightly armored and poorly provisioned. Siege craft requires a large force and time.

We had neither.

We needed to lure the Philistines out of the city somehow. An officer named Azmaveth suggested that the city would not be large enough to hold the Philistines' cattle. A raid on their livestock would be perfect to bait them out of their stronghold. In those days cattle were more valuable than gold.

Benaiah and I were chosen to take our squads and drive the cattle away from the city, making as much noise as possible. We would run like Satan himself was on our heels to a nearby valley where the remaining corps would be waiting to ambush the Philistines on either side. The plan could not have been tailored better for runners like Asahel and Benaiah. Benaiah and I began augmenting some of our older or slower soldiers with younger, faster footmen.

Joab asked for his squad to be on the front line of the ambush wings. He knew he could not keep up with Asahel and me, but he wanted to cover our backsides, and trusted no one, not even David, to do it better than him.

The lieutenants nodded and smiled in approval. This is exactly what they had hoped for from the three of us. In other squads, pairs and trios of brothers were standing shoulder-to-shoulder. They reasoned that a line of strangers could break and run, but a man would not lift his heels and expose his brother to danger. In our case, they were correct. I would die before I let anything happen to my brothers.

The morning of the assault, our commander, Shammah, addressed us. He had a shaven head that was smoother than an egg and a gruff voice.

"Find a bush," he said. "Make sure you move your bowels before the battle."

"I'm not a child that has to be reminded not to soil himself," said a soldier, who I never met.

"Are you not?" said Shammah. "Braver men than you or me have soiled themselves when their hearts started pumping and they saw red with battle rage. Today you'll do things you never thought you would, you may not even remember them."

He grabbed the soldier by the tunic. "You won't have any control over your bowels, nor any time to wipe your crease. So when you walk out in *my* formation, they had best *be empty*!'"

Looking back, I can see it was the little details like this that made our commanders great. In all my battles, I cannot count how many men I have seen defile themselves, whether in terror or exigency. Thanks to Shammah, I developed the habit of going before the battle and have never soiled myself.

Having relieved ourselves as ordered, Benaiah and I led our soldiers to the pastures outside of Keilah. Once past the tree line, we crept on our bellies across the grass past the unguarded cows. We placed our backs up against the wall that our enemies were sheltered behind. I thought I could feel their malice through the wall radiating into my back.

I struck a steer across the rump with the shaft of my spear. It bellowed and lurched forward in alarm. At that signal, our men began whooping and yelling, scaring the cows out of their wits. We did not wait to see if we were noticed, but lifted our heels toward the valley. My legs were pumping as hard as I could push them. My feet were churning up the ground, kicking up dust. Asahel kept screaming, "Whooooo! Whoooo!" He was having the time of his life.

I heard the Philistines rumble behind me like thunder. I could not resist looking behind me. It seemed like the entire Philistine raiding party was on our heels. It was true. The *whole* company was chasing twenty lousy soldiers! I guess every man in that column had his wealth in that herd and wanted to make sure personally that his cattle were returned.

I ran faster.

We fanned out to prevent the cattle from getting away. If we got to the valley, but the cattle did not, it would have been pointless. The Philistines might not chase us once they got their cows back.

There was a pause as the cows were bottlenecked into the valley. For a moment we were standing still and could see the Philistines racing to catch us. Murder was on every man's face. They saw how few of us there were, and each one tried to get to us first before there was no one left to kill. We followed the cattle into the valley, seeing the reassuring faces of our comrades ready to cut off our pursuers.

I saw Joab in the very front of the left wing. When he saw Asahel and me, his shoulders rolled as he sighed with relief, then his face hardened. I saw a pitiless gleam in his eyes. The hair on the back of my neck stood up. He looked like a real killer, and I knew my face did not look like that.

Reaching the rear lines of the ambush, we turned and pointed our spears at the enemy. Too late, they saw the hundreds of men on their right and left. The Philistines were caught in our net.

Joab was the very first to spill blood. He screamed and drove his spear into the eye of a Philistine who was still running. The Philistine's feet flew up, his body swinging on the fulcrum of the spear point inside his skull. He landed with a thud with the spear still in his head. Joab pulled, but the limp body lifted with the spear. One of the veteran sergeants stabbed at the same time he placed a foot on the fallen Philistine's skull. With his free hand he pulled Joab's spear free and left it in his hand.

Then there was a smashing sound as those with shields bowled into the enemy. I was desperate to find my brothers, but I was trapped behind David's men who fought in front of me. We fought wildly, with little training. What we lacked in experience we made up for with enthusiasm.

I lifted my spear over the heads of my comrades and poked at the faces of the Philistines. My pathetic stabs did little to injure the enemy, but I distracted them so that those in front of me could stab them through the chest. I had not yet learned to make an effective overhead thrust, but at least I was sort of in the fight.

David was a terror on the battlefield. Goliath's sword looked as light as a feather in his hand, yet it was so heavy it crumpled shields and cleaved mens skulls as if they were not wearing helmets at all. He plunged into the ranks of the Philistines, his men barely able to keep up. He seemed to be cutting down three or four men at a time with each swing.

Men flew back from his sword, as if carried by the winds of a hurricane, dead before their bodies could hit the ground. Often the lifeless bodies bowled the enemy over, sowing confusion and panic in their ranks. Men fled in terror from him, others dropped to their knees, begging for mercy, but they received none. It was awesome and terrible to witness.

A sword split open the face of the Israelite in front of me, and he fell, exposing me to the enemy directly. I was in the fight now. I knew the enemy was just a man, but I swear, when I looked at that Philistine in his war bonnet, he looked seven feet tall and breathed smoke.

I thrust my spear forward with all my strength, but it caromed off of that weird fish scale armor they wore. I thrust again, and the spear caught on the mail, slipped between the scales, and bored through his guts. I pushed the shaft of the spear toward the earth, carving a gash in his armor and flesh.

That was my first kill.

I saw his steaming entrails fall to the ground. I could even see what he ate for supper the night before. Dying but not dead, he screamed and desperately tried to scoop his innards back into his body. No longer terrifying, the man looked pathetic. I raised my spear and ended his suffering. I felt like an angel of death. The enemy held no terror to me now. They were merely men. They could be killed, and I could kill them.

I did.

I waded into that Hell like I owned the battlefield. I slashed a man across the eyes and stabbed his neck. The poor fool behind him saw me and turned to run. My spear took him between the shoulder blades. The spear became stuck, but I had seen the trick and wrenched it out with my foot on the corpse.

I felt *invincible.* I closed in on a Philistine who had killed several Hebrews in front of me. I cocked my spear arm back, but before I could thrust, another spear took him. This seemed like an outrageous insult at the time. *How dare he? That Philistine was mine!* I turned to the Israelite, and in my blood drunk state, punched him in the face. It was not until after the battle, that I realized I had struck Shammah, our lieutenant. He later laughed it off, approving of my blood lust.

Finally, I found my brothers. They had pushed deep into the mass of Philistines and stood back to back. Both had found shields, and Joab wielded a bronze sword. I picked up a fallen Philistine's shield and shoved into the enemy. Unable to use my spear in the close quarters, I whirled hacking with the edge of my shield. As men fell around me, I stabbed straight down into them.

At last, I broke through to my brothers who greeted me with a glad shout. Asahel and I cleared a swath of ground with our spears. Anyone foolish enough to close the distance to get past our spears was hacked down by Joab. They circled us as warily as a pack of wolves fighting lions.

The Philistines surrounding us were suddenly attacked from behind as our men closed in. Our army wiped out all but a handful of Philistines who were fleeing. We finished them off and stood panting. A boy brought me a skin of water, and I gulped it greedily. I saw that my hands were soaked with blood to the elbow, and poured water over them. I could barely control them for the shaking. Some of the veterans saw me and chuckled, holding out their own trembling hands for me to see. That made me feel better.

Exhausted, I leaned on my spear and looked around the valley. It was covered with bodies, mostly Philistine, but some Hebrew, hacked apart and lying in pools of blood. I never saw so much death. Maybe I should have been somber, but I started laughing.

I'm not one of them. I'm alive!

My brothers started laughing with me, and we started whooping. Our voices joined the army in a mighty shout of triumph.

4

I shall never forget the celebration of my first victory. A great hall was reserved for David and his lieutenants and sergeants by the citizens of Keilah. We looted the bodies of the slain and found silver. We carved up and roasted some of the cattle and were eating better than we had in weeks, indeed better than I had in my life. The remaining cattle were divided among us as spoil, with double portions given to those who had fought especially fierce.

Of course Adino, Eleazar, and Shammah earned acclamation among the army, but I was thrilled to find that everyone on the raiding party which drove the cattle were also to be honored, and Asahel was to be promoted to sergeant. I was now richer than I ever dreamed after one battle, but even greater than that, my uncle, David himself, singled me out by name.

"Did you all see my nephews on the field of battle?" he asked, merry with wine. "Surely Abishai, Joab, and Asahel are destined to become great warriors. You have made me proud, nephews."

I would have charged a thousand Philistines alone with my bare hands for David at that moment. I looked at my brothers. Joab smiled and looked down shyly as men clapped us on the backs. Asahel beamed like the moon.

Uriah was also singled out to receive a portion of honor. That wicked steel sword of his cleaved the necks of more than a few Philistines. Even sullen Zelek earned glory. He put a spear through a Philistine just before he was able to stab David from behind with a sword. He insisted it was nothing, grumbling he had to keep David alive to kill Saul.

At the height of the revelry, my uncle's mood grew somber. He ordered the women of Keilah, who had been serving us, out of the room and put guards on the door to keep anyone from eavesdropping. David stood, called the room to attention, and revealed to us that Saul had gotten word of our victory and was marching toward Keilah with his army. The hall buzzed as we all reacted at once.

Uriah jumped to his feet.

"Let them come!" he shouted, drawing his sword. "I myself weell geeve Saul a taste of thees!"

The men roared in laughter and approval.

"Uriah is right," said Eleazar. "With the city of gates and bars and the men of Keilah to help us, we can resist Saul."

Again there were cries of agreement, but a

concerned look passed between David and Abiathar.

"The men of Keilah," said David. "Will betray us and turn us over to Saul."

A cry of disbelief and outrage echoed through the hall. How could the people of Keilah betray us after we saved them from the Philistines?

I heard Adino say, "My spies have heard no word of this, my lord."

David clapped him on the back. "I am not without my own means of intelligence, my friend. Be assured, I have received this bad news from a highly trusted source."

"Fine," said Shammah, rising to his feet. "We put the men of the city to the sword and fight alone. There's still about six hundred of us, enough to defend the city without their help."

The men raised their voices in eagerness to fight. David raised his hands to call for silence. The room grew still. The only sound was the guttering of the oil lamps.

"I have never raised my hand against an Israelite, and God willing, I never will. Our purpose is to strike at Israel's enemies, not become their enemy."

We made to protest, but he went on.

"If we slaughter the men of Keilah, we will never be able to find a refuge among the people. Everywhere we go, we will be hunted like a man-eating lion, not only by Saul's men, but by the men of the cities. The people must learn to trust us and know they have nothing to fear from us."

The wisdom of David's words was unquestionable. The men of Keilah were jackals, but there was nothing we could do to them without making our situation worse.

"We will flee to the South," David continued. "Go to the wilderness of Ziph. It isn't the reward you men deserve, and I'm sorry. But if we are to survive, it is the only way."

He let us absorb that before giving his orders.

"Have your men ready to leave in the morning. Secure carts, oxen, and asses for the wounded. Get the provisions we will need, but make sure you trade for them fairly. Give no man any sign that we suspect their treachery. By God's grace, when Saul gets here, we will be long gone."

The march to Ziph was surprisingly pleasant. My brothers and I, Benaiah, Uriah, and Zelek all walked together. Uriah made us laugh the whole trip. He had a way of teasing you so that you did not mind. Even Joab with his hot temper and Zelek who seldom smiled were howling at jokes at their own expense.

He could take abuse as well as he could deal it out. We made fun of his accent, his clothes, we took shots at cavalry soldiers, and made very inappropriate jokes about Hittites, and no one laughed harder than he. So when he teased Asahel for the scruffy beard he was beginning to grow, or the fat Keilahite woman Benaiah had been seen with, they did not care and laughed with the rest of us.

"What about me?" I asked. "You've insulted everyone else. Take a crack at me."

He raised his hands and look of mock fear came across his face. "I see the way you handle that spear. No way I make you angry."

I laughed. "Come on, Uriah. You weren't afraid to make fun of Joab. Let's hear it."

I kept insisting, and he kept declining, feigning fear of reprisal.

"I can't." He shook his head. "I respect you too much, Abeeshai. No way I breeng up that you mother was a whore."

The group erupted in laughter. None of us could believe he had said it. I could not stop laughing to breathe. Asahel fell on his back. Joab was on his knees, clutching his sides in pain, he was laughing so hard.

"Oh! I *so* sorry!" said Uriah with a straight face.

I loved Uriah at that moment. No one ever brought up our background, but my brothers and I always felt like they were thinking about it. Now the tension was relieved. Uriah showed us that around our friends we could talk about it. Everyone knew, and it did not matter. Even Benaiah, with his famous father and honorable background, was not ashamed to call me a friend.

We settled on the hill of Hachilah in Ziph. The atmosphere in the camp was relaxed, though my uncle never let us lose our discipline. Saul was looking for us every day, and we could not forget it. Guards were posted around the camp at all hours. We sheltered in tents and ate beef from the campfire every night. During the day we drilled our soldiers.

Every day I learned something new about warfare from the heroes who followed David. Sometimes it was an individual skill, like how to use the shaft of your spear to push back an enemy that came too close to stab. Other times I learned how to maneuver my soldiers better, how to overcome a larger force with a smaller one, and how to read the battlefield.

Jonathan, the king's own son, walked into our camp alone one day. He and David embraced, tears streaming down their faces. Jonathan looked like the prince that he was. He had his father's tall stature and was dressed in fine robes. They called Abiathar forward and renewed their covenant before all of us. Jonathan confirmed that one day David would be king, and when that day came, he would be standing right beside him.

"Can you imagine?" said Joab. "David and Jonathan fighting side-by-side. The enemies of Israel will stand no chance once Saul is dead and the kingdom united under David and the prince."

Benaiah answered, "Then you and I will fight paired even as David and Jonathan. I will be captain of the host, and you and your brothers will be great captains with me."

Joab smiled, but his eyes were sad.

"You forget, Benaiah, I have no famous father like you, nor any father at all."

Benaiah dismissed that with a wave of his hand.

"The way you fought today, no one will remember that. You and your brothers are sure to become heroes in David's kingdom."

It was a beautiful dream. The way Benaiah spoke, I could almost believe it.

David made a feast for Jonathan that night, slaughtering fifty of his own cattle, and gave every man a skin of wine, though God knows where he found so much. A great table was built in a field so that all the men could feast together; there was not a tent we could all fit in. The men who knew how played music, and we built a great bonfire near the table. We roasted the cattle over pits. The air was rich with the sound of pipes and the smell of roasting beef, garlic, and onions.

David raised his hands for silence and began to tell us tales of Jonathan's exploits on the battlefield. Jonathan would counter with a story of David's victories. We lapped it up like cream. The one I remember best was the Battle of Michmash. Though he had not been there himself, my uncle's voice held us rapt as he recounted the story.

"Our armies had been hiding in holes in Gibeah. The Philistines ruled over us then and outlawed the practice of the smith. There was not a single sword or spear among the Israelites except for what Jonathan and Saul possessed. The men passed around a file and sharpened axes and mattocks to use as weapons. It was pathetic.

"Never one to hide from the enemy, Jonathan, our prince, trekked through the gorge of Michmash accompanied only by his squire. They thought to surprise the garrison of Philistines by scaling the crag of Bozez and hitting them while their back was turned. But the Philistines saw them approaching and taunted them.

"'Come on up, and we will show you something!'

"But it was Jonathan who showed *them* something that day."

At that we all chuckled and voiced our approval. The story was getting good.

"Jonathan carved a swath about an acre wide in the enemies ranks. His squire cleaned up behind him, hewing the necks and splitting the skulls of the Philistines with a wood axe. They only killed twenty men at first, but in the end, the Philistines' own fear and stupidity killed them.

"In a panic they began to trample each other to get away from *two men.* The men in the rear saw their own fellows coming at them and thought they were the Israelites. They began to slaughter each other. Some of you were there and can vouch for the truth of this better than I. But they say Jonathan made the Philistines tremble so hard, even the ground began to shake."

I quivered at the though and looked at the prince, who seemed abashed.

"Our king came out of his tent during the earthquake and heard the sound of battle. He went to inquire of the Ark of the Lord whether he should pursue, but the soldiers were already forming ranks. They who had been hiding like conies in Mount Ephraim were now straining like hounds upon the leads, frothing at the mouth to have at the Philistines.

"They chased those heathens all the way to Beth-Aven. To this day the memory of Jonathan's sword haunts their nightmares, and they pray to their pagan gods they will never have to face him again. Hail him! Champion of Israel!"

We shouted, clapped our hands, and stamped our feet for the prince. I thought I understood my uncle's friendship with Jonathan then. Who else was equal to be his friend? Who else was worthy? They existed on a different plane. I believed that David would be king, the greatest Israel had ever known. He and Jonathan would make a nation of us, drive out our enemies, and help us find goodness and peace.

The next morning we woke late, having made rather merry the night before. We saddled the prince's ass for him, laden with gifts and letters to our families. I tucked a letter in the bag for my mother, hoping it would somehow find its way to Mizpeh. Jonathan and David embraced again, slapping each other's shoulders.

"Don't worry," said Jonathan. "My father will never find you."

But I was not so sure. If Jonathan could find us

alone, how hard could it be for Saul to find us with his army? I shivered. *From the coolness of the morning,* I told myself, and we watched the prince ride into the trees.

Things did not return to normal after Jonathan's visit. We grew accustomed to eating beef every night and passing a skin of wine around the fire, though we were not allowed to lose our discipline or watchfulness. I was more comfortable than I ever had been. We were in high spirits for an army in hiding. And why not? We had just won a victory and were safe, warm, and well fed.

One night I noticed two vacancies by the fire.

"Where are Joab and Zelek?"

"Joab went to stand guard with one of his men," said Asahel. "Zelek thought it seemed like a good idea, so he went with one of his."

Most of the sergeants assigned that duty to their soldiers. It was just like Joab to take it upon himself.

"I say thees to you, Abeeshai," said Uriah. "You maybe best fighter among us. But you brother, Joab, he know how to lead men."

"What about me?" said Asahel. "What am I good at?"

"You good at getting eento *trouble*," he said.

We all laughed, but Uriah grew serious.

"You leesten to what I say to you, Asahel. You very brave young man, *too* brave. I see the way you push you way through the Pheelistines eento the meeddle of them, and you brothers have to come save you."

I blinked and looked at Asahel. I did not know that was how it happened. Asahel was grinning sheepishly, not meeting my eyes.

"You have to pay attention. No jump eento the meeddle of danger weethout theenking. One day you brothers no be there to save you."

There was a commotion from the tree line. We ran to see what was happening. We saw Joab and Zelek with two footmen leading a prisoner. He was a Hebrew. His hands were bound with a leather thong. The footmen had spears to his back, and his wide eyes darted back and forth at our naked bronze.

David himself approached my brother. "What is it, nephew?"

"My lord, we caught this one spying on us from the tree line. He says the men of Ziph have told Saul we were hiding somewhere in the woods. Saul sent him and others to find us and bring him intelligence."

The camp buzzed at this news. David had us tie the spy to a sycamore, then called us to counsel in his command tent. The tent was not packed. David only summoned his officers and a dozen of the sergeants. I felt honored that I was among those summoned, as were my brothers and friends.

"Firstly," he said. "I want to commend Zelek and my nephew, Joab, for pulling guard duty instead of leaving it to their soldiers. Men work harder when they see that their leaders are willing to share the load. Well done."

Joab smiled and Zelek nodded. All the men echoed the praise, the older men nodding in approval and clapping them on the shoulder. David continued.

"We will not stay to give battle. Saul's force outnumbers us, and I don't mind telling you, I have no heart to fight our own countrymen. We will hide in the mountain of Maon. From the mountain we will be protected and be able to see any large force coming."

"What of the Ziphite spy?" asked a man named Helez.

"Kill the jackal," answered another, a man we knew from Bethlehem named Elhanan. "Otherwise he will tell Saul which way we went."

Several shouted agreement.

David shook his head. "No. This man has done nothing wrong. From his point of view he is simply being loyal to the king. We will head out west and make sure he sees us. Then we will break to the Southeast toward Maon. That should buy us some time."

Adino frowned. "It won't be hard to track us, six hundred men with thousands of cattle."

"I have an idea," said Joab.

The room grew still. I heard Joab *gulp.* He was the youngest, lowest ranking man to speak up. "My lord, the cattle will only slow us down and make us easier to track, so let's lose them."

He drew a map in the dirt with his finger.

"A handful of men could continue to drive them westward to Lachish then sneak back to rejoin the army. The trail they leave will be impossible to miss. Maybe we can distract Saul long enough for the rest of us to escape."

There was a murmur in the tent.

"The men won't like giving up their cattle," said Shammah.

"Are they willing to die for a bunch of cows?" answered Eleazar. "It's a good plan. I like it."

"So do I," said David. "Joab, you will lead this mission. I'm giving you complete authority. Can you choose five men to accompany you?"

"Yes, my lord," said Joab, smiling at me. "They are all in this tent."

5

The army took to the road to Lachish, and we drove the cattle behind. All morning we passed Ziphites working in the field. The bumpkins gawked at us and whispered to each other. News was spreading just as we hoped. By noon the road took us deep into a wood. At a signal from David, the army silently walked into the deer trails headed south, disappearing into the junipers like ghosts.

The six of us continued to push the cattle westward, their hooves obliterating the men's tracks. Every hour or so Joab would drop something on either side of the path, a bag of parched corn or a broken strap from a shield, the kinds of things that might fall out of a soldier's pack if he was leaving in a hurry. It was a clever touch.

Joab sent Asahel back a few miles to see if Saul was following us. I was nervous watching him go alone, but we did not have enough men to send someone with him. A few hours later he came sprinting back. He told us he climbed a tree and saw a cloud of dust raised by

Saul's troops eight miles behind us.

They had taken the bait.

Joab told him to stay there, climb a tree, and come tell us when he saw them. He came back shortly with news that the army was now five miles behind us. Worse, the army was sending runners ahead to scout us out. As one came near, Asahel jumped out of his tree, killed him, and hid the body by the side of the road. We could not let Saul find out that the army was not there.

Joab had to make a decision. The sun would set soon, and the army would pitch camp for the night. If they did not find the body, they might assume that David was so far ahead the runner had not found them yet. If they did find it, they would be convinced they were close and keep pushing until they found us. The gamble would be finished.

Joab decided to keep pushing; we had to give David every chance. We kept driving as the sun set. We did not encounter another runner, and Joab was convinced they had not found the corpse of the first.

The stars came out, and the half moon lit the path in front of us. My eyes became blurry, not that there was much to see besides cows. Even Uriah, who had kept us entertained with his chattering and joking, was too tired to talk. I was even more exhausted than when Benaiah used to drill us at Adullam, though my feet did not hurt as badly. If we could get to Lachish, Saul would see the cows and be convinced that David was hiding in the city. It would buy our men a couple of days.

We staggered into the fields of Lachish around midnight. As much as we wanted to collapse right there, we knew it would mean death if Saul's army found us. Worse than that, they might first torture us to find out where David was hiding. We could not put anything past Saul.

We walked another two miles south into the forest and fell down as dead men, not even bothering to unfold our blankets. In the morning Asahel spied on Lachish and confirmed that the army was searching houses among the confused citizens. How he found the energy to run the four miles there and back was beyond me.

It took us two days to walk to our rendezvous in Maon. We gnawed on parched corn and those awful barley cakes, never bothering to light a fire. We found our sense of humor again, though now we were making jokes about the miserable conditions. We had been spoiled at Ziph. Now it would be a long time before we would eat roasted beef again. Surprisingly it was the most cheerful I ever saw Zelek. The man was a masochist and was in his element without decent food or shelter.

The camp at Maon was not much more comfortable when we got there. We slept in tents and did not have to march all day, but the food was still terrible and no one lit a campfire. We had learned to be more cautious at Ziph, and it was a good thing too. It was barely a week before Saul's army marched into Maon on our trail.

They headed right for our camp, and we scrambled like madmen to pack up camp and flee to the other side of the mountain.

It looked like battle was inevitable this time. We sharpened our bronze, some dreading the possibility of having to use it against former friends and neighbors. The whole camp was on edge. Arguments broke out over nothing.

If Saul attacked now, it all would have been for nothing, all the hiding, evasion, even Joab's brilliant diversion. We were at a complete disadvantage. Desperate, we turned to Abiathar and prayed to Yahweh. We made sacrifices without fire to avoid smoke, vowing to burn them as soon as we could.

Help came from the most unexpected place possible.

The Philistines were invading, looting and burning their way to Hebron. Saul abandoned his hunt for David, and the army dashed off to defend the land from the Philistines. We cheered after they left, some even wept in relief. The sacrifices were burned, and psalms were sung. I do not think any group of Israelites has ever been so happy about a Philistine invasion.

We got out of Maon as fast as we could and marched to En-gedi. Never staying in one place, we roamed around like the Ishmaelites of the East. En-gedi was a wild place, and I fell in love with it.

Wild ibex were there. Benaiah would take his bow, my brothers and I our slings, and we would go hunting.

The ibex were great sport and did not taste bad either. Sometimes we camped by the Salt Sea. No fish live there; I do not think anything lives in that brine. But I would bathe in the waters and come out feeling invigorated.

Our fun was short-lived. Saul left the bulk of his force in Prince Jonathan's hands and pursued us with a corps of two thousand. It was not enough to weaken Jonathan's fight against the Philistines, but more than enough to smash the six hundred of us. There was nothing for it but to run and hide.

At night we slept in dank caves, bundling up in our cloaks and blankets to keep warm. The caves were small, so we never could fit into one cave, we had to divide up and camp where there were several.

Those caves were *cold!* We slept close together to conserve our body heat. Many a morning I woke early with a full bladder but could not bear to leave my relatively warm bed and face the cold to relieve myself. I would lie for hours until I could wait no longer and was forced to get up before I found myself in an embarrassing situation. Joab found a solution and brought a small clay jug with him as a sort of chamber pot. Realizing the genius of my brother's invention, many of us copied the idea.

One night as we bunked down, Saul's army rolled in right on top of us. We crept to the edge of the cave, hoping none of Saul's men knew the area well enough to suspect where we were hiding. Fortunately, they were oblivious to our presence and bedded down in the open.

Saul was easy to pick out. He was as tall as his legend described, at least a head taller than David. I would not say he was a giant after having seen some for myself, but he was the closest thing to it among the Hebrew people.

One of the soldiers found a cave and suggested the king lie down in it. Already tense, my heart leaped into my throat.

It was the cave that David was in.

He and a handful of men bedded down there, and we had no way to warn them. We could only watch in mute horror as Saul stretched and crawled into the cave to get some rest. I considered trying to sneak over there, but of course they lit watch fires and set sentries around the camp.

None of us got any sleep. There was nothing we could do but wait and see what would happen. I knew at any moment Saul would find David and our men, kill them, and start searching for the rest of us.

Still David had a chance to kill Saul first. Maybe if the soldiers saw the king was dead, they would lose the will to fight and throw in with our cause. It was thin, but it was the best I could hope for. I did not know if God could hear me, but I prayed as quietly and urgently as I could.

It was the longest night of my life. We watched the sentries change and listened to their uninteresting conversations, the typical complaints of soldiers. The sky lightened, and the sun began to rise. Soldiers began to wake and urinate at the edge of the camp. I saw Saul himself come out of the cave nonchalantly, as if nothing was out of the ordinary.

I hardly dared to believe it. We would survive. By God's intervention or dumb luck, they had completely missed us. We grinned at each other in silent relief.

Then I saw David come out of the cave. What was he doing? Did he not realize they were still there? I turned to the man beside me to see if he was seeing what I was seeing or if I had gone mad. But his nerves could take no more. He had passed out.

David called out, "My lord the king!"

He held up a strip of cloth. It was the same pattern as Saul's robe. David must have cut it off while Saul was sleeping. Some of Saul's soldiers recovered from their stupor and surrounded David with spears.

"My lord the king," repeated David, bowing down to the ground. "Why do you believe whoever is telling you that I seek to hurt you?"

Saul was silent. Every eye above ground and below was fixed on him.

David said, "You see for yourself that the Lord has delivered you into my hand. Some even encouraged me to kill you in the cave, but I spared you. I will not lift my hand against God's *messiah.*"

He held up the cloth from his robe again as proof. David pleaded with Saul. He humbled himself and threw himself upon the king's mercy. I could not help thinking that we all were at Saul's mercy now. I trusted it far less than David did.

We waited to see what Saul would do. If he chose, he could end the lives of all six hundred of us. I resolved there and then that I would take as many with me to *Sheol* as I could. One word from Saul would fill En-gedi with blood. But none of use was prepared for what Saul did.

He wept.

"David, you are a better man than I."

What did that mean? Was he going to kill us but regretted it? Did I dare hope he would let us go?

"You have been good to me, and I have done nothing but evil to you. Even when the Lord delivered me into your hand, you still did not kill me."

The soldiers surrounding David looked confused. Did the king want them to capture David? To kill him? Or would they let him get away? Some lowered their spears. All of them were looking at each other and the king uncertainly.

Saul looked at the earth and shook his head.

"If a man catches his enemy, will he let him get away?"

Did he mean David had let him get away? Or was he talking himself out of releasing David?

The king looked up and raised his arms.

"God bless you for the mercy you have shown me. Now I know you will be king, and your hand will establish Israel. Only promise me one thing."

David answered, "My king has only to name it."

Saul's voice trembled. "Swear to me by Yahweh that you will not cut off my seed after me. Don't destroy the name of my father's house."

He lowered his head, and I thought I heard him say, "Please, spare my *children.*"

Whatever else he said was lost in his sobbing. I did not understand. Saul had David surrounded and was begging for mercy. There was no fear on David's face as he stood empty-handed before the man who had hunted him down, only pity. The soldiers had all lowered their spears.

"By the holy name of Yahweh," said David. "I will not cut off your seed. You should know the love I bear for your house, my king."

Saul nodded and thanked David. His voice was ragged. With a gesture, he ordered his troops away, and as far as we could see, David stood alone in the clearing.

We cautiously peeked out the caves. Was it a trick? Was Saul trying to get the rest of us out of hiding so he could slaughter us all? No, we could see the army marching far away with barely a glance over their shoulders at us.

We sat stunned at how closely we had brushed death. Most of us could only stare at David with wide eyes. It all unfolded too fast for us to know how to feel. Some looked relieved.

Zelek, however, was seething to the point of insubordination. He stalked around the camp shouting curses. The only reason he followed David was so he could see Saul killed, and David let him get away.

The lieutenants asked to speak to David in the cave. Alone.

They were as concerned as the rest of us about David's decision, but they did not want the rest of us to hear it. They retired to the cave, and we ordered our soldiers to get packed. We wanted to be ready when we received the order to move on.

The commanders were in the cave for hours. Occasionally we would hear a voice when one of the officers became especially heated. Finally they emerged and announced we would flee to Paran for a time. It was a short term solution, but we could not remain in En-gedi. It was obvious the lieutenants did not trust Saul to keep his word.

We were ready to go and set off at once. The march was mostly silent. I burned to talk about what we had gone through but could hardly find the words. Benaiah and Joab walked with me. Finally, I whispered to them what had been troubling me all morning.

"Has David gone mad?"

Neither looked surprised that I asked.

"He's just trying to do what's right," said Benaiah.

Joab scowled. "Does that include endangering our lives?"

"No," he admitted. "He should not have exposed us

that way."

Benaiah did not seem to be comfortable questioning David. He hastened to add, "On the other hand, it worked. Maybe God is honoring that desire to do right. How else can you explain that we're still alive? Maybe if he took his revenge, we would have been destroyed."

I listened to Benaiah but was not placated. It was too thin.

"Fine," I said. "He doesn't want to take revenge. He could have let the army move on, and no one would have known we were even there. It was a crazy risk."

"But how long can we go on like this?" asked Benaiah. "It was a risk. But now maybe Saul will leave us alone, and we won't have to keep hiding like rats."

"He should have killed him," growled Joab. "Instead of his skirt, David should have come out of the cave with Saul's head. It would have been worth dying to see that."

6

After a brief trek through Paran, we doubled back to
Ziph. The officers figured Saul would not look in the
same place twice. It was the same reasoning I once
heard from a shepherd running to the spot where
lightning had just struck. He told me it was the safest
location, since lightning never touches the same place
twice. This sounded supremely stupid, as I have
personally seen lightning strike the same tree, on the
same hill, during the same storm. I hoped Saul was
more predictable than lightning.

Our scouts ran into a group of shepherds in Carmel
which is not far from where we camped. Some of the
men wanted to take their sheep. It had been a while
since we had tasted meat, and our mouths were
watering at the thought of mutton.

David forbade us to steal. Instead he sent me and
my brothers to talk to them, reasoning our past
experience as shepherds would help communication go
smoothly. Of course Zelek, Benaiah, and Uriah came

with us.

The shepherds eyes widened and they shifted their feet at the sight of our swords and spears. We told them we meant no harm, but we did want to cull out some of their large flock to feed our troops. They had about two thousand head there. We did not have much in the way of trade; would they be willing to work something out?

They were visibly relieved. We learned from them that their herds had been looted by local brigands, hence their apprehension at the approach of armed men. Joab had an excellent solution. We would provide security and keep the thieves away from the flock, and in return we would take one hundred and twenty sheep from the thousands they had grazing in the plain.

If they could not part with the named figure, whatever they could spare would be appreciated. Surely their master would find this reasonable. But the shepherds exchanged a look of prescient frustration. We would have to ask their master who was back in Maon overseeing the shearing.

His name was Nabal, or "folly." His mother must have been a prophetess. No name could have suited him better. We soon learned what kind of man Nabal was.

We went back to camp and dispatched two squads. One went to guard the shepherds as a show of good faith to Nabal, the other to speak with the man himself. David sent Benaiah and his squad because of his noble background, a decision made out of respect. A couple of the shepherds went along as well to show him the way.

Benaiah was instructed to address Nabal by name formally and respectfully ask for anything that seemed fair to him if he could spare it. David went out of his way to be polite. You must remember David's stature at that time; his fame had spread throughout the nation. Even the Ziphites and Keilahites had treated him like royalty when we were present. They might have stabbed us in the back, but to our face they were respectful.

Nabal did not even give us that. When Benaiah returned, and I saw his face, I knew it had not gone well. The shepherds had not come back with him either. I motioned to my brothers and we jogged to David's tent to hear the story.

We caught up with Benaiah, and Joab asked, "What happened?"

Benaiah shook his head. "Sharpen your bronze, boys."

Joab raised his eyebrows in surprise. Could it really have gone that poorly?

It had.

The page ushered us into David's tent, and Benaiah gave his message to David, who was eagerly anticipating Benaiah's return. He was hungry for meat like everyone else.

"Did you get the sheep?" he asked.

"No, my lord."

David blinked. "What happened?"

Benaiah let out a long breath. "I said exactly what

you told me to, but he refused. He said he'd never heard of David, son of Jesse."

Shammah sucked in a sharp breath. No one for thousands of miles could claim not to have heard of our captain.

"He said there were any number of runaway slaves in the country, and he couldn't give his hireling's rations to strangers. Then he sent us away and threatened to loose the dogs on us."

Benaiah's voice rose in spite of himself. I could tell that the insults had chafed him the whole way back. *Runaway slave?* No wonder the shepherds had not returned with Benaiah. They did not dare.

"Did anyone else hear Nabal say this?" asked David.

"All his servants, my lord," said Benaiah. "Some noblemen in the town as well."

It may seem strange to you, living in a time of peace as we now do, but to a warrior honor is everything. A warrior who allows himself to be disrespected tends not to live very long. Your reputation is a shield to you and your men. When the enemy sees you as weak, your enemies multiply. David looked to his officers for advice.

"Just take the sheep," said Adino. "If the shepherds try to stop us, kill them."

Shammah shook his head. "Not strong enough. Nabal has to die, some of his house too."

"I agree," said Eleazar. "Nabal's story should be a

cautionary tale."

No one added that David needed to show himself strong after what happened at En-gedi, but if no one else was thinking it, I was. David cocked his head, letting their words roll around in his head. A hardness came into his eyes.

"All right," he said. "Tell the men to gird their swords. If it pisses on a wall, it dies."

The meaning was clear: every male old enough to stand. I felt no pity. At last David was talking like a warrior again. Nabal abused my friend, insulted my uncle, the future king, and deserved what was coming.

Four hundred marched out, leaving two hundred to guard the camp. We really did not need that many, but news had spread of Nabal's insult, and everyone burned to avenge David's honor. We marched toward Carmel hellbent for revenge.

The path curved around a hill, and as we rounded it, we found a woman in the middle of the road on an ass. There were servants with her leading several asses laden with supplies. The column halted. Upon seeing us, she leapt off the ass, and bowed down to the ground.

Shammah's gravelly voice rang out. "Who goes there?"

"My name is Abigail," the woman answered. "Wife of Nabal."

There was a surprised rustling in the ranks. Even David looked startled. No one had expected the man's soon-to-be-widow on the road, and it was awkward.

The woman had the same name as my aunt, and the odd coincidence made me think of her cocksure son, my cousin Amasa.

Abigail was not plain exactly, but neither was she strikingly beautiful. She had a smooth, handsome sort of face. It had the expression of austere wisdom as one who had seen to the affairs of her own house and the confidence of one who had managed very well despite many obstacles. Her sole claim to beauty was the large, light-brown eyes she fixed upon David as she looked up to address him. They arrested me by the intelligence and strength sparking out from them.

"Upon me, my lord," she said. "Upon me let this iniquity be. If I may only have a brief audience with my lord."

David consented, and the woman pleaded for the souls of Carmel. She called her husband a fool, as his name implied. She had brought the provisions as a gift, a peace offering.

"You *will* be king of Israel," she said. "Don't do something that you will look back on with grief when that day comes."

As she spoke, we all began to feel ashamed. We were ready to kill innocent people for the insult offered by one man. David blessed her and her words of wisdom.

"As God lives," he said. "If you hadn't hurried to meet me, there would not have been anyone left to piss on the wall by morning."

If David's crude choice of words offended her, she did not show it. She rose, bowed at the waist, and mounted her donkey. Our men took the reins from the servants of asses laden with fresh bread, wine, sheep already dressed to be roasted, parched corn, raisins, and figs. David turned on his heel and began to walk back to camp.

Joab was exasperated, he wanted blood.

"My lord!" he shouted. "What about Nabal?"

David turned around and met Joab's gaze.

"We do not have to kill the innocent in Maon, but let us at least kill Nabal," he continued.

"Don't you think Nabal"s servants will fight to defend him?" asked David. "Abigail is right. I was wrong. God will deal with Nabal."

He walked away, leaving Joab standing in the road. I watched as Abigail rode away with her servants. Uriah stood next to me.

"Uriah," I said. "How did a fool like Nabal trick a woman as wise as *that* to marry him?"

He chuckled. "Yes, she put us een our place, no? I tell you thees, Abeeshai, often the best of women end up weeth the worst of men. That ees why I try to be one of the worst of men."

We laughed and joined the procession back to camp.

That night Nabal threw a feast, perhaps to congratulate himself for backing the mighty David down. The next day he grew deathly ill. He never recovered. He died ten days later, and David and

Abigail were married shortly after.

David's previous wife, Michal, had been given by her father to a man named Phalti, son of Laish. David also married a woman of Jezreel named Ahinoam, who was beautiful, but otherwise unremarkable. But Abigail was the only woman ever worthy of David.

Some said that God killed Nabal to avenge David, his anointed. Others said that it was a coincidence that Nabal fell ill when he did. Joab said that Abigail must possess knowledge of poisons. To this day I wonder what really happened to Nabal. If forced to answer, I can only say that he suffered from a terrible case of foolishness, which proved in the end to be fatal.

Abigail arrived in camp accompanied by five young women. You cannot imagine the stir the arrival of unattached females causes in a camp of six hundred lonesome men. There was a perpetual cloud of loafers around their tent trying to get even a glimpse of them. How they tortured us!

None was older than twenty, and they used the men as playthings, never giving us more than a laugh and a toss of the head. Abigail watched over them like a mother hen, trying to protect them from the prurient soldiers, and there were enough in camp to keep her busy.

I tried to ignore the girls. Abigail would never let one of them court a bastard, even if I was David's nephew. Still I had the desires of a young man, and my dreams were haunted by nubile forms that giggled with flashing eyes.

I slipped off to Tekoa one day and found a brothel. It was not unusual for soldiers to seek comfort in the arms of a prostitute, and had not our ancestor Judah been known to enjoy a harlot now and then? Even today it is not considered unusual, and I saw no harm in it. Still I told no one of the reason for my absence.

The whore who met me at the door was a dark eyed girl with bad skin, but she was pleasantly round in the right places. Her dress was cut to reveal more than I had ever seen of a woman's body, and I was stirred.

She took me into a chamber and we sat on a bed. She untied her hair and let it fall to her shoulders. I looked into her eyes and saw a familiar sadness. With a jolt I realized she reminded me of my mother, Zeruiah.

I could not go through with it.

I put a coin in her palm, stammered something about not feeling well, and left without bothering to see what she thought about it. I never went back.

Laying in my own tent that night, I realized I did not just want sex. I wanted a woman to know who I was and all I could be, and I wanted her to love me. I wanted someone to see me, not as a bastard or even a warrior, but a man worth loving.

I somehow knew that taking that girl's body would be unsatisfying, that it would leave me colder and more lonesome than ever. I did not want what my mother had in the brothel, I wanted what she had with Shua.

Though little affection passed between me and my stepfather, I respected him far more than the customers who left their coins in my mother's palm and slipped away. Though I knew my own father must have been such a customer, I could never be one of them.

A day came when word reached us that Samuel, the great prophet, had died. David was disconsolate. He stayed in his tent all day playing psalms on his *kinawr*. King Saul was also reportedly deep in mourning. At one time Samuel and Saul were close, but they had a falling out at Gilgal and never spoke to each other again.

Israel will always need a prophet. The Israelites once looked to Saul, but he was not the king he once was. Bereft of Samuel, we felt lost, and wondered who could ever fill that void. At one time, Samuel had hoped his sons would follow in his footsteps, but everyone agreed they were worthless. Our king was insane, our hero was exiled in disgrace, and now our spiritual leader was dead.

The nation was broken.

The officers told us there was one way to keep our soldiers minds off women and dead prophets, and that was work. We drilled the poor slobs night and day, every day but the Sabbath. The cloth went on spears, and we pitted our squads against each other. My troops with Joab's and Asahel's faced off against Benaiah's, Zelek's, and Uriah's. If one soldier failed to perform with sufficient zeal, the whole squad ran sprints in full armor.

Then we scrambled the order of the squads and ran the drill again. It worked. Our soldiers did not have time to think about getting over Samuel's death, or the energy to chase after the fickle affections of a girl.

I shouted till my voice was hoarse. As tired as my men were, I was exhausted, but morale improved. What we accomplished by dint of savagery and the wisdom of our commanders, we could now hope to perform with skill and discipline. I made sure I kept up my own practice as well.

I learned to love the spear. Joab preferred the sword, and we sparred for hours at a time. I worked with others as well to expose myself to as many fighting styles as possible, but only Joab offered me a challenge. Even Benaiah could not touch me with a spear in my hand. I would fight two, three, sometimes four soldiers at a time. I was not trying to show off, I just wanted to improve.

Other sergeants followed our example, the whole army was shaping up. Our drills that only involved our six squads of ten now involved mass exercises of hundreds of men at a time. There was not a man among us who did not appear to be carved from stone. A former mason showed us how lifting large rocks could increase our strength, and we went from being lean and gaunt to hulking with powerful muscles.

Eleazar organized games, and we had foot races, with and without armor, javelin throwing contests, wrestling, and boxing matches. Asahel easily won all the races, but Joab defeated every contender at boxing. Uriah amazed us with his wrestling prowess, and none could throw a javelin farther than Benaiah.

Asahel became famous in the army that day. He was so fast and light on his feet, that after the trophies of honor were awarded, he performed exhibitions. Two men of equal height rested a staff on their shoulders horizontally, and Asahel leaped over it with no running start.

He challenged Benaiah, who came in second in most of the races, to another race around the entire camp. This time Asahel would wear armor and carry a heavy shield, while Benaiah wore only his linen tunic. At first the two were side by side, then Benaiah broke ahead. It was not much of a lead, he was only a few steps ahead. The men yelled, some cheering for Benaiah, others, like me, urging Asahel to run faster.

Asahel caught up with him as they rounded a corner. Their feet churned the earth as each man strove to inch past the other. Asahel drew on a reserve of strength and burst past Benaiah. He gained a small lead at first, then it grew steadily until Benaiah had no chance of catching him. His speed was superhuman, he was *flying*. His strides seemed effortless, but there was a look of sublime focus on his face.

We were hoarse from cheering as he streaked past the finish line. It was the greatest athletic feat I have ever witnessed. The men lifted Asahel onto their shoulders, even as Benaiah ran across the finish line and collapsed in exhaustion. When he finally recovered, Benaiah staggered to Asahel and lifted his fist into the air. A smile of exhilaration was on my brother's lips.

The games helped break up the monotony. Everyone was in high spirits. The champions were awarded a skin of wine and a kid to roast. Since most of the winners were in our circle of friends, we had quite a feast. We gave our soldiers a break from training for the morrow. We knew none of us was going to be crawling out of his tent early the next day.

Adino had employed spies in the towns surrounding us. He was determined not to be caught unaware again. From them we learned most of the news of what was happening in Israel and beyond, but what he really wanted to know was what was happening in the cities nearby.

One day a man ran into our camp and was almost speared by the sentry. He held up his hands and called Adino's name. The lieutenant was brought to him, and Adino immediately confirmed he knew the man. It was one of the spies he had working in Ziph, a true believer in David's cause who never had to be threatened or bribed.

"Hezrai," said Adino. "What's the matter?"

"I'm sorry, my lord," said Hezrai. "The men of Ziph have suspected me for the last few months. I didn't know it, but they've kept me in the dark. I started to notice their sidelong looks, but they tried to act friendly toward me."

"Did they attack you?" asked Adino.

"Not until tonight," he said. "I was in a tavern where I used to hear much, but it had been months since anyone told me anything worth hearing. But two men came in the door and didn't see me in the corner. They spoke loudly about telling Saul that David is on the hill of Hachilah before Jeshimon by the way. They couldn't have described the location any better. Then they said that Saul was on his way here. The other men silenced them and motioned toward me.

"I tried to look innocent, like I'd heard nothing. But the way the men were staring at me, I knew what they were thinking, that there was no way I could have missed it. Some of them drew knives, and I grabbed the bar from the door. I struck two of them before I fled. I barely escaped with my life."

Adino grabbed him by the shoulders. "Saul is coming here?"

Hezrai nodded. "Abner is with him leading three thousand men."

My heart sank. Abner, son of Ner, had been a general since before David killed the giant. He had forgotten more about battlefield tactics than we could ever hope to learn. Besides that we were outnumbered five-to-one. Adino tried not to shake Hezrai but could not keep the urgency from his voice.

"Hezrai, how far way is Saul? Did they say how

long it would be before he comes?"

There was a tense silence as we waited for his answer. Hezrai's eyes widened.

"It could be any moment."

7

We immediately left the camp, not bothering to pack, and moved into the woods. We had to get off the hill. We left campfires burning and tents standing. Saul would be able to see we had been there, but he already knew that. There was no point in wasting time trying to conceal it.

We retreated a half of a mile away, covering our tracks carefully. We lit no torches, trusting in moonlight to show us the path. It took several minutes for my eyes to adjust to the dark, and I was not the only one. Several of us were tripping over the bushes, and the silence was broken by the rustling foliage and bitten-off curses. There was no time to try to get far. Stealth was what mattered, not speed.

Through the trees we could hear the tramping of feet and the shout of military commands. We saw yellow torch light shooting through the branches as sun rays do through clouds. Everyone in the woods froze. Shammah motioned for us to lie down, and slowly we complied. I did not know where my brothers were, we left in such haste. I saw Ahimelech, the only other Hittite in our group beside Uriah, hunkered down next to me.

"Here we go again," I whispered.

His teeth showed white in the dark. His smile made me feel better. I may die tonight, but I would not die alone.

Another man lay not far from us. He turned around on his belly and crawled toward us as silently as a serpent. It was David.

"Abishai, Ahimelech, did everyone make it out?" he whispered.

We did not know.

"Were you able to bring any provisions with you?" he asked.

"No, my lord," I answered. "Only my spear."

"A few of us may be able to leeve off the land," said Ahimelech. "But no way we can provide for thees many without provisions."

David sighed and ran a hand over his face.

"I'm sorry, lads. I've gotten us into another mess."

"We would not have lasted thees long eef not for you," said Ahimelech.

David smiled gratefully, and I realized Ahimelech was right. We may not have liked the way he handled the situation in En-gedi, but David had kept his band of misfits alive, which was no mean feat.

"I'm going to sneak in to the camp tonight to deal

with Saul," David said.

Hope leapt up in my breast.

"I will not endanger any of our men. If I am caught, I will distract them long enough for the army to get away. It will be dangerous, but I need help. I may not be coming back this time, but will one of you come with me?"

"I will," I answered without hesitation. This time I would make sure Saul could not chase us anymore.

Tonight it would end.

David did not want his lieutenants to know he was going; they would only try to stop him. We relayed a message that if a commotion was heard in the camp, the army was to take advantage of the distraction and sneak away. The whispered message was passed from ear to ear throughout the forest.

We waited until the noise died down among Saul's soldiers, and David and I walked crouching toward the perimeter. We knew there were likely to be sentries by the watch fires, so we crawled on our bellies when we came in sight of the camp.

We sneaked half way around until we found an opportunity, a sentry sleeping on his watch. We walked quickly past him, far enough away that our footsteps would not rouse him, but too far from the other sentries to be seen. We slipped into a tent and put on hooded cloaks to disguise ourselves.

We stepped out of the tent and walked casually. The sentries did not question us. In a force of three thousand, you are sure to run into soldiers you do not recognize. Everyone but the sentries were sleeping. The soldiers had moved into our tents, and we could hear them snoring.

Saul was not in David's tent as we supposed. We found him in a trench, sprawled out and drunk. He tossed in his sleep, his face twisted in misery. David regarded him with pity, but I could only hate him.

David handed me Saul's spear and picked up a basin of water that had been placed there for Saul's toilet. The sentries could not see us; they were looking outward toward the trees. I raised the spear in my hands and was about to spike it through the king's chest when David's hand arrested my arm.

"Let me strike him now," I hissed. "I won't have to strike a second time."

David spoke low. "Abishai, his time will come. God will strike him down, or he will fall in battle, but he must not die by my hand."

"This is how kingdom's are won," I said.

"That is the way the heathen win kingdoms," he said. "It isn't God's way. I'm not risking our army. You can return to them and escape. I'll only risk myself."

We stared at each other.

"Please, Abishai."

I nodded.

"What will happen to us if you die?"

"God has anointed me," he answered. "Nothing can happen to me unless He wills it. I knew it in the Valley of Elah, and I know it now. But you should go. Tell the others to flee whatever happens to me."

I shook my head. "No. I will stay with you. Your fate will be my fate."

We stared into each others eyes, and much passed between us for which there were no words. I still did not understand, I only knew that I loved David. Benaiah was right, David would do what he thought was right, even if it killed him. While I did not share it, I admired the pity he had for Saul, and it made me love him all the more.

If it came to it, I would die for David.

There was another hill nearby where you could see the top of Hachilah in the daylight. I suggested that if he was going to try what he did at En-gedi, he could do it from there, and we would have a chance of getting away if things did not work out this time. We would also draw attention farther away from our men hidden on the other side of the camp. He agreed, and I felt a lot better with that valley between us.

As the sun rose, the soldiers of Saul's army were awakened by the sound of David's voice.

"Aaaabnerr!"

It was fun to watch the soldiers scrambling to get ready for an attack. Soldiers do not like surprises. I saw an old man emerge from a tent, already in armor and full of indignation. He carried an iron spear with a spike on its back end to allow him to address attacks from the rear. I could not see his hair under his helmet, but his beard was the color of the iron on his spear. This proved to be Abner.

"Who cries out against the king's army?" he said.

"Aren't you supposed to be a valiant man?" shouted David. "There's no one like *you* in Israel. So why didn't you protect the king? An assassin came into your camp last night."

We could see Abner's eyebrows shoot up from across the narrow valley. He urgently gave an order to the man next to him, who took off like the devil was at his heels.

"That's not good, Abner," said David, taunting the old general, whose eyes were dim with age and still had not recognized him. "A man who fails to protect the Lord's anointed is worthy of death. I'd be worried if I were you."

The soldier ran back to Abner, whose shoulders dipped in a deep sigh of relief.

"It seems you are mistaken," he shouted back to us. "The king is with us here and in very fine health. But thank you for your concern."

"I am not mistaken," said David.

He nodded to me, and I held up the spear and the basin. I saw Abner's face go white, and I burst out laughing. I did not care about the danger any more. We may not have killed Saul, but we bested his army, just the two of us.

The ranks parted as the king came forward to see what the noise was about.

"Do you recognize this spear and basin?" asked David. "Weren't they by Saul's pillow last night? But how could that be?"

Abner stood with his palms up, stammering at Saul, but the king ignored him.

"Is that the voice of my son, David?" he said.

"It is my voice, my lord king," answered David. "Why does my lord pursue after his servant? What have I done? What evil is in my hand? If the Lord has stirred you up against me, let him accept my offering."

David's face grew dark.

"But if it is other men, may God curse them. They have driven me out of the inheritance of the Lord to serve other gods. Do not let my blood fall to the earth before the face of God. You have hunted me like a partridge in the mountains. But to the king of Israel, I am but a dead dog, a flea."

Saul was humbled. I could see the abashed look he gave the soldiers who were watching him hopefully. They obviously did not want to be there. Who would want to fight *David?* There was regret in Saul's voice when he shouted to us.

"I have sinned. Return, my son, David. I will not do you any more harm, because my soul was precious to you. I have been a fool. I have made such a mistake."

I wanted to believe the king, but we had heard this song before.

"Will he keep his promise?" I asked my uncle.

David set his jaw, sighed, and spoke a single,

clipped word.

"No."

"Then it's a lie?" I said, my voice shrill in my indignance. "All the promises and fake tears, it's all deception?"

"No," said David. "He means it now. But I saw him like this often when I lived in the palace. An evil spirit would take him, and no one could speak to him. He would become angry and paranoid. The only way to calm him down was to play my harp and sing my psalms. When the spirit left him, he would weep and blubber, apologizing exactly the way he just did. But when the evil spirit returned, he would forget his promises and be the same as he was before. It broke all of our hearts. The only one he really hurts is himself."

"Not the *only* one," I corrected.

David laughed. "Maybe not. But I tell you, nephew, King Saul is the most miserable man I have ever met. He may be in the palace, and you in the wilderness, but are you miserable?"

"No," I said, surprised to find it was true. I had been scared, frustrated, and angry, but I had friends and enjoyed life in David's army. While it was not in me to pity Saul the way David did, I no longer felt sorry for myself.

He smiled at me. "Neither am I."

Together we watched Saul's army prepare to depart. The soldiers looked confused, and I could imagine how they felt. The object of their mission was in sight, but again the king had changed his mind. It was a great deal of work and hurry for nothing. No wonder the army was becoming so demoralized. Soldiers need a purpose, and I feared one day Saul would follow through with his resolve to wipe us out.

"Well," I said. "What are we going to do? If he's not going to stop chasing us, and we're not going to kill him, are we just going to run and hide forever?"

David stroked his beard.

"I've been thinking about that," he said. "I have an idea of how we can stop running and hiding, stay away from Saul, and have a roof over our heads again."

He slapped my upper arm.

"And you'll be able to keep doing what you do best."

"I think I'm going to like this idea," I said.

I was smiling, but David grimaced at me.

"No," he said. "You're not."

8

David was right, I *hated* his idea.

He suggested we hire ourselves out as mercenaries in exchange for gold, food, and a safe place to lay our heads. My uncle had built a peerless paramilitary group. We were small in number but had proven at Keilah that we could defeat a much larger force. The men liked the idea until he told us to whom he wanted to hire us.

Achish, king of the Philistines, our old enemy.

There was a stunned silence, then all six hundred men were talking at the same time. Shammah stood and motioned for silence. The room hushed.

"David," he said. "Letting Saul go was one thing. But fighting for our enemies against our own countrymen? You ask too much."

The men muttered in agreement, not angrily, but gravely. There was sorrow on Shammah's face, as if he would obey David, whether he was asking too much or not. All of us would go to the point of breaking and beyond if he asked us to. That was the power David had over us. We all stared at David, silently begging him not to ask more of us than we could endure.

David looked around the room.

"I've put you through Hell haven't I?"

"You have only tried to do what's right," said Eleazar. "It's hard to do that on the battlefield, but that's the kind of king Israel needs. That's why I fight for you, and not the Benjamite."

We all hastened to agree.

"But David," said Shammah. "Surely you can't think *this* is right. To fight against Israel?"

Shammah was right, it was unthinkable.

"I think I know your mind," said Adino. "If we conquer the land for the Philistines, do you think Achish will give you the kingdom as a reward? He will use you then betray you. Surely you can see that."

"That is not what I had in mind," said David. "But I want Achish to think that is my intent. Seeing you draw that conclusion encourages me that it might work."

"All right, David," Eleazar said. "What is your plan?"

Six hundred men leaned forward, hoping whatever David said would help them make sense of the crazy scheme.

David took a deep breath. "Instead of fighting on the battlefields in the North, shoulder-to-shoulder with Achish's men, we tell him that we are conducting independent raids in the South, maybe Judah. While Achish's back is turned, we will fight Israel's enemies."

Joab spoke up. "If we fight the Philistines, word will get back to Achish."

"We won't fight the Philistines," said David. "Not yet. Israel has plenty of other enemies. While Saul is busy with the Philistines, we can crush them for good."

It stirred my blood to hear my captain speak this way. Heads were nodding, and we began to smile.

"Who were you thinking of exactly?" asked Adino.

"I don't know," he said. "The Amalekites perhaps."

The Amalekites, like the Edomites, are descended from Father Israel's brother, Esau. They had been a thorn in our side since the time of Joshua, even after the prophet Samuel killed their king, Agag.

"Use the heathens' money to fight our own private war," Shammah laughed. "David, you're a bloody fox!"

"And we'll be away from Saul," said David. "I'll be safe from him, and he'll be safe from Zelek."

Everyone laughed and elbowed Zelek in the ribs, who was not amused. He rolled his eyes and muttered something about attacking the people of Ammon next. Just like that our spirits lifted. No more running and hiding, we would be on our feet fighting again. A song broke out. Asahel leaped in the air with a whoop. We were going to go to war, and this time it would be on our own terms.

David chose five of us to accompany him to Gath: myself, Joab, Benaiah, Eleazar, and Adino. He told us that I, Joab, and Benaiah were brought because we were the best fighters, Eleazar because there were few people he would rather have in a dangerous situation, and Adino because he spoke the Philistine language. Shammah remained in command of the soldiers. We put modest robes over our tunics, and walked to the city.

Gath was larger than Bethlehem at that time, easily the largest city I had ever been in. The walls were massive, but there were no soldiers at the gate. We walked in armed, and no one challenged us.

It was one thing to hear that Philistines ate pigs, but quite another to see pig corpses for sale in the market. I could not imagine anyone wanting to eat one of the hideous creatures. There were shrines to their half-fish god and other deities throughout the streets. I saw people stuffing leaves into their cheeks and sitting in a stupor. I would later learn that the herb made them see strange visions.

The Philistines are a tall people. While David and I were taller than anyone in the camp, we were of average height in Gath. Still we stood out, and people stared at our clothes, faces, and hair. The people dressed differently, especially the women. Even the prostitute at Tekoa had not shown so much flesh. My face flushed, I tried to keep my eyes on the road.

Achish lived in a mansion in the middle of the city, with a wall around the garden. Two guards were standing by the gate, eyeing us warily. We marched to the two of them.

"Tell them David, son of Jesse, of Bethlehem

wishes to see Achish," David instructed Adino. He relayed David's words to the guards, who exchanged a nervous look. One of the guards said something to the other, who disappeared into the mansion, then the guard spoke to us.

"He said to wait here, please," said Adino.

David nodded. The other guard appeared a few minutes later and spoke to Adino.

"He says we'll have to leave our weapons with them."

Joab, Benaiah, and I exchanged frowns. We did not like that. David calmly reached over his shoulder, took off Goliath's sword, still sheathed, and deposited it with one hand effortlessly in the bigger guard's hands. The guards eyes widened as he tried to take it with one hand and was forced to support it with the other, nearly dropping it. He set the sword by the gate, and they began collecting our swords and spears.

The message was clear: it is not our weapons that make us dangerous.

Achish was a fat man sitting on a throne of brass surrounded by guards, advisors, and his wives. He was eating honeyed dates and drinking wine when we approached his throne. David bowed, not on his face as he had for Saul, but on one knee. We followed his example. I was surprised to learn that Achish spoke Hebrew.

"So you have returned," he said.

Returned? What did he mean by that?

"King Achish," said David. "It is good to see you."

"So you are in your right mind again, I see," said Achish.

"I only pretended to be crazy because of the word your advisors spoke against me," he said. "I did not wish to cause a dispute in your honorable court, so I made a pretense to excuse myself."

The lord of Gath leaned forward.

"You made a pretense so you could leave to raise an army against me," he said. "I know what you and your men did to my army at Keilah."

Joab and I exchanged a cautious look from the corners of our eyes. This was not going well.

"It is true, oh king, I did fight for my people," said David. "But now my people have betrayed me. Now I fight for myself. Saul has made himself a common enemy of the two of us."

Achish squinted, leaned back, and interlaced his fingers. Seeing he had his attention, David made his proposition.

"I seek an alliance. There are men in Israel, not a few, who would follow me as king of Israel. Together we can defeat Saul, and Israel and Philistia can dwell together in peace."

Achish and his advisors consulted in their own language for a few minutes. One of them whispered in the king's ear, gesturing toward us. David looked at Adino, who winked back a him. Then Achish smiled.

"Yes," he said, playing with a date with his fat

fingers. "I have heard of your troubles with Saul. What happened between you two? Why would he throw away his best fighter?"

David put on an angry face. "He never appreciated me for the warrior I am. I am ready to follow a king who can see my potential and give me the honor I deserve."

His tone was bitter. After getting to know him in the wilderness, it was obvious he was faking injured pride. He never spoke like that. But David could read Achish and reflect back at him what he expected to see.

Achish laughed. "Very well!"

Then he leaned forward and made a fist.

"I shall take Saul's greatest champion and use him against him. I have just completed construction on a new quarter of the city. You and your men may house there until we find a better place for you."

"And I will have rations for six hundred men," said David. "Barley, wheat, and corn. And I want a hundred cows a month to feed them. Or three hundred sheep, if you prefer. But no pigs."

"Ah, yes," said Achish. "Pigs are not allowed in your strange religion. They are not, how you say, *kasher?*"

"And my men will be paid sixty shekels of silver a month each," continued David. "Seventy-five of silver for my sergeants, and fifty gold shekels for me and my officers."

Achish frowned. "My men only receive forty-five.

They will not like making less money than foreigners."

David shrugged. "My men are better. I guarantee each of them will do more than any two of yours."

Achish leaned forward and with a grin that made my stomach lurch.

"Are you so confident that your men are better fighters?"

"Yes."

"Then we will let them decide it in a contest," said Achish. "Your man will fight my man. If your man wins, we will pay you sixty. If my man wins, you get forty-five."

"Who will fight?" asked David.

"How about him?" asked Achish.

He singled out Joab, the shortest of us. David looked at Joab, who nodded back confidently.

"Very well," said David.

Achish spoke in his native tongue to his guards. One of them, a bare-chested youth, stepped forward. He was nearly as tall as David, and his knotted muscles rippled under his oiled skin.

"One more thing," said Achish. "The contest will be to the death."

David and I shot a concerned look at Joab, but he only smiled back. There was no fear in him.

"Joab," said Benaiah, laying a hand on Joab's shoulder. "Let me take your place."

"What?" said Joab. "And tell the men that you are dead, and I robbed them of fifteen shekels a month because I didn't want to fight? No, you'd better let me handle this one."

Benaiah smiled, and the two of them embraced.

"Be careful, nephew," said David.

Joab saluted him and stepped forward.

Sickle swords of bronze were given to the two of them, and a wide space was cleared in the chamber. Achish leaned forward in his throne and rubbed his chubby hands together with glee. The Philistine's sword whirled in his hands, he had obviously handled them for years. I was worried. My brother was a genius with a sword, but the sickle shape was unfamiliar to him.

The two circled each other warily, the Philistine skipping in a wide arc while my brother pivoted slowly in the center. The Philistine lunged in only to be repulsed by my brother's sword. He danced away before Joab's sword could answer. Over and over he slashed and retreated, met by Joab's defense like a wall. It was like watching waves crash into a cliff. The sound of ringing bronze echoed through the mansion.

The Philistine feinted high, then swooped under hand. Joab riposted too late. The sword carved a gash in Joab's forearm. Joab recovered, stabbed at the man's face, but missed by an inch. The Philistine dashed backward, a smug smile on his lips at having scored the first touch.

Joab fought desperately to pay him back in like coin, but the man had Asahel's speed. He was as nimble as a gazelle, flitting out of reach of Joab's sword and back in to attack. The curve of the sickle sword is deceptive, and it was an adjustment for Joab to figure its range. The man leaped in, slashed Joab's cheek, and leaped away hips first, to avoid a slash that would have eviscerated him. Achish cheered. I watched the blood flow from Joab's cheek in alarm, but then I saw his eyes.

Joab's smile was so subtle, only we who knew him well could spot it. His lips never moved, but in his eyes I saw a laugh. He had seen something in the Philistine's attack that I had missed, some weakness he could exploit. Confidence radiated out from him, and I knew the fight was over. I looked at Benaiah, and he had seen it too. He was leaning forward, smiling with his fist up.

Joab dropped his guard slightly, feigning fatigue, inviting his enemy to try that move again. The Philistine fell into the trap. The two men seemed to move as one.

As the Philistine leaped forward in an overhead strike, Joab stepped to the side, dropping his sword, and used the momentum to slice upward at an angle. Joab's sword caught his opponent above the hip and passed through his stomach and ribs.

The Philistine dropped his sword and grabbed at the entrails that were spilling out of his stomach, his mouth open as if to scream. Joab pivoted, and brought his sword down on the back of his neck. The Philistine's head and knees hit the floor at the same time.

"Yes!" I shouted, pumping my fist.

We all cheered, then remembering ourselves, looked at Achish whose mouth was hanging open.

Joab was looking at the sickle sword.

"I like this," he said to Achish. "May I keep it?"

Achish laughed. "That was a stupendous fight!"

He summoned Joab and placed a bag of gold in his hand.

"Now," said Achish, jerking his thumb to his flabby chest. "I will have the best fighters in Canaan fighting for *me.*"

After living in the wilderness, life in Gath was luxurious. The new buildings in the quarter to which we were assigned were plush, replete with new furniture bought by Achish himself. Our training was conducted in a stone courtyard, and when we finished we had plenty of leisure time. We strolled through the markets while the locals eyed us with hatred. But what did we care? We had food in our bellies and coins in our pockets.

The king forbade any to harm us, but there were two instances where we almost had trouble. The first involved David. Whenever we left the neighborhood assigned to us, we travelled in groups for safety. That day David wanted to look around, and my brothers, my friends, and I decided to tag along. He was searching for gifts for his wives, when we ran into two giants. That is not an exaggeration; they were the two tallest men I have ever seen, each easily eight feet tall.

They were loafing with what looked like half a company of Philistine soldiers. One of the giants grabbed the other's arm and motioned toward David. It looked like he was pointing to the sword on David's back. You will think I am lying to make him sound more monstrous, but I swear to you, the one pointing had six fingers on each hand. The other giant roared and charged straight for David, and his companion started after him. Their Philistine brethren grabbed them and held them back, jabbering in their tongue. It took a score of men each to restrain them.

"Adino!" shouted David. "What's going on? Have we offended these men somehow?"

"I don't know," said Adino. "The soldiers just keep telling the two big ones that the king said we must not be harmed."

"That's good to hear," said David. "Find out what's going on."

Adino walked up to the Philistines and politely addressed them in their language. One of the giants, the one with five fingers on each hand, shook the other soldiers off and stood still. He pointed a finger at David and spoke in a booming voice.

"His name is Ishbi-Benob," translated Adino. "He says that sword belonged to his brother, and that he may not be able to kill you now, but he swears by Dagon, when he meets you on the battlefield one day, he will have your head and avenge his brother, Goliath."

I walked forward and looked up at the giant.

"Adino," I said. "Tell the giant he will have to face me first."

Adino looked at the giants. "I don't think that would be such a good idea, Abishai."

It did not matter. I gave the giant a look he could not have misinterpreted. He sneered down at me and snarled something in his language.

"What did he say?" I asked.

"It wasn't a compliment," answered Adino.

We stared each other down for a good minute, then the giants turned and lumbered away. I could hear their comrades sighing in relief. I walked back to my friends who were staring at me incredulously.

"What is it?" I asked.

"Are you crazy?" asked Benaiah. "You didn't even have your spear."

"So?" I asked.

"Look at their swords," said Joab.

I looked and saw massive swords of iron on their hips, only slightly different from the one on David's back. I smiled and turned back to my friends.

"One day I'm going to have one of those swords on my back." I predicted. "And I'm going to get mine the way David got his."

"Abeeshai, you crazy!" laughed Uriah. "But eef any of us can, eet's you."

The second incident involved the brother of the guard Joab killed, who swore to avenge his brother. Our standing orders were to defend ourselves if necessary, but we should try to avoid any altercations if possible. It did not sound like this Philistine was going to give us a chance. Joab and I were in the marketplace one night discussing the dilemma.

"Maybe we should kill the fool and be done with it," he said.

I frowned. "David wants us to avoid a fight."

"That may not be possible," he answered. "It was a fair fight, but the pig eater won't let it go."

I smiled and leaned over to clap him on the back.

"If I were killed in a fight like that, would you let it go?"

He smiled back.

"I guess not."

We must have been very distracted by our conversation, because I do not remember going down the alley. We did not even see the old crone and nearly jumped out of our skins at the sound of her voice.

"Have you fortunes told, young lords?"

She spoke Hebrew very well, though her voice sounded like a file on metal. Her robe was tattered and dirty, and she had lost several teeth. A breeze that was too light for me to feel tousled her thin, white hair, causing it to float upward. Her eyes blazed with the light of the mad, as though seeing many futures had taken a toll on her mind.

My brother and I looked at each other uncertainly. Soothsaying and witchcraft were outlawed in Israel, and

David would not like it. But my brother and I were mystified. We never had our fortunes told and were curious. Besides, we were not in Israel, and David was not there. I shrugged at my brother.

"Are you a witch?" he asked the woman.

She cackled at him. "I am considered a holy woman here."

That made me nervous. The law giver, Moses, had taught us not to worship other gods, and I doubted this "holy woman" was a prophetess of Yahweh. Was not this the same thing as idolatry? Whether or not he shared my doubts, Joab reached into his purse and held a silver coin out to her.

"Tell our fortunes," he said. "And give us a blessing."

The old woman barely looked at the coin as she laughed again, as though she was more pleased that we would give her permission to work her magic than she was to be paid for it. She squatted in the alley and began drawing shapes in the sand with her finger, all the while intoning incantations. A diagram took shape, into which she placed objects from her satchel, a fish bone, a feather, and other things that I did not recognize and was afraid to ask what they were. She took a vial and poured a thick liquid that looked very much like blood over the sand. We were mesmerized.

"You are bastards," she said, smiling. "The sons of a whore."

My hair stood up. It is obvious to me now that she

could have gotten this intelligence on any day in the market. But at the time, the only explanation I could credit was that the devil was whispering in the woman's ear.

"Yet you will not be remembered as bastards," she said. "You will be known as powerful warriors. You will travel far and win many victories. Death will not find you on the battlefield, but on the battlefield you will find a fate worse than death."

"Will we be captured?" asked Joab. "Tortured?"

"There are many kinds of torture," she said. "But I do not mean the kind you are thinking. Though you will feel anguish for a time, never shall you fall into the hands of David's enemies."

She pointed a bony finger at us.

"Stretch out thy weapons," she commanded.

Joab drew his sword, and I stretched out my spear. We crossed the bronze before us, his sickle sword resting upon the head of my spear. The old woman grabbed the blades and pulled her hands back sharply, cutting her palms deep on the edges. She held her fists over them, letting the blood drip on the axis of the blades. Her incantation rose in volume. "Moloch Mot Araphel, Moloch Mot Araphel." A cold wind whipped through the alley.

"These blades will always thirst for blood," said she. "As long as you wield them, your enemies shall never be safe from you. You shall be avengers, and these shall ever be tools of vengeance. You shall find no rest until your enemies are in their graves. And your rage shall give you strength."

My hand and arm tingled as she spoke. She lowered her fists, and I looked at the blood on my spear. Joab was looking at his sword and smiling. Did he really believed that the old woman's spell on his sword would lead to glory on the battlefield? Part of me knew she was probably telling us what we wanted to hear, but the woman spoke with conviction, and it was hard not to be swept up in it.

"We should go," I said to Joab and the old woman. But when I turned to include her, she had vanished.

9

The guard's brother would have to wait, because we were going on a raid. David, with Adino's help, made sure the Philistines were under the impression that we were going to attack the southern settlements of Judah, but in reality, we marched south to attack the Amalekite bands that ravaged Israel's southern border.

We were playing close to the edge of a cliff. If any of the Philistines got word of our actions, it could cost us our lives. That night as we camped on our route to the cities of Amalek, David held counsel with his leadership, and the problem of secrecy was brought up.

"All it takes is one Amalekite," said Adino. "Just *one,* to run away to Gath. In fact, he doesn't even have to go to Gath. He, or she mind you, just has to survive long enough to tell one other person. Then that person tells another, and before you can stop it, word will reach Achish."

Eleazar spoke. "David, I know you don't want to hear this, but we must kill everyone, men and women."

David opened his mouth to speak, but was interrupted by Shammah.

"Let us not forget, this is what Yahweh commanded Joshua and our fathers. I know it is difficult, but it may be the only way our land can rest from their evil works."

"The Amalekites are not above killing Hebrew women," reminded Eleazar. "Children too. Sometimes what they do is worse than killing them."

The fire illumined David's pensive face. He was backed into a difficult corner. He was convinced God wanted him to take the fight to the enemies of Israel, but to do so he would have to choose between endangering his men and fighting in a way that few would have willingly chosen.

He looked at the priest. "Abiathar? What does God expect of us?"

The priest looked as if David had caught him unprepared. Abiathar's head swiveled side to side as he looked at the faces of the men, and he took a deep breath.

"There were times that Joshua destroyed every living thing when he came into this land," he said slowly. "But that was when God expressly commanded."

"What does God command now?" asked David.

"I don't know," said the priest. "When my father was alive, he said that our nation suffered because our people did not wipe out the inhabitants as God commanded. In fact, the reason God took His hand away from Saul was because he would not destroy Agag, the Amalekite king."

"It's strange," said David. "That God would become Saul's enemy because he was merciful."

"Saul wasn't merciful," said Eleazar. "He was *greedy.* I was there. He held Agag for ransom from the scattered tribes of Amalek, and kept the best livestock for himself."

David frowned.

"David," said Abiathar. "Perhaps it is time that you finished the work that Saul began. The cities of Amalek are destroyed, but until every man and woman of the Amalekite tribes are dead, we will never have peace."

David nodded reluctantly.

"What about the children?" asked Shammah.

Once it had snowed when we were children, and Asahel had stuffed snow down the collar of my tunic. That was close to the experience I felt now, like ice was crawling down my spine. Killing women was bad enough. But children? *Chara.*

"The little children will be spared," said David. "They will be too young and ignorant to give the Philistines any useful intelligence. We will give them enough provisions to make for the homes for orphans in Beersheba."

We caught the Amalekites by surprise. We attacked

from the East early in the morning, with the rising sun at our backs. The defenders organized hastily, but not in time to prevent us from entering the city. We slaughtered the guards and poured in through the gates. The fighting was in the streets, up close and dirty. The Amalekites were fierce fighters, taller even than the Philistines, and as strong as bulls.

Asahel, Uriah, and I led our squads down a street parallel to a street that Joab, Benaiah, and Zelek were clearing. About fifty Amalekites formed ranks to repulse us. They charged us shield first, threatening to crush us with their superior size and number, but we had drilled against this very tactic.

Uriah's squad of ten men was in front of mine. Uriah urged his men to hold as the enemy ran to them. When the Amalekites closed within a few feet, Uriah's men slipped behind my squad who had taken a knee concealed by the men in the front.

The enemy's momentum was thrown off. As they staggered forward, my men struck the enemies' legs with their shields and stood, lifting them off their feet and depositing them on the earth in front of Uriah and his men, whose spears were waiting.

We plunged our weapons into their second squad as Asahel broke his squad into two wings of five that flanked them, completely surrounding the larger force. It was a microcosm of a move performed by larger armies, and small units, used to charging wildly, could not deal with it.

Many of the men abandoned their spears for swords in the confines of the streets, but I kept mine. I had adopted an overhand thrust which was faster and allowed me to throw the spear without changing my grip if needed. There was no grace to the killing, only deliberate, monotonous work.

I resembled a boy I once saw who had discovered an ingenious method of slaughtering steers with a small pickaxe. The cows were trapped in a chute as he walked the line sinking the spike into their brains. *Pop! Pop! Pop!* Just like that, my arm methodically drove the spear into the Amalekites, who were equally trapped and just as doomed as those dumb cattle.

Three Amalekites broke off and ran down a side alley. Asahel, blinded by the thrill of the chase, sprinted like a devil after them. His men did not notice and continued to hack at the enemy in the street. Feeling fear for the first time that day, I fought my way out of the melee and ran after my brother.

I rounded the corner into the alley in time to see Asahel catch up with the first man and cut him down from behind. He did not slow but continued to chase the other two, who turned to square off against him. Asahel parried a clumsy swing easily and buried his sword in the chest of an Amalekite, as the other raised his sword to cleave my brother's skull.

I screamed savagely and hurled my spear. It caught the Amalekite in the throat and hurled him to the ground.

Asahel turned to see where the spear had come from and smiled at me. I was livid with anger.

"Don't *ever* run off on your own like that again," I screamed at him.

He hung his head and grumbled, "I could have taken them by myself."

"This one was about to split your stupid head," I said, pointing to the man who was gurgling as he tried to breath from his ruined windpipe.

We gathered the others who had finished off the company of Amalekites, and we rushed to the adjacent street to see how Joab, Zelek, and Benaiah were doing. They had come across a larger group of Amalekites and were surrounded by over a hundred men. Several of our men lay dead in the streets.

Cut off, Benaiah and Joab were fighting back-to-back against the Amalekites. The two were holding their own, and bodies of the slain were all around them. Benaiah's sword was a terror to behold, and Joab was an artist with his. My brother dispatched men as if he were squashing insects, swatting aside sword and spear thrusts with contemptuous ease.

Zelek was fighting fiercely to come to their rescue. The men could not keep up with him. I raised my spear and screamed. Our men took up the battle cry, and we descended on the Amalekites like a storm. The enemy was terrorized by our appearance. Most turned to run away, getting trapped by the walls of the houses.

A few stood and fought like men, forming a line of

shields to block our assault. As I stabbed the first man in the chest, I saw Asahel leap over their heads. He turned and slashed their legs as he landed. They fell in a pile at our men's feet, who quickly finished them off.

An Amalekite surprised me from the side, swinging at my neck. I caught the blow on the shaft between my hands. The sword skidded down the shaft and cut off my left finger. I kicked the man in the chest to knock him back, and thrust my spear upward under his leather girdle, lifting him off of his feet over my head.

For a moment he was wriggling on my spear like a fish. In the fury of losing my finger I smashed my spear to the earth, man and all, and he landed on his head, which flattened like a ripe melon. I expected the red blood that squirted out if his mouth, nose, and ears, but I was surprised at the grey matter that came mingled with it. Even more gruesome, his eye shot out of its socket, held in place only by a pink tendril.

We cleaned up the remaining soldiers easily. Joab thanked Benaiah, and they embraced. A quick clap on the shoulder was all he had time to give the rest of us. I dimly realized that I had almost lost both of my brothers that day, but I would only realize it fully later. When your blood is pumping in battle, you may think clearly, but you have no time to feel.

After I wrapped a bandage around my hand, we rejoined our company and gave our reports. The soldiers had been wiped out, and now we must go from house to house, killing the rest. The first house I entered was occupied by a woman. She spoke wildly to me in a strange tongue and waved a dagger at me.

She screamed as my spear took her, a scream the raised the hackles on my neck. I pulled the spear out. I can see her now, the linen of her dress and her dark curls spoiled by her blood forming a pool around her. I left and walked to the next house.

I felt nothing. That would come later.

We gathered the children by the gate. Almost all of them were wailing, tears and snot streaking their dirty faces. The oldest, a girl of about ten, had stopped crying and was staring at us with hatred. One of the men handed her the reins of an ass laden with food for the children. Adino was busy elsewhere, and none of us could speak their language. The only thing for it was to point north toward Beersheba and hope she would get the idea. She began to trudge down the road. Other children followed crying. Some sat in the dust at first, then realized what was happening, panicked and bolted after her.

We looted the houses, stuffing our bags with gold, silver, clothes, food–anything we could get our hands on. We herded the cattle and sheep together, and loaded the asses and camels we found with the haul.

I had never seen a camel before. They are great, ugly beasts, not as fast as horse, though their endurance is legendary, and more trouble than I thought was worth. They bit, spit at, and charged us. I was ready to kill them and be done with it, but some of our men knew the trick to tame the beasts, and managed to load them for the journey.

It was getting dark, and our officers discussed our sleeping arrangements for the night. We could camp by the road, but there were plenty of good houses for us to sleep in right there. We said we wanted to get out of that place, none more loudly than me. I did not admit it out loud, but I would have rather slept on the cold, hard grass than spend the night with the ghosts of the people I had just killed. I did not know it then, but I do now.

The ghosts follow you.

We set the city to the torch and marched away. A half mile away, there was a hill in the road. No order was given, but we all stopped and looked back at the blaze. The sun had set, and the fires lit up the night. It was the largest fire I had ever seen. You could not even see the stars above the city. I stared at the enormous flames, hoping they would be hot enough and bright enough to burn away everything I had seen and heard and done.

We came back to Gath, and David delivered his bogus report to Achish, as well as his share of the loot. The king was delighted, convinced that David could never go back to his people after attacking them. For Achish it was a kind of loyalty insurance. Little did he suspect that our deeds would endear us to the Israelites more than ever, taxing on our consciences though they may be.

Adino continued to expand his ring of spies, listening for any hint that word had gotten out about the Amalekites. Of course, news spread of the city's destruction, but the identity of the attackers was still a mystery. Fortunately everyone blamed Saul's army, the Moabites, the Egyptians, or even Amalekite bandits within their own country. But no one seemed to suspect David.

Still tension remained between us and the Philistines, which was fine with us. They hated us, and we hated them. The only Philistines who pretended not to hate us were the whores, and only a few men were willing to risk a romp in one of the brothels. A man might be greeted with a smile, but we did not trust them not to cut our throats the moment we closed our eyes. Mostly we kept to ourselves.

My brothers and I had not forgotten about the threat of the brother of the guard Joab killed. Everything was quiet in the streets, but somewhere there was an assassin without a face or a name who intended to murder Joab. We lodged in the same house, and Asahel and I seldom let him out of our sight. Joab laughed it off, but he never went anywhere without his sickle sword at his waist.

One night as I lay in bed, unable to sleep, I dressed and went into the salon. Asahel was already there.

"Can't sleep either?" I asked.

He shook his head. "I keep thinking about what I did to those Amalekite women and children."

"It's best not to think about that," I said.

"But I thought that we would be doing good fighting for David," he said. "He's always preaching about following God and doing right. I knew I would have to kill on the battlefield. But that...I don't know."

"That's what happens in war," I said. "When we decided to become warriors, we made that decision, whether we realized it or not. It's what we have to do to survive."

He turned away.

"I don't know if I can do it again," he said.

I placed my hand on his shoulder.

"Now is not the time for weakness."

He looked hurt, so I tried to soften my words.

"One day this will all be over. You will marry and have children of your own. Your wife and children will live in peace because of what we did today. *Then* we can be soft. Then we will never have to kill a woman, or turn a child out in the cold. But for now, we must harden ourselves."

"Maybe," he said. "But I don't think I'll ever get used to it."

I squeezed his shoulder.

"I hope you don't."

He smiled and looked at me from the corner of his eye.

"Thank you, Abishai. I can't talk about these things

with Joab. They don't seem to bother him. I guess they don't bother you either, but with you…I don't know. It's just different."

I knew what he meant. Joab did not seem to have any hesitation wiping out the inhabitants of the town. To him they were all the enemy. But Asahel was wrong about it not bothering me.

I was about to tell him so when we heard a commotion in Joab's chamber. I grabbed my spear and ran into the room. Asahel raced ahead of me. We saw Joab wrestling with a man on the floor, and he was holding his wrist. In the man's hand was a curved dagger.

With the blunt end of my spear I struck his hand. He held the dagger tightly. I struck again harder, and it clattered to the floor. Asahel and I grabbed the man's arms and pulled him away from our brother. He struggled, but we held him fast. He stopped and began jabbering in his language, probably cursing us in the name of his heathen gods.

My brother stood and wiped his mouth. He picked up his sword and pulled it out of its sheath. The man started struggling again, and began to cry. I could not understand his words, but his tone was pleading. Joab held the naked blade up to his face and smiled.

"I've been waiting for you," he said. "This is the sword that killed your brother, and it has *thirsted* for your blood."

With that he slashed from the collar bone to the hip.

I felt the body go limp in my arms. Blood spilled onto the floor. Asahel and I dropped the corpse. It seems strange to me now that I did not even consider taking the man prisoner and turning him over to our superiors. We were utterly pitiless in those days, especially toward a man who would attack our brother.

We told our lieutenant what happened, who told David. They ordered us to stand before Achish. David could not afford to break the peace with the Philistines. We put on our finest clothes and accompanied David to the king's mansion. If Achish was distraught at the man's death, he did not show it.

"Mtiniti was a fool," he said with a dismissive wave of the hand. "It sounds like your men killed him in self defense."

"I assure you, my lord, that's what happened," said David. "My men have been doing their best to avoid conflict with your people. Please, do not be offended with us over this unfortunate incident."

"Of course not," said Achish. "You have served me well, David."

David cleared his throat and stepped closer.

"I may have an idea to prevent any further unpleasantness. My men and I could relocate to Ziklag. The Philistines there could take our place in the new quarter."

Achish rubbed the beard on his fat neck. "That would make my life much easier. People have complained about your presence, through no fault of yours, my friend."

"Oh king," said David. "We are at your service. If you so command, my men and I will stay at Ziklag, and be ready when you call."

Achish smiled.

"Then I do so command it."

10

Ziklag did not have the fresh, new feeling of our quarter in Gath, but there were no Philistines there to stare daggers at us. There were also no distractions. The marketplaces, brothels, and taverns were empty. Smiths took over abandoned forges and began to manufacture and repair weapons. Drilling resumed in deadly earnest. Although the men took advantage of the space and seclusion to send for their families, it was a town dedicated to our war.

I was impressed by David's wives. No one heard them complain about being stuck alone in a town filled with soldiers. Ahinoam made herself busy setting David's house in order, and Abigail became a motherly figure to us bachelors. She had her maids prepare homey meals for unmarried soldiers, and repair clothing that was torn or worn through, usually pitching in with her own two hands. More than Abiathar, she listened to men spill feelings of homesickness, concern for their families back home, and the pangs of conscience we all felt.

As I said before, she was the only woman worthy of David.

We continued to raid cities of the Amalekites, Gezrites, and Geshurites, wiping out the inhabitants, looting, and burning the cities. Adino had the idea of planting evidence to make it look like the Gezrites were attacking the Geshurites, the Geshurites were attacking the Amalekites, and so on.

We began to carry the corpses from one battle in a cart to lay them at the aftermath of the other. We also made sure that we left no artifact to show that any Hebrews had passed that way. The fires often accomplished that for us, destroying any evidence we could not take with us. The plan worked well, and soon we would come to a city to find it was already destroyed in retaliation for an attack ascribed to the inhabitants, but which we had in fact carried out.

Our enemies were doing our work for us.

We grew rich with plunder. There were more cattle and sheep in Ziklag than there were people. Once again we were eating meat every day, but we did not grow fat with all the training, marching, and fighting. I filled a whole room full of silver and gold, rich carpets and tapestries, lapis, jade, amethysts, topaz, as well as fine clothes of silk, linen, and wool, though I had nowhere to wear them.

Still we felt like outlaws. Our reports to Achish were works of complete fiction, and if he ever found out, we would be fighting Philistines again. We could not return to Israel. The capricious demon that tormented Saul would turn him on us without warning, and we would be hunted like the ibex in En-gedi. What was worse, we were starting to get used to the killing of women. We celebrated after every victory as though nothing bothered us, but there was always an edge to our revelry.

We marched out from Ziklag and spent the night in the woods so we could attack at dawn with the sunlight at our backs to blind the enemy. Our armor was piled in carts to preserve our strength while marching, but we carried our weapons. David always wore his armor on the marches; he wanted his men to see that it did not fatigue him.

A wagon of corpses slain in the last battle followed well behind to keep the foul smell away. Woe to the poor soldier who drew that duty! The cart was often led by a soldier who had committed a particularly egregious offense. Asahel was punished this way once for breaking ranks and reported that the smell nearly made him vomit. What was worse, maggots had crawled up his arms when he was loading the bodies.

He never broke ranks again.

We slept in the woods with no fire to betray our presence and woke well before the sun rose. We ate a cold breakfast and strapped on our armor. David prayed, with Abiathar mediating, for strength, wisdom, and safety for us, his men. We quit our campsite, with none of the usual camp litter that might reveal our identities, and formed ranks. We flew no banners, pennants, not even a guidon. We marched silently, lest the merest sound reveal our attack too soon.

The Gezrites by this time were wary of attack, and were posting more guards than we had seen before. David tried to make the attacks seem random and avoided patterns that might help our adversaries guess where we might attack next. This time the Gezrites set sufficient guards to sound the alarm and mount a counter attack well outside their walls. I was glad, I liked the battlefield where I could stretch out my spear, but I would be content to kill them wherever I was obliged to fight.

The city in my mind probably has an unpronounceable name in their dirty tongue. It does not matter, as we were never told the names of the city to preserve secrecy, and once we got there we did not care. We did not even know what race we were fighting until we saw them. None of us hated them, except maybe Zelek, who hated everyone. They were like vermin who had infested the house and needed to be exterminated. It was no more personal than that.

The Gezrites arrayed a thousand men against us, not an army, just the local brigade, and held more within the walls as a reserve. On that occasion our company had the honor of being in the center, with Shammah leading the first squad next to David himself.

The enemy was equipped with swords and spears, but also axes. These were not axes you would use to chop down a tree. They had actually designed axes to be used in war, some with broad blades like a duck's bill and others with narrow, chisel-like heads, and used them to great effect. A few clever warriors would put a spear head above these devices, making a kind of hybrid weapon. Their warriors had long hair like a woman's, but one side of their heads was shaven. I heard that they often painted their faces for war, but in their urgency they had not had the time.

They were still too close to their walls, and if we attacked now we would be exposed to fire from their archers on the wall. So we waited to draw them out. There was a long silence as we stood. We were not stupid enough to fight near the wall, and they were not stupid enough to leave its protection. The waiting was torture.

Standing still before a battle with your enemy arrayed before you gives you a chance to imagine all sorts of horrible fates for yourself. A man's instinct is to run away or to charge into battle and get it over with. We knew the Gezrites would flinch first. Their sergeants were walking the lines, struggling to keep their younger, more eager and nervous, soldiers in check. Finally one of them broke, unable to take anymore, and burst from the lines with a shout.

As I mentioned Asahel did that once at a different battle, which was how he ended up driving the corpse cart. When Asahel had broken ranks, our soldiers were too well disciplined to follow him. But when the Gezrite lost his nerve, all of his comrades followed him, and his commanders lost any semblance of control. The Gezrites surged toward the middle of our front. This was exactly what we wanted. Our two wings flanked them like the closing of two hinged gates, and the battle was as good as over. The only thing left was the work.

We let them close on us, then the officers ordered us to lower our spears with exquisite timing. The fools practically killed themselves for us. Once our spears were lowered, they could not stop even if they had the presence of mind to do so. It was not uncommon to see two or three men impaled on the same spear.

We learned to carry extra spears. Rather than try to wrench your spear free of multiple corpses, we would reach an empty hand behind us, our mate would plant his spear in our palm and reach behind him until the last rank picked up a spare. This happened so frequently that we incorporated it into our field drills, and the men were efficient in its execution.

The overhead thrust of the spear, which I adopted for myself, I made a sort of policy for my men, contrary to the technique used by the rest of the army. Eleazar had shown me the advantages of the technique, and I schooled my squad to perfect it. Though we aimed for the gaps in the armor, my men were strong enough to drive their spears clean through the enemy's chest armor. Armor is fine for stopping slashes and cuts, but useless against the thrust. I learned to ignore the wild swings of my foe and focus on blocking his thrusts, and I almost always walked away with nothing more than superficial cuts on my body.

The Gezrites were undisciplined savages, but they had courage. They saw rank after successive rank crash against our shields and fall like stalks of wheat under the scythe. How they kept charging without losing a step, I shall never know. But I saw waves of Gezrites stumbling over the bodies of their own brethren to claim their portion of death, which we gave to them liberally.

Word spread that whoever was attacking the cities was not sparing the women, and several women joined the men on the battlefield. Some even shaved the sides of their heads to look like men. I was grateful for that. Though killing women was always distasteful, it somehow felt better that they had a chance to fight for their lives. There is something noble in facing your fate on your feet with bronze in your fist, rather than cowering behind your door waiting for your doom to find you. But in the end, the women on the battlefield were just as dead as those behind the walls.

David was always in the front swinging that behemoth of a sword. He was an absolute nightmare. The transformation that turned my gentle, psalm-singing uncle into the blood drenched monster we saw on the battlefield was horrific. If the angel Michael had fought for us himself, he could not have outdone him.

He forsook the shield, blocking only with the sword, wielding it sometimes with one hand, sometimes with two. Whether he slashed or stabbed, no armor could resist his crushing blows. Helmets crumpled like papyrus under it. Our men gave him a wide berth to swing the weapon, and dozens of the foe littered the ground at his feet.

Joab's sword was like a living thing, whistling through the air, ringing off of shields and helms, then whirling back in tight arcs to bite into the flesh of the enemy. I saw him smash the face of a Gezrite with his shield while simultaneously stabbing another in the throat, then pivot to cut the neck of the first. Benaiah was with him again, battling at once three Gezrites who stood in a semicircle around him.

A spear lanced toward Benaiah's unprotected back, and Joab caught it on his own shield. Still busy with the other three, Benaiah trusted Joab to deal with the spear, which he did. His sickle sword cut the wrists of the Gezrite, then slashed across his eyes. I saw the two of them rely on each other hundreds of times in this way. In battle, trust in your comrade is crucial to the kinds of feats we performed, and Joab and Benaiah's bond was wrought of iron.

Zelek was a butcher on the field, hacking at the enemy like they were overgrown brambles in his garden. At camp he was quiet, but on the battlefield he spewed an incessant stream of curses in his tongue. Whether he was speaking to himself or the Gezrites I never knew, but the effect was terrifying to the enemy. When they fled from him, he ran after them in a fury, cutting them down from behind.

Asahel had developed his own style of fighting that took advantage of his speed and agility. Though not as strong as Joab and I, he would leap up into the air and bring his spear down with all his weight. I warned him that if an enemy had the presence of mind, he would simply spear Asahel in mid-flight.

Fortunately for Asahel, the Gezrite would be too stunned by the display and stand gaping until it was too late to raise his shield. Asahel's spear would knock the man over and nail him to the ground. Planting his foot in the body, he wrenched it free and perform the feat on another hapless enemy.

One of the greatest dangers in battle is to become too fixed on the enemy in front of you and forget the enemy to the side or the rear. I made that mistake in this battle. I had just planted my spear in a man's chest and had my leg up to kick him off. While my leg was still raised a shield bowled into me from the side and lifted me off my feet and onto the ground. The straps of my shield were knocked off, and the wooden disk flew away.

I could not breathe, the wind was knocked out of me. The Gezrite who struck me rushed in with his comrades to finish me off. My spear was still stuck in a man's chest, and I was defenseless. I cursed myself. How could I let myself be defeated by such an obvious attack? Now I was going to be killed by lesser warriors than myself. I cringed and threw my arms up defensively.

One of our men rushed in and beat back the Gezrites with his steel sword. I recognized the sword, it was Uriah! I pushed myself off the ground, still unable to breathe, found a discarded spear, and thrust it under the armpit of the man closest to me. Uriah smiled at me. I shall never forget his face, his pale skin speckled with bright red blood. There were flecks of blood and gore in his beard as well.

"Are you all right, my friend?" he asked.

I croaked that I was and pulled my own spear out of the man who was graciously holding it for me with his ribs.

"Thanks," I said to the dying man, and Uriah's laughter bellowed across the battlefield, terrifying enemy and ally alike.

We rejoined what was left of the battle. The reserves had joined the field, creating a new front for us to fight. Worst of all, the archers came with them. There is very little you can do against arrows until you close the distance. We listened for the orders from their officers and threw up our shields.

Most of the time, the first volley from a company of archers flies high as this one did. The arrows swished through the air over our heads. Barely a handful landed among our men, and only one was fatal. Eleazar led his company to smash the archers's flank. It was vital that they prevent a second volley.

Fear made the archers' hands tremble, and only a few were able to loose another hasty shot at the charging heavy infantry. When they reached them, the archers were practically defenseless. Their infantry had all rushed in to fight us instead of leaving a retinue of foot soldiers to protect the archers as they should have. To me this kind of negligence borders on betrayal.

The archers had short swords, hardly more than daggers, but few knew what to do with them. Eleazar's men rolled over them, like a bull trampling a dog, and rounded to surround the remaining infantry. The battle was over before noon, but it always felt like we had been fighting for a week once fatigue set in. It was crucial that we finish our work and leave before this happened.

The bodies of our slain were replaced with corpses from a previous battle. Adino had lost track of most of his spies and was more paranoid than ever. We never worried about picking up the fragments of our broken weapons since they were indistinguishable from the bronze weapons of any other army in Canaan.

Once again the dirty work of going from house to house must be performed. Having everyone purging the city was unnecessary, and it took a toll on the men, so the companies performed the task by turns. After that battle, it was my company's turn, so we rounded up our men and made for the gate.

In between each house, I would check on the men to

make sure they had not taken on more than they could handle. I would poke my head in a door, often to find my man herding children out of the house or with his sword buried in a woman's abdomen. We would nod curtly to each other. No words were exchanged. Their eyes were hard and cold as the daggers of ice that hang from the trees in winter.

I heard a woman screaming in one of the houses. This was not unusual in of itself, but she had been screaming for too long. If my man had done the job, she would not be alive to scream anymore. I ran to the door and began to search the building. The screaming had stopped, but I could hear the woman weeping.

I found one of my men, Ishai, raping a Gezrite woman. Her eye was swollen, and her face had been cut by the knife Ishai had in his hand. He had beaten and tortured her. As I stormed into the chamber, he smiled at me–actually *smiled*, as if I would approve of this behavior.

His smile infuriated me more than anything else. I took a single step and drove my spear behind his collar bone until it was half buried in his body. I drew my sword and cut the throat of the woman.

I sat on the bed. My head and shoulders felt so heavy, I could barely lift them. I did not look at the bodies of the two I had just murdered, but I could not ignore them. I felt them. I tried to ignore the sounds of death outside, but they cut their way through the walls into my brain, as loud as my own guilty conscience.

He actually smiled *at me.*

The implication was clear. He welcomed me into his wicked company as one of his own, a man like him. To a degree, I knew it was true, and it made me feel filthy. If my mother could see me now, what would she think?

I was a killer, but never a liar. I went to Shammah and told him what I had seen and done.

He nodded gravely. "That was right, Abishai."

We sat down at the gate and he passed me some water.

"I once told my son to wring the neck of a chicken for supper. I came out and found him tormenting the poor creature, pulling its feathers out, breaking its legs, its wings."

"What did you do?" I asked.

"I beat him, of course," he said, as though it should be obvious. "He was confused, because I told him to kill the bird. He wondered why it would be wrong to hurt it when it was not wrong to kill it."

"What did you tell him?"

"I told him that killing the creature was necessary, but causing unnecessary suffering is cruelty."

I sighed. "I suppose Ishai's father never gave him that lesson."

"Ishai was a foul man before he joined us," he said. "And was a foul man after."

"His mates are not going to like it," I said.

Shammah scowled.

"His mates are likely to be as cruel as he was," he said. "Better they know what happened and be afraid to make the same mistake."

He stood and laid a fatherly hand on my shoulder. It almost made me weep. I cannot say why.

"We kill," said he. "Because we must, not because we are cruel. You understand this, which is why I need you to lead villains like Ishai and his friends. I need you to restrain their cruelty."

I nodded and rose like an old man, my hands braced against my knees.

We set the town on fire and left, leaving Ishai's body to burn next to the woman he had tortured. I hoped that her ghost would hunt his, and that he would be tortured as he had tortured her in life. Instead they both decided to haunt my nightmares, and it was I who was tortured by my own guilt.

As we made camp, I laid down on the grass and looked at the stars on a moonless sky. Beyond the usual fatigue of battle, I felt a great weariness of soul. There was a purity on the battlefield, two sides striving for mastery, one receiving death and defeat, the other life and glory, and I loved it. But the fell deeds we performed afterward left me feeling defiled.

I went to Abiathar and asked him to intercede for me to Yahweh. I prayed that God would grant us a chance to come out of the shadows, to fight our battles honorably, and to forgive us for all we had done. When I finished, Abiathar spoke to me.

"You know, Abishai, you're not the only one who feels this way. Lots of soldiers are praying the same prayer."

"Couldn't David answer that prayer for us?" I asked.

"He wants to," said the priest. "Even he is asking God to help him see a way out of this."

"Will God show him a way?"

The priest chewed his lip while he considered.

"I don't know."

Neither of us could know, but looking back now, I can see that events were set in motion that would give us all the answer to our prayers. We would fight honorably again, and today the people sing of David's victories over the Amalekites, Gezrites, and Geshurites. But few understand the emotional and moral cost of those victories. No matter how I justify it, I can never wash away the stain of our deeds in the southern desert.

11

Word reached us of an Amalekite gang of bandits that headed past us toward Judah and Moab. We decided to patrol eastward to see if we could find their trail. It was risky because the chances of being spotted were greater, and it was never as lucrative as taking a city. Still we liked these kinds of raids. When we caught the bands in the wilderness it was never as messy as spoiling their cities.

We found their trail in the land of the Kenites, with whom our nation had a peaceful relationship. We followed the trail north toward Judah. Fearing exposure, the officers expressed reluctance to pass into the land of Israelites, but the thrill of the chase had taken David. He compromised and promised if the trail went too deep into the land of Judah, we would break pursuit before we were discovered. We reached the outskirts of Judah which was not as expansive as it is today. In a nameless village a day's walk from Beersheba, we saw their handiwork.

Men and women were mutilated, flayed, burned. Remembering it now, I would not wish to defile your imagination with a description of the perverse tortures they enacted on my tribesmen and women. Everywhere was the acrid smell of burnt flesh and hair. Men vomited at each new revelation of our enemy's depredation. Bloody footsteps led away from the scenes of horror.

The footsteps of Amalekites.

At first, we were relieved not to find the corpses of the children, assuming they were taken as slaves, a common practice. We hoped to catch up to them and rescue them. Perhaps some of us could take the orphans to Ziklag and raise them as our own children. But any hope of a rescue was soon shattered.

It was Joab who discovered the bodies.

The Amalekites reserved their most wicked violations for the children, gathering them into one house for their final orgy of torture. Judging by the evidence in front of us, the smaller and more precious the child, the more they desired to make him suffer.

I knelt and ran my fingers through the hair of a little girl. She must have been three years old. My hand was trembling. Behind me men were racked by sobs of anguish. I did not lose control, but wept tears of white hot fury. I exchanged a look with Joab. His face was a mask of pure hate.

Those too overcome with grief to march stayed to bury what was left of the twisted bodies. The rest of us flew after the Amalekites. I wanted to see them suffer as those children had. I wanted to watch their faces twist in a rictus of pain and horror. I wanted to return every heinous act they committed back to them tenfold.

Along the way we came upon a squad of local Hebrew soldiers. They stiffened at the sight of our weapons, but we assured them that we only wanted intelligence. Had they seen the Amalekites come this way?

"Yes, we saw them," said one of the sergeants with a smirk. "They tried to attack Hebron, but we knocked them back from the walls and crushed them on the plains. They're all dead now."

Our shoulders drooped. Zelek kicked the dirt with a growl.

David nodded, a gesture at war with his discontented scowl.

"They are dead," he said. "Well enough."

"Who are you?" asked the sergeant.

"A man of Judah," said David. "Like you."

The march back to Ziklag was somber. We were all disappointed that the Judaeans killed the Amalekites instead of us. We felt robbed of our vengeance. Those Judaeans had not seen what we had seen.

However much the Amalekites suffered before their deaths, it was not enough.

One afternoon a messenger came to us from Achish. They always sent the same Philistine soldier, Ittai of

Gath, because he spoke Hebrew well. Poor and without a family, he was, like us, an outsider in his home country. We began to get used to him, even fond of him. After he delivered his message to David, we hectored him with playful insults.

"Ittai," said Joab. "Do something about your breath. It smells of the pigs you've been eating."

Ittai towered over my short brother.

"You can smell it all the way down there?" he said. "Fancy that. Your long Hebrew noses have a *powerful* sense of smell."

Joab's laugh bellowed with good humor.

Asahel chimed in. "These Philistines all wear that silly fish scale armor to emulate their fish god, but only Ittai carries it so far as to have a face like a fish."

Ittai smiled. "A fish always has its mouth open. That sounds more like your face, you jabbering ape."

The rest of us laughed at Asahel's expense. Ittai always had a quick wit and returned our jests with a good nature. He was a decent fellow for a barbarian.

He went on. "Typical of you Hebrews. You can only face us when you outnumber us six-to-one."

"You outnumbered us at Keilah and we thrashed you," said Asahel.

I elbowed Asahel in the ribs and scowled at him. He had gone too far.

Ittai's smile never faltered. "Be glad I was not there. I'd have shown you what a Philistine can really do and shut up your boasting for good."

"Any time, you Gittite swine!" roared Joab with a twinkle in his eye.

The two began to tussle in the road. We laughed and cheered, some for Joab, but some for Ittai. Soldiers began to gather to enjoy the sport. A messenger interrupted to tell us an assembly of the officers and sergeants was called. Joab had to break away just as he was trapping Ittai's shoulder in a hold.

"You got lucky. This isn't over, you filthy pagan," Joab shouted.

"Name the time and place, Jewish scum."

Benaiah clapped him on the shoulder.

"Good to see you, Ittai."

Ittai's smile flashed brilliant as he dusted himself off.

"Chara, Benaiah," said Uriah. "Maybe you should buy heem a cup of wine before you keess heem."

Benaiah punched him in the arm.

When the men were gathered, David relayed Ittai's message to us: Achish was summoning our forces. We would march north in the morning.

Joab frowned.

"We're going to Gath?"

"Not Gath," said Adino. "Aphek."

David sighed. "Achish has marched on Gilead and summoned us to join him in his fight against the Israelites."

We reacted in alarm. Everyone started talking at once. How could we fight our own people? David raised his hand for silence, and we complied restlessly.

"We knew this would happen sooner or later," he said. "We have a plan."

Eleazar spoke. "We aren't the only ones keeping secrets. Achish hasn't told the other four lords of the Philistines that he has employed us."

"It seems the Philistines don't like the idea of fighting with us, any more than we do fighting with them," said Shammah.

"Nonsense," said Uriah. "I would *love* to fight weeth them."

A chuckle went around the room.

"You know what I mean, you dirty Hittite," said Shammah with a laugh.

Eleazar continued. "We will sow discord among the Philistines, get them to rebuke Achish for our sakes. To Achish we will continue to be humble and respectful, but around the other Philistines we must seem aloof and untrustworthy. They will pressure Achish to get rid of us, and we will 'reluctantly' sit out the battle."

"So," said Adino. "When we get to Aphek, be as obnoxious as you can."

Uriah looked at Joab from the corner of his eye. "That should not be so very hard for you. Just be yourself!"

We arrived at the fountain of Jezreel in back of the Philistine camp. The months we spent in Gath had schooled us on how to best irk the Philistines, and we put them to good use. We did not do anything overt, but we put as much insolence into our body language as possible as we strutted around the camp. We made a point of sneering at them and muttered under our breath about "filthy heathens" just within earshot of them performing their religious rituals.

It worked. The Philistines glowered at us with even more hatred than they had at Gath. Even better, I ran into Ishbi-benob, Goliath's brother, once again. Before I sauntered over to him, I thrust my spear into the dirt so there would be no excuse for us to come to open hostilities.

Yet.

"Hello again, Ishbi-benob," I said.

He sneered at me, and to my surprise, answered in Hebrew with the thick accent of a man who had recently learned the tongue.

"Hello, puny man. You come to fight me?"

My eyes never left his. I was conscious of having to tilt my head back to look up at him, but I would not back down.

"Not yet," I said. "We'll get our chance."

He gestured to my mutilated left hand. "You have no so many fingers as last I see you."

I shrugged. "After seeing your ugly brother I realized that having too many fingers is not seemly on a man. Better to have too few than too many."

He looked puzzled until one of his comrades translated for him. He scowled.

"You say many insult for one so small."

"And for someone who's supposed to be a giant you look small to me."

I turned my back on him.

"I'll see you again soon, freak," I said without looking as I walked away.

I heard a growl, then heard his mates jabbering at him in conciliatory tones, obviously trying to cool his blood before there was an incident.

Our naked contempt did the trick. Or maybe it was unnecessary, as the Philistines hated us before we even got there. Before David could even see Achish, he was politely asked to leave. The other lords were furious that we were there in Achish's name, and they refused to fight with us.

David feigned a reluctance to leave and an eagerness to remain and fight the Israelites. When the king assured him that his dismissal had nothing to do with our service, David led us out with a head hung low for Achish and a wink for us.

David had outfoxed the Philistines again.

We camped in a field by the road back to Ziklag. I was ready to settle down for a night of sleepless rest when the watchers reported a sizable force headed our way. I girded my armor back on to meet the threat and shouldered my spear. As I jogged to where the commotion was coming from, my friends and brothers met me. We exchanged concerned looks. Maybe our ruse did not succeed as well as we hoped.

The men approaching proved to be a company from the tribe of Manasseh. The army of Israel had discovered us again. They outnumbered us more than ten-to-one. It would be a tough fight if David gave the order to defend ourselves, which I doubted he would do.

Two of their officers came to treat with David unarmed.

"I am Jozabad," said one. "And this is my companion, also named Jozabad."

Uriah whispered to me. "The mothers een you country surely are creative."

I dug my elbow into his ribs and shushed him.

"We have come to join you," said Jozabad.

David looked as surprised as I felt.

"I am grateful. But Saul needs every man he can get in his fight against the Philistines. I would fight at his side myself if he would permit me."

"The king has gone mad," said the second Jozabad. "The demon vexing him grows stronger every day. We have even heard rumors that he is consorting with witches."

There was a stir in our ranks at that. King Saul had made witchcraft a capital offense. It was unthinkable that he would have stooped so low. Then I remembered the crone in the alley at Gath.

"I will not fight for a devil worshipper. I would stand beside a man who worships the God of my fathers."

There were shouts of agreement from the men behind him.

"If you will not fight for Saul," said David. "Fight for Israel. Fight for your people."

"*You* are the hope of our people," said Jozabad. "The spirit of God has laid this on my heart, David. Do not turn us away."

David looked to his lieutenants. They were nodding. He smiled.

"We are staying in Ziklag. The city is ours, and now yours. Welcome to our company, my friends."

We and the men of Manasseh cheered. The Jozabads' milky white teeth flashed in the dark as they embraced David in turn.

"Ziklag," said the second Jozabad. "Would there be room for our wives and families there?"

"Room to spare," said David. "Many of my men have moved their families there. They are welcome."

"We will meet you in two weeks," said Jozabad number one. "God bless you."

"May He lift up your head," said David.

The three of them struck hands, and the army of Manasseh marched away. David turned to find a worried look on Adino's face.

"Why do you worry, Adino?" he said. "This is a blessing to us. The men of Manasseh will make us stronger than ever."

If I had any chance of getting a good night's sleep, Adino ruined it by what he said next.

"If the men of Manasseh found us," he said. "Who else knows where we are?"

We set out early the next morning. We marched at a quickened pace, sensing something was wrong. Still it took days to reach the city. Our conversations were few and brief when we made camp for the night. Something in our hearts told us we must reach Ziklag as soon as possible.

Before we reached the city, I heard Benaiah gasp. I followed his gaze and saw the smoke laying heavily in the trees the way it will on a cloudy, humid day. It might have passed for a fog but for the smell of wood ash in our noses. David's wives and the maidens had been left behind with our wounded when we left. No order was needed to compel us to break into a run.

We dropped our packs, running only with our weapons. Asahel darted to the city like lightning and ran from house to house. When we made it to the gate, he was already standing there. His skin was smeared black from having run into the burning buildings.

"They're not here," he said, a puff of smoke escaping from his mouth as he spoke. "Everyone's gone!"

12

Whoever it was had taken all of our plunder, but we cared little for that. Our families and friends were taken captive. Some of the wounded soldiers were missing arms or legs, helpless to defend themselves and worthless as slaves. What would happen to them? I thought of Abigail, who had become a second mother to us, and yes, the teasing girls she had brought with her.

Ahinoam had also become a fixture in our lives. One of the men had even remembered that she had come from Jezreel, and picked a bouquet of the local flowers for her while we were camped by the fountain to keep her from getting homesick. Now we wondered if they were alive or dead.

David tarried long enough to enquire of Yahweh via Abiathar and almost started a mutiny among the men with wives and children. I could see that he was beside himself with worry just like the rest of us, but the men were talking murder.

"Stone him!" shouted one. "This is all David's

fault! Bash his brains out!"

My spear point at his throat shut him up.

"Choose your last words carefully," I said.

Joab stood beside me with his hand lightly resting on the hilt of that wicked sickle sword. The man gulped, and a small trickle of blood ran down his neck. There was no more talk of mutiny.

Abiathar was wearing his priestly ephod.

"Go," he said. "If you pursue, you will overtake them and recover everyone."

David looked so encouraged that I did not want to point out that he had not said we would recover them *alive.* We raced south like wildfire. We wore no armor to slow us down and did not stop to rest. The fastest of us got to the Besor River first and plunged in, swimming with our weapons in our hands.

We bounced on the balls of our feet as the others swam over. About two hundred were too exhausted to continue. Among them was the pile of dung who had wanted to stone David.

"You accuse David of endangering your family," I shouted. "But you can't even keep up with him on the rescue?"

I struck him on the jaw, and he fell. I had no time to look back at him, or even think of him again. The rest of the men were already resuming the chase. I found myself toward the front of the pack again, but well behind Asahel and Benaiah.

Asahel would race ahead, turn, and run backward,

facing us while we caught up. As he was doing so, I saw him stumble and fall. I thought he had simply tripped over a divot in the earth or some brush. But when I caught up, I saw he had tripped over a young man.

The boy was obviously foreign, a slave, and was lying unconscious even after Asahel had fallen over him. The boy's head had been shaved clean by a razor, but not recently; there was a few days stubble upon it. He was girded with a linen kilt but wore nothing else.

We gathered around him, and someone put a skin of water to his lips. He woke up choking and greedily emptied the skin of water. When he opened his eyes, his irises looked as black as his pupils, making his them appear large and expressive. I handed him mine to replace the empty one. He was still too weak to speak.

"Does anyone have any food?" shouted David.

"We have no time to nurse a sick boy," some fool said.

"Did you think he might know where the raiders went?" snapped Joab.

We found a cake of dried figs and some raisins and urged the young man to eat. He ate as if he had not in days, and in a few minutes, he recovered. He spoke in a language that was strange to me, but his tone was grateful.

"The boy is speaking the tongue of the Amalekites," said Adino.

"Can you translate?" asked David.

He nodded.

"Ask him who he belongs to and where he is from."

Adino dutifully rendered the question in the Amalekite tongue.

"He say's he's an Egyptian, a servant to the Amalekites."

Adino switched to the Egyptian language and asked the boy about what he had seen. We learned the Amalekites were raiding the Cherethites when they decided to invade Israel. They pillaged towns belonging to the tribes of Caleb and Judah right up to the Salt Sea. They were on their way home when they spied Ziklag. It was the easiest of all, the ripest and lowest-hanging fruit. When the boy took sick three days ago, his master left him for dead.

"Can he show us which way they went?" asked David.

After Adino translated David's question, the boy spoke back in his tongue, trembling in fear or anger, perhaps both.

"If you swear to God you won't kill him, he'll take us right to them."

The boy led us near the enemy's hideout. When we were about a mile away, David took a dozen of us to gather reconnaissance. From a copse of trees we spied the Amalekites celebrating their success. Our cows were roasting on their spits. Skins of our wine were being drained down their gullets. They were chanting and singing and laughing in their harsh tongue. The Egyptian watched his former masters with wide eyes and crouched lower.

Joab pointed. I followed his finger with my gaze. There was Abigail, serving wine to the Amalekite raiders. Her dress was torn, and there was a livid welt around her eye. I looked at David. His eyes burned with anger. His body squirmed restlessly, as if he could barely restrain himself.

We crept away and gathered our men together. They were all on their feet waiting for us. David pointed with his spear in the direction of the Amalekites.

"Let's go," he said.

We ran silently at first. When the enemy came in sight I raised my spear and shouted my battlecry.

"Vengeance!"

The men took up the call, and we rolled in like a sandstorm. The Amalekites were startled, but slow and stupid with drink. We cut many down before they could find a weapon, before they could stand, before they could *think.* The camp was in utter confusion. Some of the better fighters soberly formed ranks to make a hasty stand. We gave them the warrior's death they had earned.

I fought in a rage. The point of my spear rent hearts in two, tore apertures for guts to escape through, and made bloody ruins of men's faces. A man dropped to his knees and raised his hands in supplication. I rammed my spear down his throat and twisted as I pulled out. A black fountain of blood and bile spilled from his mouth.

Another turned to run away from me, and I shoved my spear into his back. He fell on his face. As I strode past, I wrenched my spear free, ignoring his scream.

I heard the stampeding of feet as hundreds fled on camels. I hurled my spear into the back of an Amalekite, and he toppled from his saddle devoid of life. Asahel raced after them in a blur.

He gained on one of the beasts and leaped, grabbed the man by the collar, and yanked him from his seat and onto his back, raising a small cloud of dust. The supine man cowered with his hand in front of his face. It did no good, Asahel thrust his sword in his chest.

Four hundred escaped on camelback, but over a thousand lay dead at our feet. Amid the apocalyptic sea of carnage, men were relieved to find their women and children. David was embracing Abigail. Friends were enjoying tearful reunions with their mates. They had all been spared.

Unbelievably, they were all alive.

We marched home richer than ever, the plunder of the Amalekites heaped on carts. Even the men who had stayed at the Besor got a share, over the protest of more than a few. We left the stinking carcasses of the Amalekites for the birds and jackals.

David divided up the newly acquired spoil and sent it to the chieftains of the tribes of Israel. Some of it belonged to them anyway. Besides, if they were to learn of our presence in Ziklag, we should take the opportunity to win their favor. With the treasures, David sent a message: "Behold a present for you from the spoil of the enemies of the Lord."

When the army of Manasseh arrived and heard the tale, they were beside themselves with envy and asked when they would get a chance to have at the Amalekites for themselves. David answered that first they must help us rebuild the burned quarters of our city. This they did without complaint. When the repairs were done, our home was as good as new, better even, thanks to our newfound riches heaped upon the spoil we had taken before.

As our force had grown, David took the opportunity to promote his leaders. The Three, Adino, Shammah, and Eleazar were made captains.

David also made overtures to Cherethites, kin to the Philistines to whom we were employed. He supposed they might not be averse to making league with us against their common enemy, the Amalekites, who raided their towns, especially after we had just dealt them such a decisive blow.

The Cherethites fought for Achish for years, but they would fight for anyone with enough coin. David charmed them as he charmed us all. The fierce Cherethites liked David's brash mode of warfare, and I think they would have fought for us for free, or even paid for the privilege.

David made Benaiah the captain of our Cherethite mercenary division, a promotion which pleased us all. We all knew his ambitions, indeed we all thirsted for glory. But our ambitions did not make us competitive to the point of envy. When one was promoted, we all celebrated.

Best of all, we would not have to skulk in hiding to wage our secret war. That meant no more purging the inhabitants of the cities we attacked. No more screaming women on the point of my spear. Let Saul hear of our deeds. We knew the whole country was in our favor now.

Ziklag began to resemble the cities in Israel. The newly constructed houses had a distinctly Hebrew touch, and in the streets my native language was spoken by thousands of men, women, and children. Abiathar made a synagogue for us to sacrifice, pray, and study Moses' Holy Law, although as bastards Joab and I were forbidden to worship with the congregation.

One day Ittai came to pay us his routine visit. He gaped at all the new construction, and even more at the number of people inside the gates. We surrounded him immediately but did not draw our weapons.

"Why are there so many people?" he asked.

"We received reinforcements," said Benaiah.

"They aren't Philistines," he said.

"No."

Joab spoke without humor. "We've got a problem Ittai. We can't let you tell Achish what you've seen."

It was a problem. I liked Ittai, we all did. He was one Philistine I did not want to kill. But Joab was right, he could not return to Gath.

Ittai looked thoughtful. He knew his life depended on his answer. He smiled.

"I suppose there's nothing left but for me to join you."

Joab smiled back. "I was hoping you'd say that."

"What will we tell Achish?" I asked.

Ittai shrugged. "Let him think I fell into some mischief on the road. I wouldn't be the first messenger that hasn't returned."

"Won't your family miss you?" asked Asahel.

Ittai shook his head. "Never had one. There's nothing for me in Gath."

Joab and I nodded. We could understand that.

"Who knows," he said. "Maybe I can even teach you sheep-humping, donkey-faced farm boys how to fight."

Joab dropped to a crouch. "We can have a lesson now, you pig-eating, uncircumcised heathen."

We laughed and cheered as the two clenched each other and went down right there in the road. Someone went to inform the commanders of Ittai's defection. We knew he would be accepted on our recommendation.

We began to send out part of our force while the main body remained to protect the city. We would not be caught unaware again. At that time we, the Cherethites, and the soldiers of Manasseh remained in each of our original commands; we did not restructure the units. Sometimes our men deployed, sometimes theirs did, and more often at first, we sent a mixed force of those who had been with us since Adullum and the newcomers.

The purpose of this was to show the men of Manasseh how it was done, but also to build camaraderie between the groups. We knew from first hand experience that nothing brings strangers from different backgrounds together faster than shedding blood on the battlefield together.

My brothers and I had more leisure time than ever, and we hated it. I volunteered to march out with groups from Manasseh, and of course my brothers and friends, now including Ittai, came with me. We took the place of men with families, who were all too happy to let us go for them and spend time at home.

Joab, Benaiah, Uriah, and I were often given the position of brevet lieutenant on these forays. Our skill and experience were respected, a concept I was still getting used to. Zelek was not yet ready to lead, and Ittai was new. As for Asahel, he was a phenomenal fighter, but he lacked the circumspection to lead much more than a squad.

In return, we gave our share of the loot to the men who stayed home. We did not need it; we were rich from the booty of dozens of previous raids. Our small, private war transformed into a major military operation. We employed smiths, cobblers, tailors, and cooks.

While life was exciting, it took on a comforting rhythm.

"The game is up. Saul has found us," Asahel said as he dashed breathlessly into my room.

I shot to my feet in alarm. I was drinking wine and nearly spilled it jumping from my couch.

"Are you sure?"

He nodded. "There are thousands of men at the gate. Benjamites by the looks of them."

My heart sank like a millstone. The Benjamites were King Saul's own tribe. They must have rallied around their kinsman and come to stop us from usurping his throne, though that was the last thing on David's mind. I girded my armor on and hefted my spear.

We stood upon the wall and looked out at the host that came up against us. There were the Benjamites just as Asahel said, but there were also men of Judah and Gad. You could tell their tribes by their clothes, but also each tribe had their own weapons unique to their style of fighting.

The Judaeans, men of our tribe, carried swords, shields, and spears as we did. The men of Gad carried short swords paired with small bucklers which fit their swift method of fighting. The Benjamites carried javelins, bows, and great war slings capable of hurling hand polished stones as far as an archer could shoot an arrow. These concerned me the most.

A captain from each tribe walked out apart from the

armies to hold a parley. David, Adino, Eleazar, and Shammah, walked out the gate to meet them. I strained my ears to hear them but could not make out a word at that distance, even though Ziklag had gone deathly silent. Every man among us was straining to hear as I was. Conversely the men arrayed outside the gates were chatting nonchalantly.

"They don't look very worried," said Asahel.

"Why should they be?" said Zelek. "They outnumber us at least three-to-one."

"Maybe they no come to fight," said Uriah. "Maybe we geeve them bribe and they forget they find us."

It was a hopeful thought, but it did not seem likely.

"If they think we'll die easily, they'll be disappointed," said Joab. "I'll take twenty with me or more to *Sheol* before I go down."

"Well, it's been fun," said Benaiah. "I can't think of anyone else I'd rather make my last stand with."

He and Joab clapped each other on the shoulders. I agreed. He, Uriah, Zelek, and even Ittai had become brothers to me as much as Asahel and Joab were. Still, I hoped it would not come to that.

David struck hands with each of the captains and walked back to the gate.

"What does that mean?" asked Ittai. "Are we going to fight?"

"Maybe he surrendered, and we'll be taken as prisoners," suggested Benaiah.

Joab hissed. "I'd rather die."

David, Shammah, Eleazar, and Adino were smiling when they came through the gate. David looked up at his soldiers standing on the walls, looks of anxiety and bewilderment on our faces.

"Don't worry," he shouted. "They haven't come to fight."

I exchanged a puzzled look with my comrades.

"They have come to join us."

13

David now possessed an army equal to that of the Philistines or Saul. Our soldiers numbered over thirty thousand, and more joined us day by day. Ziklag's population swelled to over seventy thousand. David's stature was equal to any king in the land, though he allowed none to call him king while yet Saul lived. I looked for Jonathan to join us, but the prince remained loyal to his father even as his friendship with David remained firm and true. How he found footing to walk that fine line is a mystery to me, but Jonathan simply did not know the meaning of treachery.

It was good that our army had grown. The Amalekites, Geshurites, and Gezrites had formed an alliance. Tired of falling prey to our raids, the heathen bands joined forces. They were intent on wiping out our army. Though our identity was no longer a mystery to them, they had yet to learn of our whereabouts. David decided to make good use of our newfound strength and deliver a decisive blow to the alliance that would allow our southern tribes to dwell in peace for generations.

Scouting parties were sent into the wilderness of Paran. For two months we hunted them over mountains, forests, and deserts. The skirmishers of Gad and the slingers of Benjamin made excellent scouts. The Gadites were as light of foot as gazelles, and only Asahel and Benaiah could accompany them without slowing them down.

I loved to spar with the Gadites. With their short swords and bucklers they closed in, making it difficult to use a spear against them. The Benjamite archers were wonderful to behold on the practice range, but the slingers outshone and outshot them by far. My brothers and I tested our skill against theirs, but we were no match for them. We had used our slings as shepherds to hunt and kill the predators that stalked our flocks, but they had trained as warriors to use their slings against men. Arrows pierce, but the polished stones of the Benjamite war slings *crush.*

Around that time Asahel received ill news. Shua, his father, had died. He had taken ill, and there was nothing the physicians could do to restore his health. I cannot say that I grieved for him. He never showed any affection for Joab or me. But it was hard for me to see Asahel in pain. He had always been the most carefree of the three of us, but now a cloud passed over him.

And of course, I grieved for my mother. It was my responsibility as the eldest son to take care of her now that she was bereft of her husband, so I wrote a letter to ask what her wishes were. She had left Moab to stay at our ancestral home in Bethlehem with the uncles that were too old to go to war.

Her letter in response what not what I expected. After hearing of the raid on Ziklag, she felt safer in Bethlehem. Besides, she had been homesick when she was in Moab. I sent gold to Uncle Eliab to keep her comfortable. Although I missed her terribly, I was grateful to be able to concentrate on finding and destroying the enemy alliance.

Multiple parties scoured the wilderness until at last our quarry was located. They were gathered almost by the Red Sea near Midian, over fifty thousand strong. Our army would have to march deep into the enemy's territory. David's plan was to tempt the enemy into giving chase to a small company of five hundred and lure them into an ambush set by the remainder of our force. One thousand would be left to defend Ziklag. David would lead the ambush and entrusted the brigade of five hundred to his newest captain.

Joab.

The day we marched out men were kissing wives and children and embracing those friends who would stay behind. We expected many to return, but some would not.

Ittai was offered a place on the wall in relative safety, but he refused. He, Uriah, Zelek, Benaiah, Asahel, and I insisted that we would fight and, if necessary, die by my brother's side.

David stood on the wall by the gate, so as to be heard by all of us. A hush fell over the thousands of men in marching formation and the women and children who had come to see them off. A baby cried, heedless of the solemnity of the moment. But for that, the only sounds were the wind and the ringing of David's voice.

"Long have the Amalekites persecuted our people. They have burned our farms, raped our women, and enslaved our children. When Moses led us to this land, it was the sons of Esau who first attacked us at Rephidim. The battle was sore, but Moses lifted his hands over our fathers, assisted by Aaron and Hur, and they prevailed by the power of Yahweh!"

There was a shout and David had to raise his hands for silence.

"Saul, our king, God grant him long life, smote them when they attacked my people in Judah. Some of you were there and remember chasing them from Havilah to Shur. I was still tending my father's sheep when Samuel cut their king Agag in pieces and broke the back of that nation."

The older warriors grinned at each other, and I wished I could have been there with them. One old warrior stripped his sleeve and was showing his scars to his mate, talking under his breath about that battle.

"Moses and Joshua are now dead, and our great king is occupied with war against the Philistines in the North. It falls to us to finish that mighty work they began. And not just the Amalekites, but the Geshurites and Gezrites that have plagued our people must also be destroyed. Moses was old when first our nations met in battle, and I am yet young. All my strength will I spend, even my life is forfeit if that's what it takes for us to win the victory."

David held up both hands.

"But should my strength fail and my arms grow weary, will you lift them up as Aaron and Hur did for Moses? Will you help me win this battle?"

A great cry rose from thousands of throats. We would have fought the enemy with naught but our fingernails and teeth at that moment.

"Then march with me! And together we will make our nation sure. For Israel!"

Again we shouted until our voices were hoarse. We marched through the gates at a pace that was nearly a sprint, so eager were we to get our hands on the enemy. The women sang and the maidens danced and played timbrels. I felt something crush beneath my shoe and saw that palm leaves and flowers were strewn in our path. The men of the garrison looked from the walls, burning with envy that they were not coming with us. I would not have traded places with them for all the gold in Egypt.

On we marched until Ziklag was out of sight. When we could no longer hear the voices of the women singing, David began to sing a psalm. His voice rang out sweet and powerful. I swear to you that the very birds hushed to hear his voice, but we were caught up and could not refrain from joining in.

A reverent silence followed the psalm, so that the sound of men's tramping feet echoed through the wood. Joab nudged me and pointed at Ittai. It was the first he had ever heard one of our psalms, and Joab asked him what he thought of it. Ittai pursed his lips, as if choosing his words carefully.

"I liked the parts about your God's mercy and him being a refuge and destroying our enemies. But your God is fearful! If I fall in battle I should be afraid to meet him."

"You find our God cruel?" asked Joab.

Ittai shook his head. "Not cruel exactly, only just. I think your God will scrupulously mete out what every man deserves. That's what I'm afraid of."

Joab and I had to smile at his candor.

I confessed, "So am I."

We marched in the day and camped at night, resting long enough for every man to have a good night's sleep, even if he had watch duty. It would not do to have the men weary on the day of battle. The men wanted to push on when we gave the order to pitch camp.

They were up before the sun, their tents packed and breakfast gulped down, bouncing up and down like children in their eagerness to set off. This was exactly what David wanted. He would rather the men go slowly and have a surplus of energy than have their spirits worn down with fatigue before they set eyes on the enemy.

Finally we settled a good two miles from where we knew the horde to be camped. Asahel took some of the Gadite scouts who discovered the camp to make sure it had not moved. They discovered the coalition had increased in size to now over sixty thousand, twice our number. We found a wide crest of land shaped like the letter *bet,* forming a bowl with sides that sloped high enough to conceal our numbers. It would be a long, mad dash to lure them there.

"Asahel," said Joab. "Is there a group of them that is isolated? A place where one might think their numbers were smaller than they are?"

Asahel scratched his neck and looked thoughtfully into the treetops.

"They're camped in a valley. Some of the Geshurites are camped at the mouth. If someone approached alongside the western ridge, he might think there were only a few hundred there."

Joab rubbed his hands together.

"Then we'll attack from that side. If we attack that large of a force with the five hundred of us, they'll be convinced it's a trick. Better they think we were too stupid to see how many there were before we attacked."

"When the truth ees we are far more stupeed," said Uriah. "Attacking them when we know full well there are seexty thousand!"

We laughed, but Uriah had a point. Our mission was

hardly better than suicide. We knew there was a good chance that most of us would die. But death was less a concern than failure. With David leading us, we did not believe we could fail.

"Remember," said Joab. "The archers will have to wait until all the enemy have arrived to reveal their position, or they'll be outflanked. We have to hold them in that bowl until the moment is right."

Joab picked Gadites to compose half our force, swift and lethal as arrows. They wore their hair longer than the rest of us, not as women do, but in shaggy manes. Add to this their beards and long jaws, and when the light of battle came to their eyes and they snarled in battle rage, they took on the countenances of lions. The other half were the swiftest men from Judah and Manasseh, whom I would command.

We left in the middle of the night and marched slowly, conserving our strength, a long circuitous route that took us to a path parallel to the ridge. We slowed as soon as we spotted the camp, creeping up silently to preserve the fragile advantage of surprise. It was just as Asahel said. From that angle we could only see two, maybe three hundred men. There was no indication of the vast army hidden behind the spur.

The guards were lax. When we got within twenty yards, Joab began to walk casually. It was improvised, not part of the plan. We followed suit, and the guards took us for their allies.

When Joab approached the first watch fire, he

calmly drew his sword and slashed the Geshurite across the face. His mate watched aghast, mouth hanging open, and did not so much as evade the spear that I shoved into his guts. The Geshurites were so surprised, we killed at least twenty before they defended themselves.

We fought our way into the middle of their camp and were now in view of the pass. In my periphery I could see more men than I thought possible in one place. But there was no time for fear. Again and again I worked my arm as a wave, my spear riding upon its oscillation to punch holes in the flesh of the men before me.

The Gadites were a horror, darting swiftly from foe-to-foe as rats from hole-to-hole, nearly too fast to follow with the eye. Few had time to swing their weapons at them. They would hit a man on his blind side, deal a mortal wound, and vanish like smoke. Those swift enough to swing a weapon met only the sturdy bucklers in their left hand. They would block and strike simultaneously, leaving no chance for their enemy to counter.

The Geshurites' comrades realized what had happened and charged to reinforce them. I found myself fighting not a Geshurite, but sinking my spear into the groin of an Amalekite. We polished off the remaining Geshurites, and I commanded my soldiers to close ranks and plug up the pass. The spears of the second rank chewed at the enemy's ragged front. The enemy must have thought we had lost our minds. We pushed them away with our spears and shields for a time, but quickly found our feet churning the clay for purchase as we were pushed back by the sheer weight of the bodies the enemy threw at us.

"Now, men," screamed Joab. "Retreat!"

His eyes blazed white out of the grime on his face. "Run for your very lives!"

He hoped some of the enemy spoke Hebrew and would sense our panic, which was only half faked. Asahel and the Gadites sprinted for the bowl while the rest of us tried to keep up. My arms and legs were pumping furiously, my heart throbbing in time with them. Never had I run that fast before. I knew this was a race for my life.

Two miles does not sound far, but it is when you are sprinting. I set a pace that I thought I could maintain, but found my legs aching. My feet and knees felt like they would break from the strain. Even in my back the muscles felt like they were going to snap. I had run farther before, but never that fast. I felt like I had been running a long time–too long. Where was the bowl? Had we gone the wrong way?

There! When it came in view, it broke my heart. It looked to be *another* two miles away. I dimly realized this was my mind playing tricks on me. Thoughts invaded my mind such as, *I have a good enough lead. Surely it won't hurt to stop for a* little *while.* I battled them as fiercely as I would any combatant; they would kill me just as surely if I gave in to them.

At last I stumbled into the bowl as the red sun began to rise on the burnt orange horizon. The Gadites panted like dogs from the exertion, and I was worse. I gulped the air like a man dying of thirst swallows water, and still I felt like I was suffocating. The muscles adjacent to my shins felt like they had after my first march with Benaiah. All of us were sweating like sponges being wrung out. Only pride kept me from doubling over; I stood erect, even though I desperately wanted to collapse.

I looked at Asahel. His breathing was calm and even. There was barely a trace of sweat on his brow. How I hated him at that moment!

Fortunately the enemy was in worse shape than I was and were yet three hundred yards behind us, giving us a moment to catch our breath. One of them was farther ahead of the others, ecstatic with the thrill of the chase. He was heedless of his peril as he sprinted toward us alone. Joab decapitated him with an effortless, shoulder-level stroke, and for a moment, it looked like he was still running headless, carried by the momentum of his final dash.

Joab raised his bloody sword toward the charging horde.

"Hold them here men. For Israel," he cried. "Vengeance for Israel!"

The men of Judah and I stood on one side and Benaiah and the men of Manasseh on the other. Our shields funneled the mob into the Gadites in the center, where the enemy was pulverized. The first ranks of the enemy hit our shields, and pushed by the charging men behind them, slid irresistibly toward the churning swords of the Gadites, Zelek, Ittai, Uriah, and most fearsome of all, Joab. In the bottleneck we had created, they had no space to swing a weapon, but we gave each other plenty of room to use our own.

Men were so tightly packed together, our men's swords would kill two or three with each swing. Just as often they had to cut downward to deal with enemy that had tripped over their comrades' corpses. Those of us in the wings stabbed into the crowd with our spears from behind our shields. We did not kill as many as the center ranks in that stage, but we kept them too busy to notice they were being pushed to their doom like cattle stampeding off of a cliff.

The main body of the enemy caught up with the rest. From where I stood I could not tell if all sixty thousand had shown up to deal with the five hundred of us, but I could not see the end of their ranks. They stretched out like an ocean of murder. I ordered the wings to fall back to a defensive position, and we circled behind our shields the way a small company does to make their last stand.

Maybe this would be ours.

The enemy flooded into the bowl and quickly surrounded us. Their shields crashed into ours with a sound like a thousand cymbals from Hell. The forward ranks pushed like oxen straining to plow a rocky, fallow field. We attacked from within the wall of brass, and the enemy was mowed down like dry wheat. The first rank stepped into the void, and our circle widened.

"Don't get too spread out!" cautioned Joab.

The swords and spears fell heavier on our shields, a maniacal drumming that our spears could not completely quiet. No matter how many we killed, more took their place. I scanned the ridges around us quickly but saw no sign of our army. Had they forsaken us? Had they seen the horde's numbers and lost heart? I could not believe it, only where *were* they? Why had they not yet come to our aid?

A mace dashed open the skull of one of my first-rankers, scattering gobs of brain. It was wielded by a stout, bare chested Gezrite champion covered with knotted muscles. The stone head of the mace had been polished until it gleamed like metal. Without even cocking it back, he swung a backhanded blow at another. Our defense cracked like an egg, and the enemy poured through the breach in the formation. I put my spear through the Gezrite's heart and tried to fight them back, but it was too late.

The time for group tactics had passed, and the battle devolved into several battles in miniature. We fought three or four together. We spread out into the bowl, and each carved out a patch of dirt for us to die upon with as many of the enemy as we could take with us.

I stayed with Asahel, fearing that in his recklessness

he would sell his life cheap. We fought, just we two, with our spears keeping the enemy in a wide circle around us. I would swing to check the advance of the group, then strike, quick as an adder into the closest man. Behind me I heard my little brother laughing without a care.

Uriah, Benaiah, and Joab claimed another area and laid heaps of the enemy upon the grass. I could not see Zelek or Ittai. One of our Gadites stood alone, completely cut off from us. He spun and darted among the enemy for several minutes, cutting deep gashes in the enemy and then dodging away. I called for him to fight toward us that we might stand together, but I do not know if he heard me.

A sword slashed his hamstring, and he went down. I could not see what blow finally claimed him. The enemy surrounded him and viciously hacked away at his body as he screamed out in pain and defiance. Here and there our men began to fall to the numbers of the Amalekites, Gezrites, and Geshurites. I was beginning to think that none of us would make it out of that bowl alive.

That is when I heard his voice.

"We've got them now, men!"

David!

"We must come to their aid. For Israel! And for your brothers down there dying!"

That was when I saw him standing on the ridge, addressing a host of my brethren at his back. My heart lifted at the sight of the gleam of their bronze. David stretched his gargantuan sword one-handed toward the fray.

"Attack!"

14

The slingers and archers attacked first. Into the press of the enemy they fired, close enough to take some of the pressure off of us, but not so close as to put us in danger of being hit. Together arrows and slung shot are devastating. The arrows whisper like a chorus of winds, but the stones are silent. The arrows pierced the enemy, and the stones crushed him.

I saw a man who had taken arrows in his legs and shoulder keep fighting until a shot punched into his ear and he dropped like a stone himself. Conversely another was buffeted by a half-dozen stones, and yet he kept fighting until an arrow sank into his chest.

We were still outnumbered where we stood, but the weight of their numbers was lightened as the barrage thinned their ranks. We took courage and began to drive them back again. Shammah and Eleazar had shut the back door on them, trapping them in the bowl.

Joab shouted, "Reform! Reform!"

We fought our way back toward each other. There

were Zelek and Ittai. I breathed a sigh of relief, even as my spear connected with the face of a Geshurite with a thrust that unhinged his jaw.

Shields had been laid in the bowl ahead of time for the Gadites and any man who lost his, and there were many of us who had. Several of our men had picked up shields from the enemy dead on the run. We had prepared a nasty surprise for our foe, and now was the time to use it.

"Now!" barked Joab.

We formed a circle, the tallest men in the center and shortest outward. We linked our shields to create a dome of bronze around us.

"Now!" echoed David.

Our slingers and archers fired all around our position. The stones hit first, and through the gaps between the shields I could see them work their carnage.

One man was struck in the knee and went down, only to be pelted in the face. Another sprinted straight toward us with a pike when he was arrested by a shot to the face. His head was stopped, but his legs flew up. The force of the blow paired with the momentum of his charge slung the man in a graceful backflip, in which he landed belly down. Many were brained by the missiles, but some suffered only broken arms, legs, ribs, or collarbones.

Then the arrows landed.

The Benjamites had painted the shafts and

fletchings so they could find their own arrows. They were competing, keeping score, every man firing furiously to claim more kills than than his mate. I saw arrows pierce throats, puncture skulls, burst eyeballs, and pass clean through limbs and torsos.

Have you ever heard a heavy rain pound the roof in waves? The sound throbs louder, then softer, then louder again. That was the sound, only these raindrops had sharp bronze tips, and the hail stones crushed bones. That flood of homicide poured into the bowl for several minutes. Very few hit our shields, as they were not aiming at us and did not have far to shoot.

I have seen the archers and slingers fire on command, load slings or nock arrows, then at the command, loose their missiles as one. Normally they fire precisely in unison, but not that day. After the initial command, no orders were called. The Benjamites simply fired cartloads of stones and arrows without ceasing, one after the other, each trying to outdo the rest in firing the most.

Finally the barrage stopped, and we lowered our shields. I cannot say how many hundreds–perhaps thousands lay dead at our feet. From where we stood, it looked like half the horde was gone. There were none who were not dead or dying near us, and we were obliged to cross acres of corpses to join the fight.

"Don't run!" commanded Joab. "Your feet will slip on the blood! Form ranks!"

Joab was right. Even marching in formation, our

feet slipped on gore- and excrement-covered bodies and limbs. When we came across one that was still moving, we sent him off with a downward thrust and kept marching. The rest of the army descended from the flanks, even the Benjamites who expended all of their ammunition. We could see them slugging it out a few score yards away. It was surreal, approaching it so slowly.

Calmly we marched into Hell.

David's mammoth sword was insatiable. The Hebrew soldiers at his side were notionally there for his protection, but they had little to worry about. The enemy came at him ten, twenty, sometimes thirty at a time. It did not matter. No one could touch him. They fell before his sword like summer wheat before the reapers. Had fire and brimstone fallen to consume them, they could not have been more terrified. The sweet voice that had entranced us with its singing not a day before now roared with a terrible, inhuman ferocity. Men shrank, then fled from him, often impaling themselves on their own weapons or those of their own men.

One man, an Amalekite giant of at least seven feet, stood his ground with a wicked polearm. His weapon had a fell spear point atop a duck bill blade, and a chisel-like spike protruded from the back. Its thick shaft was plated with bronze langets. The mob cheered for him and edged forward, hoping this monster would be the equal to David. But our host's captain turned their hope to despair.

David raised his sword above his head in a feint. The brute fell for the ruse and raised the shaft above his head, thinking to take the blow on a langet. Quicker than thought, David spun, swinging the sword in a horizontal arc cutting through flesh, bowels, and spine. The giant fell in two pieces to the utter disbelief of both sides. The enemy goggled at their hero's demise and were only brought back to their senses when David mowed down a half dozen more, and their panicked flight resumed.

Ittai wore his fish scale armor and a feather-crested Philistine war bonnet. He showed us the mettle of a Philistine that day. He was slower than the rest of us, but his movements were deliberate and sure. His heavy iron sword dealt such crushing blows to the enemy, I wondered that he even bothered to sharpen it. Over the sounds of battle I could hear the ghastly crash against armor and the crush of bones.

Zelek's alien curses resounded through the bowl. I never saw him display any particular skill; he mastered his enemies through sheer fury. The heat of his obscenities baked the lacquer right off the enemies' shields. Their tongues were similar enough that some of the meaning of his swearing was understood, and their faces grew pale. Zelek seemed to compose this stream of profanity to flow seamlessly with the movements of his sword. He punctuated every thrust with an exclamation and sent them to Hell with his curses ringing in their ears.

Benaiah's spear was shivered in two, and he wielded the upper stump without pausing. It never occurred to him to pick up one of the many weapons left by the slain at his feet. It would only slow him down. He would smash into an enemy's shield with his own, sling it upward, and simultaneously shove his shortened spear upward into his guts. A yank downward produced an inimitable sound as the bowels, cut free from their knotted confines, would spill onto the earth in hideous, steaming piles.

Uriah made good use of that fantastic steel sword of his. Lighter and stronger than any weapon on the field, its fullers made a whistling sound before it bit through the armor of the foe. I saw a spear lick at his face, but he slid to his knees and blocked upward with his shield, thrusting mightily into the chest of his attacker.

Another seeing him down and thinking him at a disadvantage, swung downward with an axe. Uriah rolled backward onto his feet, dodging the axe by a whisker. The enemy was unable to bring it to bear before Uriah's sword cleaved his windpipe.

I saw a Benjamite slinger take the field with nothing more than his sling. It was loaded with a fist-sized shot, but he used it like a club. Helmets were crushed and shields were splintered by this weapon. He kept it constantly in motion, whirling it around him in wide circles. When the foe shied away from him, he loosed the stone nearly point blank, turning a man's face into a bloody crater. Then he would simply find another spent shot upon the field.

Once he mistook a severed head for a stone in the heat of the moment. It ineffectively splattered against the chest of an Amalekite. The Amalekite was horrified and ran off, but the slinger was disgusted, not at the macabre of the head, but its lack of utility. He had expected the breastbone to shatter and was disappointed. He flung the head into the enemy ranks and found another stone. I can only imagine the reaction among the enemy when that head landed.

Asahel leapt across the battlefield as a deer skips through tall grass. His spear was an extension of his graceful self. I saw him vault high into the air, seeming on the verge of flying. In mid-air he twisted back and thrust his spear into the chest of an Amalekite running up behind him. He had lost his helmet in the fray, revealing the white streak in his hair.

In the ugly carnage of the battleground, he was beautiful. He had given up on trying to grow a beard, and his clean-shaven, leonine jaw made him look more youthful than other men his age. He did not sneer or grimace as we did in battle, but his face was serene, smiling. Instead of shouting, he laughed on the battlefield as if it was great sport. Again he soared nearly into the clouds, his spear held in a two handed grip, point downwards, and drove it through two men at once, nailing them to the earth. Not bothering to free his spear, he bent, took another, and resumed the dance.

Do not think I stood spectating the whole battle, for I had plenty to keep me busy. I must have been exhausted to the point of delirium, but I do not remember feeling it. The enemy seemed to slow down, every thrust or swing seemed to take half a minute to reach me.

What in practice had taken deliberate planning, I now performed without conscious thought. I observed the attack, countered, and killed before I realized it. A Geshurite lunged toward me from behind. I do not know how I knew he was there; I did not see him. No time to swing my spear, I thrust backward with the butt of my weapon. It caught him under the chin, crushing his windpipe and knocking him off his feet.

My spear developed a mind of its own. It was a thing possessed, and shot forward of its own initiative. *Sshk! Sshk! Sshk! Sshk!* It fell and again, *Sshk! Skrrrissshh!* Half a dozen were dead before the first could fall to the ground. A man came at me huddled behind his shield, only his eyes were showing through the bronze, so I stabbed through his eye and felt my spear split the back of his skull and scrape across the back of his helmet.

The man next to him turned to flee, shouldering his shield so as not to expose his back. I stabbed him in the calf and he went down. I flipped him onto his back to finish him off, and he crabbed backward on his hands and good leg. I stepped on his stomach to hold him still, plunged my spear through his armored chest, and twisted.

For all this, my valor could not outshine Joab. His sickle sword claimed nearly as many of the foe as David's. Into the thick of the enemy he spun, like a ghoulish top removing limbs and heads in his path. I saw them press in upon him only to be knocked back by the concussion of his shield. Heaps of slain he left in his wake. But it seemed he had found the valor of the horde. They refused to be cowed but surged toward him again and again to no avail.

Finally, the enemy had their chance. Joab's sword sliced off the burly arm of an Amalekite. Rather than being unmanned by the amputation, the man howled with rage and swung his shield at Joab's blind side. The bronze rim of the shield cracked the base of Joab's skull, and he crumpled to the blood matted grass. I was too far to stop what would happen next and cried my brothers name. The one-handed Amalekite raise his shield to deliver a fatal blow to my unconscious brother.

There was a silver streak of light. A sword flashed as it flew through the air end-over-end. It struck the Amalekite between the shoulder blades like a thunder bolt, and he fell dead.

It was Uriah, who had seen my brother's peril and acted. Now disarmed, he shoved the Gezrite next to him to the ground and sprinted to my brother's aid, without bothering to look again at the Gezrite. Right behind him, Benaiah stabbed the man with his shortened spear and followed. Uriah plowed through the lines shield first like a bull, reached down, and shouldered Joab with one arm. Dropping his spear, Benaiah pulled Uriah's sword from the Amalekite's back, picked Joab's from the ground, and followed Uriah to cover him.

I fought my way toward them. There was no way the two of them could get through alone. But Uriah kept pushing toward our men on the far side, thinking only of defense. Benaiah stabbed and slashed with both swords in every direction. Several times a man would raise his weapon to strike Uriah from behind, only to fall dead at Benaiah's hand.

I killed more men trying to reach my brother than I did in the whole battle. Hundreds of them stood between us, but no thought of breaking off the chase entered my mind. That was my *brother*.

At last they broke through. Our men parted before them, some shoved aside if they were too slow to get out of Uriah's way. By the time I broke through myself, Uriah was already in the hands of physicians.

"Eet's all right, Abeeshai," said Uriah. "He was only knocked out. The Pheeseecian splashed some water on hees face and he woke right up."

Joab was sitting aright on the grass with a dazed look on his face. Tension that I had been unaware of rolled off my shoulders. I told him what I had seen, how our friends had saved his life. He looked up at the Uriah and Benaiah with gratitude.

"I never hoped to have two friends as fine and true as you," he said.

He stood shakily and embraced them in turn.

"How do you feel?" asked Benaiah.

"Not as dizzy as before," he said. "I'm all right."

"Well, let's go," said Uriah. "We're going to meess the fun."

I started to object, but the hand Joab placed on my shoulder was strong.

"Yes," he said. "If Ittai lasts the whole battle and I don't, I'll never hear the end of it."

A relieved laugh echoed through our circle.

"You'll need this," said Benaiah, and he handed him the sickle sword.

Joab took the sword and allowed himself a moment to take in the graceful arc of the weapon, the gleam of the bronze reflecting in his eyes.

"A fine blade," said Benaiah.

"Yes."

Our men had become discouraged seeing one of their champions carried off the field unconscious. At the sight of Joab the light of hope returned to their eyes, and rekindled courage burst from their chests in a deafening battle cry. Joab flourished the blade and stepped back into the theater of battle. The very men we had just battled through saw us coming and quailed. Their fear made our mouths water.

We could smell it.

Joab pointed his sword at them and walked calmly forward. For every step he took, the enemy stepped backward. Annoyed at their cowardice, he charged with us right behind him.

The battle was over, and so commenced the slaughter.

Joab cut the enemy down with three times the ferocity he displayed before. The four of us charged four hundred and were more than a match for them. We had robbed their hearts of courage; they barely fought back in their mad scramble to retreat. But our army had them surrounded. There was no escape.

Asahel saw us from across the field and loped to our side. Ittai and Zelek followed. The seven of us herded the throng like sheep while the other soldiers dealt with the larger group of the army.

At last a group of them found their spines, and we battled like men again. They tried to use their superior numbers, but whenever they tried to flank us, we cut them down.

My spear and shield were black with gore. My whole body was covered in blood. I felt neither hunger nor thirst. Fatigue was forgotten. I did not know if I was hot or cold.

I had one desire at that moment: to destroy every mother's son of them and spill their blood on the earth.

A couple dozen were all that were left. They dropped to their knees and threw their hands up. Joab spit on one and slashed. Both of the man's hands flew off of his wrists. He was still staring at the bloody stumps in disbelief when Joab's sword split his skull.

We finished them off as they groveled, wept, and

tried to wriggle away. Our army was mopping up the last of them. David strolled over to us and laughed to see the destruction caused by only seven men, which was ironic considering he had probably done at least as much single-handedly.

There were cuts all over my arms and a deep gash in my thigh. *When did that happen?* My hands felt raw, and when I looked, my nine fingers were scored and abraded. Two of the fingers on my right hand had been smashed somehow, and were swollen and purple. Still I felt no pain. That would come later.

"You're bleeding," said Asahel, pointing to my head.

I felt and found that my cheek had a gash punctuated by a clip in my ear. I did not remember receiving any of these wounds and shrugged them off.

I felt nothing at first, but then I heard the hoarse battle cry of my comrades.

"Da-VID! Da-VID! Da-VID!"

They were chanting my uncle's name in victory. A blast of exhilaration swept through my chest, and I joined the call.

"Da-VID! Da-VID! Da-VID!"

My brothers and friends were shouting too, pumping their fists in time with the chant. There were tears in Uriah's eyes, and Ittai was grinning from ear to ear. I marveled that Asahel for once looked solemn. The sun was setting behind the six of them, my comrades, my *brothers,* turning them into dark silhouettes bathed in reddish gold. I thought my heart would burst with love for them and joy that they had survived this day.

David raised his hands, and the chanting died down. He looked into every man's eyes with gratitude, and love shone out from him like the noonday sun, which we gave back in equal measure.

"Give thanks to Yahweh, men," he said. "For He has given us VICTORY!"

At that the bowl thundered. And when the thunder died down, it yielded to the pious melody of a psalm.

15

The bowl was carpeted with corpses, mostly Amalekite, Geshurite, and Gezrite, but many Hebrew. We began to extract our dead from the field, searching for missing hands, limbs, and heads that they might be interred whole.

A woman once told me her husband could not go into *Gan Eden,* the paradise, until he found the nose his murderer had cut off in a final act of spite, and that he was doomed to wander the earth until it was found. I hoped this did not apply to my missing finger. At any rate, we did not want our brothers to be missing anything important at the Resurrection of the Dead.

This was when the weariness set in. After a battle you feel wrung out physically and emotionally. To say I felt sluggish is understatement, even my fingers felt heavy. I laid down in the grass, heedless of the pool of blood at my elbow. Just to raise my head seemed a monumental effort. Even in my old age, I know no weariness that great. But move I must, for I needed to bathe, and our army was to camp a few miles away near a little stream. I tied a bandage to my leg and fell in line.

The other men seemed afflicted with the same fatigue. It took hours to walk the short distance. When we arrived, the sky had been dark for hours. We collapsed on the grass. Few had the energy to wash, and I was not one of them. I think I was asleep before I could even shut my eyes.

When I woke, the sun was high in the sky. My brothers and friends had slept heaped together with me. Our bodies were sticky with sweat, dirt, and blood. At last I removed my armor and clothes and waded into the bracing water. It took hours to scrub the gore and grime from my skin. I opened many of my wounds afresh, unable to discern between the dried blood of my enemies and my own scabs.

Worst of all was my beard. It seemed to trap crusts of dirt and gobs of blood, clinging to them as a coin in the claws of a miser. I was glad my helmet had covered the hair on my head. But for a strip of blood-matted hair at the nape of my neck, it had been spared the defilement and only needed to be washed of dirt and sweat.

I knew I needed to eat if I was to regain my strength, but had hardly enough motivation to trudge to the victuals cart. Bread, honey, and figs were being issued. When the first morsel touched my lips, my stomach began to speak. Only then did I realize how hungry I was; I had not eaten in over a day. When I finished my breakfast, I was still sore, but my energy returned.

We stayed by the stream for a week to allow the army to restore its strength and recover all of our dead. I hated the long, dreary march to the camp but now saw the wisdom of the decision. Even miles away, when the wind blew in the right direction, we could smell the decay from the battlefield. Those who went there to recover a fallen brother or mate experienced the full strength of the odor.

When I went to lend a hand myself, I retched on the grass. Not only was the smell overpowering, but the sight of stiff bodies corrupting in the sun, the jackals tearing the flesh off their hands, and birds plucking their eyes and rooting in their abdomens for a morsel, it proved too much for me. I wiped my mouth and stood on weak knees to get back to work.

I realized something seeing those corpses. They were no longer men, no longer human. When you refer to a living person, you say "him" or "her". When we spoke about a corpse, we referred to "it." The body is not the person, and when the person has departed, it leaves a shell. Even the bodies we recovered, even though we called them "him," were no longer men. It was the first time I began to wonder about the *nephesh,* the soul, where it came from, and where it went.

In the valley where the horde camped, the few who had not joined the battle fled, taking little with them.

We found food, silver, wool, ivory, asses, and cattle among other things. We looked like an enormous caravan of merchants as we travelled back to Ziklag.

The Battle of the Bowl increased not only our wealth, but our prestige. My friends and brothers and I had covered ourselves with glory. We all were promoted officially to the rank of captain, and Joab, who was already a captain, received prizes of valor. The feast went on for two days in the great hall, and prizes were given to each hero from the battle, including the Benjamite slinger who had used his sling as a mace. We were surprised to learn his name also happened to be Ittai.

"How did he come by a Philistine name?" wondered Ittai, our friend.

We were stumped. The man was definitely a Jew, and his name was not Hebrew in the least.

Benaiah shrugged. "Maybe his father married a Philistine."

Whatever the mystery of his name, the man fought like a devil.

Great platters of beef were served, as well as all kinds of fowl stuffed with rice or grain, lamb, dates, figs, apricots, almonds, honeyed bread with butter, and olives. Cups of wine were kept full. Music rang in the hall, often performed by David himself. For two days we laughed, bragged, cheered, and took moments to mourn and acclaim our dead. When I retired to sleep, I was surprised to find the sun was coming up. I slept like a bear in winter, and when I returned, the party was still in full swing.

The feast might have lasted a week or more if not for the Amalekite messenger. I was still there, sitting in a place of honor between my brothers, when he was brought into the hall. He carried a sack with him. His clothes were torn and his face was dirty, but he was grinning like the cat which had eaten the nightingale. He fell to the ground and bowed to David as one might a king.

David was annoyed. To him there was one king in Israel.

"Get up," he said. "From where have you come?"

The man's smile slipped, and he stood and brushed at his tunic with his hands.

"I escaped from the camp of Israel."

David leaned forward, eager for news. Saul had been at war for the Philistines for months, his army was engaged up north near Gilboa when last we heard.

"How went the matter? Please tell me."

"The people of Israel have fled from battle, and many are fallen and dead."

His smile crept back across his face, and my skin crawled.

"And Saul and Jonathan, his son, are dead."

A gasp echoed through the room. David stood to his feet.

"How do you know that Saul and Jonathan are dead?"

Grinning at his stupefied audience, the man continued.

"I happened to be passing by Mount Gilboa."

David grunted with disdain. It seemed he was thinking what I had been thinking: the man had probably followed the battle to loot the corpses.

"And then I saw him," he continued. "It was Saul, leaning on his spear. The Philistine chariots and horsemen were on their way to finish him off. He saw me and called me to him. He asked me who I was, and I told him I was an Amalekite. He said to me, 'Wait! Please, kill me. For I am in anguish.'"

The man's smug smile widened.

"So I stood upon him and killed him. I fled, because I knew one of the soldiers would kill me for it. I took his crown and bracelet and brought them for you."

He produced a golden diadem and bracelet from his bag with a look that showed he was expecting to be rewarded handsomely. Adino took it from him and brought it to David. David reseated himself and held the crown in his hand, turning it in the lamplight.

"Then it's true," he murmured.

David began to weep and rent his robe in mourning. As I looked around the room, others were weeping too. Few of us had warm feelings for Saul, but we had still hoped he would lead our nation's army to victory. How many in the room had brethren among Saul's host, perhaps fallen at Gilboa?

Jonathan had been our hero to all of us since we

were children, and his death was a tragedy to the whole nation. But worst of all was seeing our David beside himself with grief.

I thought back to that day in Ziph. It was just as David had said. Saul had fallen in battle, but David's hand had not stained itself with the blood of the *messiah*. To his credit, he did not even take satisfaction in his death.

David composed himself and returned his attention to the Amalekite, who was beginning to look nervous. His news was not being received in the manner he thought it would.

"Where did you say you were from?" David asked.

"I'm the son of a stranger," he said. With a gulp, he added, "An Amalekite."

David laughed bitterly, as if to say he would *have* to be an Amalekite.

"How were you not afraid to stretch out your hand and destroy the anointed one of Yahweh?" he asked.

David commanded one of the soldiers who drew his sword and walked over to him. The man began to back away, but Joab and I grabbed him from behind by the arms.

"He-he *wanted* me to do it," he protested. "I put him out of his misery. I did it for you! *Please!* I thought you would b-"

His babbling was cut short as the sword skewered his chest. He went limp in our arms. Blood oozed from his mouth and nose. We gave his corpse to the guard to get rid of the stinking thing. The guard dragged him out by a leg, to be buried I suppose. We forgot him as soon as he was out of sight.

David often composed when he was emotional. He picked up his harp and began playing softly. Even in his grief–*especially* in his grief he was a master. He began to improvise lyrics to a dirge.

"The beauty of Israel is slain upon thy high place.
How are the mighty fallen!

"Tell it not in Gath, publish it not in the streets of
Ashkelon
lest the daughters of the Philistines rejoice,
lest the daughters of the uncircumcised triumph.

"Ye Mountains of Gilboa, let there be no dew,
neither let there be rain upon you, nor fields of
offerings.
For there the shield of the mighty is vilely cast
away,
the shield of Saul, as though he had not been
anointed with oil.

"From the blood of the slain,
from the fat of the mighty,
the bow of Jonathan turned not back,
and the sword of Saul returned not empty!
* * *

"Saul and Jonathan were lovely and pleasant in their
lives,
and in their death they were not divided.
They were swifter than eagles!
They were stronger than lions!

"Ye daughters of Israel, weep over Saul,
who clothed you in scarlet, with other delights,
who put ornaments of gold upon your apparel.

"How are the mighty fallen in the midst of the battle!
O Jonathan, thou wast slain in thine high places.

"I am distressed for thee, my brother Jonathan.
Very pleasant hast thou been unto me.
Thy love unto me was wonderful,
passing the love of women.

"How are the mighty fallen,
and the weapons of war perished!"

As the song ended, we were crying like children.
David's grief for Jonathan, and yes, even Saul, was
shared by all of us. I looked at Zelek. His face was
stony, but tears were running down his face.

"I thought you would be happy when this day
came," I said.

"So did I."

We left the food on the platters untouched. No one

was in the mood for food anymore. We had just celebrated a great victory but were now in mourning. It was not in David's nature to hold a grudge. He yet remembered Saul for what he had once been, the champion of Israel, our king.

We would learn later that the Amalekite scum had been lying. He had not even killed Saul. Witnesses saw Saul take his own life, falling on his own sword. His squire, following him, fell on his sword in turn. If the fool had told the truth, he might yet be alive. But in his greed, he thought David would reward the one who killed Saul. He rewarded him all right, and exactly how he deserved.

Several of Saul's other sons died that day as well. The Philistines hung their bodies to on the wall of Beth-Shan. Saul's men stole the bodies and burned them in Jabesh, burying their bones under a tree. Saul's head was nailed to the wall in the temple of Dagon like some hunters do with an impressive trophy. His armor was paraded through the cities of the Philistines and put on display in the temple of Ashkelon.

How are the mighty fallen!

To them, it was a sign that their gods had triumphed over our God. They thought it was a great day for the Philistines. Not one of them divined how killing Saul was the beginning of their ruin and that the new king would make them wish for the days of Saul to return.

Killing Saul was the biggest mistake the Philistines ever made.

16

Our grief began to subside long before David's and gave way to a hopeful expectation. Saul was dead, his princes were dead, and there would be a scramble for the throne. David was anointed by Samuel and held Saul's crown in his possession. The wheel of history was turning before our eyes. The time seemed manifest for David to claim his destiny as king of Israel.

"Saul's army is still regrouping," said Joab, ever the tactician. "If David moves swiftly, Saul's heirs won't have time to lay claim."

Benaiah agreed. "Saul's house is divided. Look at how many of us are here."

"David has the support of the people," said Asahel. "Our victory over the Amalekites has been spread across the land. Surely none would dare defy him."

I marveled at how grown he sounded.

"Such wisdom!" I said. "Maybe our uncle hasn't made so terrible a mistake in naming you lieutenant."

The boy actually blushed. I should not call him a

boy; he had just turned twenty. And yet I cannot think of him any other way. With his smooth chin, he looked for all the world like the child I remembered tending sheep.

At least to me.

"Shouldn't you three be practicing?" asked Ittai.

I cringed. David had declared that the men of Judah would learn to shoot the bow in honor of Saul and Jonathan. That meant me and my brothers.

"He's right," said Benaiah. "It's time for your lesson."

Unlike my brothers and me, Benaiah had grown up with the bow and had taken it upon himself to be our tutor. He was just as strict a trainer as he had been at Adullum. For hours he made us loose shafts at a bag stuffed with straw. The skill did not come naturally to us, but we were improving. Just yesterday I had actually been able to pull the string all the way to my ear before the arrow fell off the string.

A great improvement.

A footman ran up to our group.

"The counsel has been summoned," he said.

Joab grinned. "Perfect timing!"

Benaiah's eyes narrowed. "You're going to have to make up practice some time."

David had been locked up in the synagogue with Abiathar all morning, seeking God's counsel. He grasped the exigency of the time as well as we had. We expectantly waited to hear his decision.

"My brothers," he said. "For sixteen months we have bided our time here. I refused to lift my hand against Saul because he was the anointed of Yahweh and because I loved him. But now the king is dead, and others will hasten to claim his throne. But there is only one man anointed by God to rule over Israel. In His wisdom he has chosen a man that I would have considered unworthy, a lowly shepherd from Bethlehem."

We chuckled at his self-deprecation.

"Though I be humble, I will not shrink from the task the Lord has set before me anymore than I shrank from the Philistine at Elah. We will march to Hebron. There we shall declare before all that David is king of Israel. Will you follow me?"

We jumped to our feet with a roar. For years we had followed David, waiting for this very thing. We left the counsel in a swarm of activity. Households began packing their belongings right away. We ordered our soldiers to prepare to march. The streets of Ziklag were buzzing. There was a smile on every face. We were going to Hebron to crown our new king.

Word was sent out to all the tribes to meet at Hebron and declare for David. It took two days for the first convoy to be ready. Others were still packing and would follow when they could get their households together. I had always traveled light until I came to Ziklag. Now it took an oxcart and three asses heavily laden to carry my treasures. I had become a man of considerable property. My brothers and friends and I packed at a furious pace. We were afraid of being left behind. We did not want to miss David's triumphant coronation.

Ahinoam and Abigail rode in the front of the procession with their husband. They beamed proudly, the soon to be queens of Israel. Others had brought their families as well. Psalms of victory and thanksgiving were sung the whole way. The caravan had the atmosphere of a festival.

Our camp by the road was crowded. I have always loved to sleep outdoors; it reminds me of my days as a shepherd. Now the campsite rang with the laughter of women and the raucous play of children. Abigail made some pottage and distributed it among the bachelor soldiers.

"When are you boys going to find your own wives to cook for you?" she asked.

"Have you grown seeck of caring for us already, Abeegail?" asked Uriah, feigning an injured tone.

She laughed. "Never, Uriah. You all are welcome at our table any time. But wouldn't you like to have a woman of your own to keep you company?"

"Who would want to marry the likes of us?" said Zelek.

Abigail smiled warmly. "Big, strong, handsome heroes like you shouldn't have any trouble finding families who would take you for sons-in-law, nor girls who would be happy to marry you. If you need help arranging the match, just let me know."

"Sounds good to me," said Asahel with enthusiasm.

Abigail giggled and went away to spread her homey cheer to other soldiers.

"Do you think she's right?" I asked. "Do you think anyone would marry us?"

"Abigail's right," said Benaiah. "We're heroes now. The women will fall at our feet!"

That sounded nice, but I was not so sure.

"Easy for you to say," said Joab. "You have a noble father. Who wants a bastard for a son-in-law?"

"Or a foreigner," added Ittai.

Uriah stared into the fire and nodded once.

"I weell do eet. I weell ask Abeegail to arrange marriage for me. No more I come home to empty house and sleep alone. I want cheeldren before I am too old."

"What kind of wife will Abigail find for you anyway?" said Zelek. "She was married to Nabal. I wouldn't trust her to pick a spouse for me."

"Don't listen to them, Uriah," said Ittai, then he imitated his accent. "Eef you are lonely, then go get you wife. I weell pray to your God that you cheeldren do not look like their father!"

When we arrived at Hebron the people lined the road and cheered. David rode an ass at the front of our procession. The women and children laid palm branches in the path before us. I recognized a face among the women. It was Gomer, the old servant who had watched David grow up. I had not seen her since that day in the cave. Tears of joy were streaking down her cheeks. Those of us who had been with David since Adullum exchanged a wide-eyed look and a shake of the head, as if to say, *Can you believe this is really happening?*

On each side of the road were scores of thousands of soldiers, standing in rank according to their tribes. The largest tribal armies were of Zebulon, Asher, and Naphtali, each of which were bigger than our total force at Ziklag, and in far greater numbers than King Saul had been able to muster.

David led us to the sepulchers of Abraham, Isaac, and Jacob. He called forth Abiathar in his ephod, and sacrificed a bull to Yahweh. From his lips came this psalm.

"The earth is the Lord's, and the fulness thereof,
the world, and they that dwell therein.
For he hath founded it upon the seas,
and established it upon the floods.

"Who shall ascend into the hill of the Lord?
Or who shall stand in his holy place?
He that hath clean hands, and a pure heart,
who hath not lifted up his soul unto vanity, nor
sworn deceitfully.

"He shall receive the blessing from the Lord,

and righteousness from the God of his salvation.
This is the generation of them that seek him,
that seek thy face, O Jacob.

"Lift up your heads, O ye gates,
and be ye lift up, ye everlasting doors,
and the King of glory shall come in.
Who is this King of glory?
The Lord strong and mighty, the Lord mighty in
battle.

"Lift up your heads, O ye gates,
even lift them up, ye everlasting doors,
and the King of glory shall come in.
Who is this King of Glory?
The Lord of hosts, He is the King of glory."

An awed hush followed the hymn. David had come to claim his kingship, not in pride and audacity, but humility and reverence. He knelt, and Abiathar took a ram's horn and poured oil upon his head. He laid the diadem which had been Saul's upon David's head, oil still dripping from his beard and the curly locks of his head.

The crowd cheered for a long time. David was majestic in his grave acceptance of the crown. Abiathar laid his hands upon David's head and blessed him in the name of Yahweh. David stood and addressed the crowd.

"My brothers and sisters, I am humbled by this

honor that God has given me. As a simple soldier I have tried to serve you, fighting the Philistines, Amalekites, Gezrites, and Geshurites. As your king, I will serve you still. I will defeat our enemies by God's grace and drive them from our lands. One day our land will know peace. And may God establish here a kingdom that will last for all time."

The throng burst in frenzied applause. The speech was shorter than the psalm, but it was perfect. I could see the love for our king in my own heart reflected on every face. Timbrels and pipes began to play, and the people rejoiced.

I can still see him. He was thirty years old that day, and no gray had yet crept into his hair or beard. His hair was dark and slick with oil, and his eyes were sharp. His skin seemed to glow, and his crown flashed in the light of the sun. David's psalm ascribed all glory to Yahweh, but at that moment, it was David whom God exalted.

For the next three days we feasted as men from all over the nation came to pledge allegiance. They brought camels and asses laden with bread, meat, flour, figs, raisins, wine, and oil. They drove oxen and sheep into the pens to be slaughtered for our celebration.

Most importantly, they brought soldiers. The tribes of Judah, Simeon, Benjamin, Ephraim, Manasseh, Issachar, Zebulon, Naphtali, Dan, Asher, Reuben, Gad, and even your kinsmen of Levi sent thousands of men, though David would not employ the Levites in battle.

With the Judaeans came my cousin, Amasa. He had grown since we had last seen him, but he was the strutting rich boy he ever was. I did not know if he would actually fight with us in battle, but he presented himself with the other soldiers. We exchanged a perfunctory greeting, but had little else to do with each other. Of course he stood by David as kinsman now that he was king, but where had he been when we were fighting in the wilderness?

A young man named Zadok had formed a militia and fought independently of Saul or David. He now came with twenty-two companies of soldiers, commanded by stalwarts like himself. We were glad to have him, for we heard of how he had harried the Philistines.

We had grown from a band of six hundred outlaws to an army of six hundred *times* six hundred.

David's first act as king was to honor the men of Jabesh-Gilead, who had stolen Saul's and his sons' bodies from the wall at Beth-Shan and buried them. The people loved him all the more for that. Saul was our first king and would always be loved. Maybe you think David was just being canny, yielding to public sentiment for political gain, but you were not with us at En-gedi or Hachilah. David loved Saul and would always love him.

For three days the lamps never dimmed, the wine never stopped, the food never ceased to be served steaming before us, nor did the music fall silent. One could go from mansion to tavern, from the great hall to the street, and the celebration was already there. No place was exempt from the riot of noise and color. No one was turned away from the feast, from the captain of thousands, to the judge who sat in the gate, to the widow, to the crippled beggar. All were made fat and merry.

The apex of the celebration was centered at David's table in the great hall of Hebron. My brothers, friends, and I would not tear away from it. We slept in our chairs with our heads on the tables, afraid of losing our places if we went to an inn to sleep. Over fifty officers who were at Ziklag rubbed shoulders with those who had just arrived, many who had been on campaign with Saul against the Philistines. Joab found himself sitting next to Zadok, and it was not long before the two of them were arguing battlefield tactics.

One of the men of Judah who had been with us in Ziklag stood to address David. His name was Amasai, and he had a reputation for being loyal and eager to serve my uncle. David lifted his hands to let Amasai speak.

"My lord king," said Amasai. "What do you intend to do about Abner?"

David smiled. "Abner served the king honorably since I was a boy. There's no captain with his experience in all of Israel. Now that Saul is gone, we should have no quarrel. If he wishes, I would have him lead my soldiers, but if not, I would be happy to pay him a pension for his years of service."

"You don't understand," said Amasai. "He has declared Saul's son, Ish-bosheth, king of Israel. He made a coronation in Mahanaim."

"What?"

The room buzzed with this new intelligence.

"It's true, lord," said a man from Ephraim. "Word was sent to Ephraim and some our men declared for Ish-bosheth as well."

Several others stood confirming the report. The same thing had happened in Gilead, Asher, Jezreel, and of course, Benjamin, King Saul's tribe. Adino looked troubled. Eleazar was stroking his beard thoughtfully. Would David follow through with his decision to become king, or cede the right to Saul's offspring?

David rose to his feet, and the hall grew still.

"There is but one anointed king in Israel. At one time that was Saul, and I respected that, for it was decided not of man, but by Yahweh Himself. Now it is time Abner learned to respect God's decision. He rebels not only against his rightful king, but God's holy will."

He stretched out his hands to include us all.

"I will not neglect the duty that God and you, His people, have laid at my feet. Never have I lifted my hand against my loyal countrymen, but I will now strike those who seek to supplant me. You have named me king. Will you now follow me into battle?"

Over a hundred men shouted and pounded their fists on the tables. Our blood was like fire. For days we had celebrated our love for David, now we would prove it, even to our doom.

David raised his hand. Again the room was silenced.

"I intended to strike outward, to rid us of the Philistines for good. But Abner has decided I must first make our nation sure from within. It grieves me to have to fight our own brethren. But once we are united, we will at last be able to claim the land God promised our fathers."

His voice crescendoed, carrying our hearts with it.

"So prepare your armies. For tomorrow we will begin the war that will decide the fate of Israel."

17

The armies of Benjamin, Gad, Ephraim, and Asher returned to their lands to drive out the men who turned to Ish-bosheth, augmented with armies from the other tribes. David was leery of sending men to fight their own kinsmen, preferring to use our Cherethite mercenaries and the Pelethites who also decided to fight for David's gold.

But the captains of the Hebrews insisted. They were angry that their whole tribe had not come over to David's cause, for the whole nation had heard by now that Samuel had anointed him before he died. They were eager to prove their loyalty to David's cause.

Joab took me aside as the preparations were being made.

"I know where Abner will be," he said.

"How could you know that?" I asked.

"He will take Ish-bosheth to his father's house at Gibeah," he said.

The prospect of finding the rebel general first was

exciting, but I was not sure.

"But Amasai said that they were at Mahanaim," I said.

He shook his head. "They will return to Gibeah, the seat of Saul's reign. Abner will try to use it as a symbol, a sign that links Ish-bosheth with Saul's kingdom. I'm sure of it."

I nodded. It made sense.

"You should tell David," I said. "Or Adino or Shammah."

He lowered his voice.

"*I* want to go to Gibeah. The man who kills Abner will be remembered forever."

He grabbed my shoulders.

"Will you go with me?"

Of course I would. We told David of our plan, and he assented. Asahel and all of our friends insisted on being included in the adventure. Benaiah left his mercenaries at Hebron and commandeered a company of Judaeans. The next day we set out, the seven of us, each leading a hundred men. It was not many to face down Abner, but it was more than we had at Hachilah.

When we arrived at Gibeah, we went from house to house. We did not break in and search. These were, after all, our countrymen. We asked politely if Abner and his army passed through there.

Some seemed nervous and said they did not want to become involved in a feud over the kingdom. Others seemed eager to help, but they had not seen Ish-bosheth's army and did not know where they were. One old man was downright belligerent.

"Filthy rebels," he said. "I was loyal to Saul, and am loyal to his son, the *rightful* king."

"Haven't you heard that Samuel, who anointed Saul in the first place, anointed David to be king?" asked Joab. "If you accepted Saul's anointing, you should accept David's."

The old man scowled. "The kingdom should go to the king's son."

"Would you have accepted Jonathan as king?" he asked.

"Jonathan?" The man's eyes lit up. "Now he would have made a grand king! A peerless warrior he was. And the king's son."

"Well, I was there when Jonathan told David he would follow him as king," said Joab.

"That's a dirty lie," said the man, and he spit a gob of phlegm on Joab's shoe.

This was going badly. Joab had a violent temper, and the hand resting on the hilt of his sword made me nervous. I tensed, anticipating trouble. But instead of drawing the sword, my brother reached into his purse and handed the man a gold coin.

"What's this for?" he asked.

Joab smiled. "For your courage, grandfather. I hope I have a tenth of it at your age. I respect your loyalty and the strength of your conviction, as I'm sure King David would. Please accept this as a peace offering. We will trouble you no further."

The man softened, but closed his door on us with another scowl. I let out a breath I had not realized I was holding.

"That was well done," I said.

"He's just a crazy old codger," said Joab. "If ever I live that long, I suspect I'll act the same way."

"We should let the men rest," suggested Zelek. "The sun will be setting soon. We can start fresh tomorrow."

"There is a pool not far from here," said Benaiah.

Joab nodded, and Benaiah led us toward the water. The sun was yet high enough to be seen over the trees. It was warm, but not hot. The perfect blue sky was reflected in the sparkling water.

And there, on the other side of the pool, was Abner with his men.

"Form ranks!" shouted Joab.

Abner started at the sound of Joab's voice then saw our brigade of soldiers. He began organizing his own soldiers. We drew up and hastily formed ranks. Abner commanded about a thousand soldiers, but we had whetted our swords on Amalekites for over a year. To us there were far too few of them.

After arraying his men and marching around the edge of the water, Abner walked out from his men, flanked by two officers. He obviously wanted to have a chat before the fight.

"You think he wants to surrender?" said Benaiah.

"I hope not," said Asahel.

He stared at the soldiers with a hungry look. He came for glory. He wanted blood.

Joab turned to us. "Asahel, Abishai, with me."

The three of us walked out and met the famous general. I had not laid eyes on him since Hachilah. Up close I could see that age had not robbed him of his strength. His hair may have been grey, but he was lean and fierce looking. His muscled arms bore the scars of countless battles. His two lieutenants, both Benjamites, looked greener.

"You must be Joab," said Abner. "You have the look of your uncle. You know, I was there when he cut the head from the giant. What a day that was! Pity his ambition has led him to usurp the throne."

"David is the anointed king of Israel," answered Joab. "And he still admires you, as he did when he was under your command. Swear fealty to him and join us."

Abner crossed his arms

"I am still loyal to the house of Saul," he said. "I cannot follow the son of Jesse."

"Then lay down your arms and command your men to go home, or every one of them will die."

Abner chuckled with a dark smile. "I promised these men that they would see battle, and they have been bored stiff. It would be a shame to send them home now. Why don't we let them play a little?"

Joab pressed his lips together.

"So be it."

We turned our backs and began to walk away, and I

noticed Asahel was not beside me. I turned and saw him standing not a foot away from one of Abner's lieutenants. He was smirking, but Abner's man was glaring up at him with a face chiseled from flint.

"Come, Asahel," said Joab. "You'll get your chance."

Asahel threw his shoulders back, looking down his nose, and turned his back on him. The Benjamite's face flushed crimson.

When we rejoined our ranks, we cinched our armor tight, donned our helmets, and picked up our shields. Joab unsheathed his sword with a flourish. Sometimes we used our voices to frighten the enemy with a battlecry, but this time Joab elected to unnerve them with silence. He told us to keep quiet until we heard his voice. Across the field we saw men's spears tremble and heard their armor rattle with fear, even as they gave a feeble shout.

We stood still as mountains, silent as death.

Joab pointed the wicked crescent of his bronze sword at the foe and we jogged toward them. The enemy countered by linking their shields. We closed within twenty yards of them and increased our pace to a run. Ten yards. Now the battle cry.

"DAVID!" Joab voice thundered, and we all took up the call.

Abner's men flinched violently at the sudden burst of sound. During the first moment of the battle, in the fury of closing with the enemy, a dozen of our men beat aside the shields of Abner's men and took them by the heads in a one-handed grappler's clench, forgetting their spears. Soldiers of both sides took out their short swords and buried them in the ribs of their opponents. Twenty-four men died before you could count to ten.

The sight of their brethren dying unnerved Abner's men, but whipped ours into a frenzy.

Once as a boy, I saw a pack of wolves come across the carcass of a cow. The cow disappeared under a churning, milling storm of fur, but skin and entrails flew up from them as if being torn apart by some diabolical maelstrom. That is the only thing I can compare to the battle.

In five minutes, more than fifty of their men died. We lost only seven more in the whole battle. There is nothing like the feeling of routing the enemy. At first they step back, jostling the men behind them.

Then panic takes them, and they begin backpedaling in fear, often tripping over each other. They lie pathetic, whimpering on their backs as they are killed by the downward thrust, delivered with all the attention one devotes to swatting an insect.

That is when the enemy takes true flight, turning their unprotected backs to us. Like a pike in a school of minnows, our spears thrash into them in a feeding frenzy.

No longer a battle, I find myself in a hunt, and our sport is men—men not without valor, but who have found themselves grossly outmatched. All fear our men may have had for their lives is forgotten. We now shared one concern: that any should get away. It did not look like any would; over three hundred more fell in the chaos of that rout.

Joab sprinted through the battle, his head swiveling, eyes searching. He only swung his sword when absolutely necessary, casually ending lives while barely noticing them. Let his soldiers have these piddling kills. He was on the hunt for the real prize.

Abner.

Then Abner appeared from behind a copse of trees far to the rear of the battle. He had started at the fore of his ranks and must have fled the field. Joab sneered at the cowardice. We expected more from the legendary warrior.

But Abner still had some ability to command. He stood on a knoll called Ammah and rallied his soldiers to him as the sun began to set behind him. They scurried like biddies to their mother hen and reformed their ranks. Joab raised his sword and called for us to regroup. Some of us did, but others continued to cut down the enemy who were scrambling to get to their comrades on the hill. Their sergeants had to pull some of them away bodily.

We panted in excitement, waiting for Joab to give us the order to finish them off, when Abner called to us.

"Joab!" he called. "Shall the sword devour forever? Don't you know it will be bitterness in the latter end? How long will it be until you call your men off from chasing their own brothers?"

Zelek smirked. "Well, *he* doesn't sound so confident anymore."

"Yeah," said Ittai. "I wonder why."

"We can end this now, Joab," urged Benaiah. "Ish-bosheth is nothing without Abner."

Joab frowned and looked into my eyes.

"What would David do if he were here?"

He turned back to Abner. "As God lives, if you hadn't spoken up, we would have chased you down until tomorrow morning."

Joab took a ram's horn and trumpeted the withdrawal. At last the final remnant of our men fell in.

"Let them go, boys," said Joab with a smile. "Victory is ours."

The men cheered as Abner's men began to slink away.

"Sergeants," I called. "Count your men. Give us a number of wounded and killed."

The sergeant's looked into every man's eyes, not trusting to hear the sound of their voice alone. Every man must be accounted for.

"I weell take the tally," volunteered Uriah.

I thanked him and walked to my brother.

"What about the glory of capturing Abner?" I asked.

His mouth twisted in what might have been regret.

"He was willing to retreat," said Joab. "And I think our king wants us to settle this with as little bloodshed as possible. These are our people. I'll settle for taking the field."

"You've grown," I said. "You showed restraint today."

He stared at the hill where Abner's men had retreated, now long gone.

"I've learned from watching David. I never understood why he kept letting Saul get away, but I think I'm beginning to."

I had never heard him talk this way before.

Uriah ran up to us, clearly distraught. "Nineteen are meessing. We have recovered eighteen dead."

"Do we know who's missing?" asked Joab.

"Asahel ees meessing in action."

We stood silent. Surely I had heard him wrong. I thought back to the battle, mentally retracing my steps. I could not remember seeing my youngest brother.

Joab seized Uriah by the shoulders. "Have you questioned his men?"

"Benaiah ees doing so now," he answered.

Before he could finish we ran to Benaiah, who was debriefing the squad which had been fighting with Asahel. Seeing us coming, he answered the unspoken questions on our faces.

"He went after Abner," he said. "This one said he saw him fleeing and took off. None of the men could keep up with him. They had their hands full with the men in front of them."

My hands were around the soldier's throat before I knew what I was doing.

"You let my brother go after Abner alone?" I said slowly through clenched teeth.

The man held his hands up apologetically. I could see the shame on his face. I was not being fair, but I did not care. I was out of my mind with worry and needed someone to blame. Anyone but myself.

Benaiah laid a hand on my shoulder.

"It's not his fault, Abishai."

I released the man, but continued to stare daggers through him.

"He saw him disappear behind that copse of trees," said Benaiah.

Joab and I took off before another word was spoken. Benaiah called orders to our men which I barely heard, and he and our companions sprinted to join us at the trees. I have run for my life several times, but until that day I knew not the meaning of haste. I sprinted until my lungs were aflame, afraid of what I would find behind that cluster of trees, but compelled to go nonetheless. I ran into the trees through a goat track and broke into a clearing.

There lay the cold, still body of my baby brother.

Those who have seen as many battlefields as I know death when we see it, yet I would not believe my senses. I knelt and searched his body frantically for wounds, finding a puncture under his fifth rib. From the shape of it, Abner had stabbed him with the butt spike of his spear. The spear had passed clean through his chest and out his back. His ruined lungs were no longer straining to breath.

He was gone.

I cradled my little brother's body in my arms and wept as I have never before. As I looked into his face, I saw the grinning, beardless boy who was always moving. I saw the man who had grown into a virile warrior, peerless in his beauty. I saw the baby who had given my mother the only joy she had ever known, unmarred by shame. An inhuman cry escaped my lips.

Joab was kneeling beside me, stroking Asahel's white-streaked hair and shaking with sobs. He cupped Asahel's face and kissed his forehead tenderly. Benaiah arrived and seeing our grief, knelt down next to Joab and wrapped his arms around him. His fingers were enmeshed with Joab's hair as he wept in his chest. It was the way my mother held him when he was small and he fell and scraped his knee. Joab collapsed onto his shoulder.

Uriah came next.

"Oh!" he groaned. "Oh, no! No, no, no!"

He wrapped his arms around me, and I felt his tears soak my shoulder. When he broke from the hug, his pink face looked raw. Asahel had been a brother to him too, a brother to all of them.

Zelek pulled his sword out in a rage. He attacked a pine tree, screaming in rage until he had no more strength and sat on the ground. He pressed his lips together, trying not to cry, but great tears rolled down his face.

Ittai only stood silently, watching us with liquid, red eyes. It was hard for him who had grown so close to us so quickly. He shared our grief but did not wish to intrude.

Other soldiers came and mourned with us. It must have been unsettling to see their commanders so stricken. Our bearing was undisciplined and unmilitary. We had forgotten our soldiers, forgotten the war, forgotten everything in our anguish.

Joab stood and wiped his eyes. He sniffed and spoke as if struggling to breath.

"We should take him to Mother."

I nodded, and Joab lifted his body from my arms. The sun had already set, but we were mindless. Taking my brother's body home felt like the most important thing in the world. Joab and I walked all night, and the men followed us without a murmur. Never before had we broken off a campaign to return a fallen comrade, but no one questioned the decision.

This was Asahel.

I kept my hand on Joab's shoulder to remind myself that he was still there. Joab was grieving, but there was strength in it. I had none of that strength. My brother was dead, and it was my fault.

We arrived in Bethlehem before the sun rose. We walked to the little cottage my mother had once shared with Shua, and we roused her from her sleep. She came to the door quickly, sensing something was wrong. Part of me wanted to let her sleep, to spare her a few more hours of pain, but I felt she would never forgive us if we did not tell her immediately.

She opened the door, looked at the body, then at us for answers. Was he wounded? Would he be all right? But she found no comfort in our eyes.

"Asahel! Ah!" she cried. "Aaahhhh!"

She laid herself over the body and wailed, and threw herself on the floor as if struck and wept. Her unbound, grey hair hung in front of her face. I saw a lost child in an old woman's body. I fell to my knees and wept with her. She looked into my eyes, her eyes glistening, and smoothed the hair from my brow. Would she be so tender toward me when she knew that I had been there and done nothing to stop it?

"Mother, I'm so sorry," I tried to say.

My diaphragm was spasming as I found myself choking on the words. Joab laid Asahel's body on the floor. I wiped my eyes and nose.

"Abishai," he said. "It wasn't your fault."

Oh, how I wanted to believe him! He pressed his lips into a thin, hard line.

"It was mine," he said. "I thought I could be merciful. I won't make that mistake again."

He turned to my mother and spoke with eyes lined red.

"We know who killed Asahel."

My mother stopped crying for a moment and looked at my brother with an expression of disbelief.

"I'm going to kill him."

18

That wretched war would continue for seven and a half years. We captured villages and cities throughout the tribes that had declared for Ish-bosheth, and many surrendered without a fight. Each day David's kingdom grew stronger, and it was only a matter of time before Ish-bosheth lost what tenuous grip on the kingdom he had. The only thing that held it together was Abner.

We hunted for Abner for months, but he had returned to Mahanaim, too deep in enemy territory for our small force to dislodge. Our friends stayed with us on the hunt, but eventually they moved on with their lives. They mourned for Asahel as Joab and I did and longed to avenge his death, but they were not obsessed with it as we were. Ittai, Benaiah, and Uriah found brides during that time and built homes and domestic lives apart from their military duties, whereas Joab and I wanted nothing but to put an end to Abner, son of Ner.

Benaiah's wife was a sweet-faced girl named Rebekah. To Benaiah she was truly beautiful, and when they were together it was obvious they were happy. She bore him a son not long after they married, whom they named Jehoiada, after Benaiah's father. Benaiah asked me if I wanted to hold him, but I had only held one baby my whole life. I reluctantly accepted, but it brought back too many memories of my brother.

Uriah married a gangly teenaged girl named Bathsheba, who was in awe of all of us, famous heroes to her by now. She worshipped Uriah, who in turn treasured her above all else. Although he never let his marital duties interfere with his soldiery, for he held military duty sacred, he treated his young bride like a queen. Joab confessed to me that he did not understand what Uriah, who with David's recommendation could have his pick from a score of women, saw in the shy, unremarkable girl. But I knew Bathsheba was only late in blooming and had the makings of a true beauty when she came of age.

Ittai was not the only Philistine who had chosen to take David's side. He married one of his own people, a handsome, dark-eyed girl named Sidka. Sidka could make fish taste better than I ever thought possible by slowly cooking it in the smoke of hardwood, and I spent many nights at their table. Not long after Benaiah and Rebekah had little Jehoiada, Sidka gave birth to a baby boy.

They named him Asahel.

David's household was also increasing. Ahinoam and Abigail had each given him a son, and David had taken other wives as well. Talmai, king of Geshur, became afraid of our king's growing strength, and sealed a treaty with him by giving him his daughter, Maacah. It was she who bore David's third son, Absalom.

David ended up having six different sons by six different wives in Hebron, and Joab predicted trouble between them, as well as trouble for the kingdom in the future. One does not have to know much about political intrigue to know that a king with six different sons by six different wives can lead to in-fighting, but none of us could have foreseen how violent the future would be.

It was Sidka who tried to take Zelek, Joab, and me under her matronly arm. While all of these women became sisters to me, Sidka was genuinely concerned for us. All of us were above thirty years of age, and she worried that we would remain wild bachelors forever without a woman's gentling influence. Zelek was just too cantankerous to be yoked with a wife. Joab was too consumed with finding Abner. As for me, when she prodded me about finding a wife, I simply stretched my spear out before me.

"This is my bride," I said.

I was not far from the truth. Whether by the Philistine witch's enchantment or by the strange species of chance that only happens on the battlefield, my spear survived scores of battles where other weapons were destroyed, their shafts snapped or points dulled beyond repair. Sometimes soldiers become superstitious about such things, and will treat weapons, clothes, or jewelry like good luck charms, refusing to set foot on the battlefield without them.

I never went *anywhere* without my spear. Even when I slept, that is when I could sleep, it sat in my chamber within arm's reach. At times I imagined I could hear it whispering to me in the dark, and one night I would have laid an oath that I had heard Abner's name spoken aloud.

Joab and I campaigned incessantly. None of our men could maintain our operational tempo, so we would volunteer to go out with other battalions. While most of our friends were marrying and trying to get sons by their new wives, we fought. Ostensibly we claimed to fight to make David's house sure, but we were hunting for Abner.

Whenever business called us back to Hebron we were restless. Our friendships began to feel strained. We did not joke and relax when in Hebron. Our friends implored us to spend some time at home, but somehow it felt wrong knowing that Abner, our brother's killer, was out there somewhere.

Every battle was another step toward Mahanaim; every man we killed was one less we would have to fight through to reach our target. I remember little about those battles. We fought in a haze, though it did not dull my ability to kill, nor Joab's to command. Afterward breathless soldiers told me of extraordinary feats I did not even remember performing. We accepted their exuberance in stony silence. None of it mattered to us.

We began to shun the company of others. Only we two could understand each other's need for vengeance. We became peevish and snapped at our soldiers and even our friends. Zelek seemed downright cheerful compared to us. We did not go to the priest, and we ate our meals alone if we ate at all.

One day we came back from hunting down a troop of Ish-bosheth's men. Again Abner was not there, and we were ready to take another battalion out to find him. Our men were giddy from the combination of the ecstasy of victory and the weariness from weeks of marching and fighting. The atmosphere in Hebron was more gay even than usual. Our friends met us near the gate with smiles and embraces.

Benaiah looked concerned.

"Were either of you hurt?" he asked.

We shook our heads.

"Just the usual scratches and bruises," I said.

"We worried," said Uriah. "You two keep trying to ween the whole war by you selves. You should wait for us, so we can watch you backs."

"If I wait for you, someone else will kill Abner before I get the chance," said Joab.

At that the others exchanged a concerned look.

Ittai changed the subject. "Abishai, Sidka thinks she's found the perfect girl for you. She wanted me to invite you for dinner this Sabbath to meet her and her family."

I groaned. "Won't she ever give up playing match maker?"

"She gave up on me months ago," said Zelek.

Uriah smirked. "That because whenever she say you name the weemen run away screaming!"

Everyone laughed, and even Joab and I had to smile at that. Uriah could always cheer us up.

"She wants to know when you and Bathsheba are going to have a baby of your own," said Ittai.

Uriah's smile faded. "I hope soon. I try, but so far nothing. She worries, but I say to her, is early yet. And the great matriarch Sarah not have Isaac unteel she ninety. But that only make her cry!"

The confusion on Uriah's face made us all laugh again.

"I wouldn't bring that example up again if I were you," said Joab.

It was good to see him smile again.

The crowd around us was buzzing. I looked past my friends' shoulders and saw David riding an ass. The most beautiful woman I had ever seen was riding next to him. Her hair held a dark, coppery luster and spilled from a golden crown to hang at her waist. I caught the tail end of someone saying something about the war being over soon. David spied us and came over to speak to us.

"Joab and Abishai again?" he said. "No one fights harder for my kingdom than my two nephews. How went the patrol?"

"We found the rebels in Succoth, my king," answered Joab. "Most of their corpses are still there."

"Well done," he said. "Now please, take some well deserved and much needed rest. I command you both to stay in Hebron over the next month. I don't want you injured or killed out of misplaced zeal."

Joab's accepted the order with a blank face.

"Yes, my king."

David turned his ass and rode away with the woman.

"Did the king marry again while we were out?" I asked.

Benaiah shook his head. "The king's *been* married to her. That's Michal, Saul's daughter."

Michal? My head snapped to get another glimpse of the woman for whom David had killed two hundred Philistines.

"Phaltiel's been keeping her warm for heem all these years," said Uriah. "That must have been an awkward reunion."

"David hasn't been exactly cooling down with his six other wives," said Zelek. "However much he pined for her, it hasn't kept him idle. That house gets more crowded all the time."

Uriah shook his head.

"Seven wives. *Chara!* How does he do eet? I have my hands full with just the one."

"That's why he's the king," said Ittai. "He can handle the jobs lesser men like us never could."

Joab was chewing on his lip.

"I don't get it," he said. "She's been with Phaltiel all these years. What made him turn loose of her now? Was he afraid of David?"

The group became very quiet again, and once more they exchanged nervous glances, each silently willing the other to break the news to us.

"It was a stipulation," said Benaiah. "For Abner's defection."

I have never been struck by lightning, but I cannot imagine it feeling any different than I did at that moment. Joab and I stood gaping at our friends.

"What?" said Joab, still not comprehending the weight of the news.

"Ish-bosheth and Abner had a falling out," said Ittai. "Over a woman of all things."

Zelek continued. "Abner sent word to David. Said he wanted to join our cause. David's only condition was that he return Michal to him. Abner brought her and left two days ago with twenty men."

Joab was trembling.

"I've been searching for my brother's murderer for years, and he walked in here, and you did nothing?"

The four of them looked at the ground.

"He was David's guest," said Uriah. "David made a feast for heem and hees men. What could we do?"

"Besides," said Benaiah. "Abner did not murder Asahel any more than you murder those you kill in battle. Asahel was a casualty of war. We are just as angry as you, but don't let your bitterness blind you. I beg you, brother."

"You are no brothers of mine," spat Joab. "Or you would have avenged one of our own when his killer came into our town."

The four of them looked injured. Tears came to Benaiah's eyes. I said nothing.

"Joab," pleaded Uriah. "You can't mean that."

Joab softened. "I'm sorry, Uriah. All of you. I didn't mean that. I'm just *so angry.* I will not go to battle with that man, no matter what the king says."

He looked at Benaiah whose gaze was still on the ground.

"Benaiah," he said.

Benaiah looked at him.

"I'm sorry. I was wrong to say that."

Benaiah pressed his lips together and nodded, and they clasped hands. I was glad Joab had singled him out. Benaiah and Joab had a special bond, and Joab's words cut him the deepest. Still I was confident no words could sever that bond.

I thought back to our recent encounter with the king.

"So that's why David commanded us to stay in Hebron," I said.

Joab's eyes snapped in my direction, and I saw that I had realized the truth first for once.

"I know you don't want to hear this, but maybe it's for the best," said Ittai. "Abner has already turned Ish-bosheth's own tribe against him. All of Benjamin has allied with David. Ish-bosheth is nothing without Abner."

"Maybe you're right," said Joab, but his voice was absent. Abruptly he spun and walked toward David's house.

"Where are you going?" shouted Benaiah.

"I'm going to speak to the king," he answered.

I jogged to catch up, and we left the others in the street. When I looked over my shoulder, they were looking at each other as if trying to decide if they should come with us. We did not wait for them.

Joab and I were admitted into David's salon immediately. He was sitting on a bench with Michal. I have said that Abigail was the only woman worthy of David, and it is true, but her beauty was not a tenth of Michal's. Even in my state of agitation, it was difficult not to stare. David did not seem surprised to see us come.

"So you heard?" he said, shifting in his throne warily.

"Why did you send him away?" asked Joab. His tone was close to insubordinate.

"Abner is doing important work for me," said David. "He has already turned Benjamin to my side. When the others see his defection they will turn as well."

"They might turn if they learned of Abner's death," answered Joab. "It would dishearten our enemies."

"I will not kill a man in cold blood," said David. "Abner came here in p-"

"He came to deceive you!" interrupted Joab. "He has seen your comings and goings. How difficult will it be for an assassin to catch you alone, or an archer to find a spot to take a shot and disappear now that this spy has observed your movements?"

David ignored Joab's interruption.

"I do not believe that is Abner's intent, and you will trust my judgement. You and your brother will stay here for a month. You will not chase Abner down. Is that clear?"

Joab contained his anger as best he could. "My king, it is not wise to let your enemy-"

"I said is that clear?" said David, this time allowing his anger to show.

Chastened, Joab pressed his lips together and spoke with effort.

"Yes, my king."

David spoke with regal command. "Joab, you are one of my best commanders. But I will not have my wisdom questioned. Enough of our brothers' blood has been spilled, and I will not spoil a chance to end the bloodshed because of your personal feud. Now, go."

We turned to leave. As we opened the door to the salon, David spoke again.

"Asahel was my nephew. I wept the day I learned of his death. But he was a casualty of war. Now that the war is ending we must put it behind us."

We looked over our shoulders at David, said nothing, and walked out.

Put it behind us? There was no chance of us forgetting the man who had slain our brother. I thought David understood something of loyalty. But if he thought we could just walk away from Asahel's killer, he knew very little of his sister's sons.

When we were back on the streets Joab spoke to me under his breath. "I will not let Abner get away. David is doing what he must. The others are too soft or too afraid to do what must be done."

He looked over at me.

"Can I count on you?"

I stopped walking and looked into his eyes.

"Always."

Few in Hebron use the small gate near the well of Sirah. The street leading to it is hardly more than an alley. It is quiet and unlit. We sent Abner a message that David wished to meet him there after dark alone. It was the perfect place to stage a murder.

I hid in a corner near the gate, and Joab sat opposite in an adjacent dark corner. Abner came with twenty men the last time he visited Hebron, and it might take both of us to kill his guards. We agreed before hand that should he ignore the the condition to come alone, the important thing would be to cut Abner off from his men and trap him. If necessary, we were willing to trade our lives for the revenge which had consumed us for the last seven years.

The corner grew darker as the sun slipped behind the tops of the houses in Hebron. I could no longer see my brother hiding in his corner. Lamps were lit in nearby streets as people began to make their way home. Merchants had long packed up their wares, leaving empty stands to face the cold night naked and alone. I saw a scrawny cat stalk the lane, looking for rats that were emboldened by the dark, but other than that, not a creature stirred in the alley.

I clutched my spear, careful to keep its bronze head in the shadow lest any glimmer of reflected light betray my position. Once again I imagined that it whispered to me, as if it too had been waiting these seven years to slake its thirst for Abner's blood. I stroked the shaft as one does when gentling an ass, silently reassuring that soon it would be satisfied.

Abner arrived alone and unarmed. He stepped through the gate and glanced furtively around the shadows. I moved swiftly to block the gate, though my knees were stiff from squatting in the corner. Abner whirled with the sudden movement, then again as Joab stepped out to face him.

"Joab," he said, his face passive. "I knew I would have to face you one day."

Joab said nothing but gestured toward the well, as if inviting a dinner guest to have a seat at the table. Abner walked into the alley with Joab, and I stood at the portal, one eye on Abner, the other looking to see if any had followed us or noticed from an adjacent street.

Abner spoke to us. "I want you both to know that I begged your brother to stop chasing me. I didn't want to kill that boy. But I couldn't have outrun him even on my best day, and he wouldn't let me go."

There was no pleading in his voice, only a deep sadness.

"Do you have a brother?" asked Joab.

Abner shook his grey head. "All sisters."

"Then you can never know the pain I've felt these seven years," said Joab.

"Maybe so," said Abner. "Maybe not. One of my sons died in battle."

For the first time his voice betrayed emotion. He thrust an accusing finger at Joab.

"You killed him."

I was stunned. We did not know Abner had a son, much less that Joab killed him.

"It was five years ago while you were looking for me. I felt an anger so hot I would have to kill you a thousand times to satisfy it. Then I blamed myself. It should have been me. If I hadn't gotten involved in this stupid squabble, he'd still be alive."

I fought the tears that were beginning to come to my eyes. Abner's words were striking too close to home. But rather than pity him, I only grew angrier at him.

"I went all dead inside. Drank wine and *shekar,* hoping I wouldn't be able to feel anything anymore. I even thought about killing myself. I don't know if that's what it's like to have a brother killed, but that's what it's like to have your son killed."

Joab grabbed his cloak and drew his sword, pressing the point to Abner's chest. I held him by the arm and shoulder so he would not run away.

"Do you think your lies will soften me the way they did my uncle?"

Joab's voice trembled, whether from rage or uncertainty, I do not know. But the sword was steady.

Abner laughed. "I don't care if you believe me. I'm not going to lie, beg, or reason to save my worthless life. I have no weapon and I'm too old to outfight or outrun you. I've lived too long as it is, and I'm ready to join my son. You're the one who has to live with it. So get on with it."

"This is where you stabbed him," said Joab. "Here, under the fifth rib. Now feel what he felt."

Joab slid the sword point slowly between Abner's ribs. Abner grimaced, but did not move or make a sound. Joab took the sword handle in both hands and twisted it deliberately. There was a moist, sucking sound as air from his lungs escaped from the wound.

Abner gave a Joab a pitiful look, turned to include me, and dropped to his knees. Joab wrenched the sword free, and Abner fell on his face. I walked trembling into the alley. I watched his shoulders heave one final, agonal breath, and then it was still.

I dipped my fingers in the warm pool of blood spreading from his body. The blood looked bright even in the dark. On a strange impulse, I put my fingers to my mouth. The taste was the same as the meaty, metallic smell. I realized that I had violated an injunction of Moses' Law, to eat no manner of blood. But it seemed such a small thing after the other, greater law we had broken that night.

I am not sure how I thought it would feel, but I felt no relief. I will not lie to you, I did take some satisfaction from seeing him die. But the pain of losing my brother had not diminished by a scintilla. If anything, I felt it more acutely seeing the ragged wound that looked so much like Asahel's had. My brother's ghost did not appear and smile at me as if to say, "At last the job is done, and I can rest in peace." I felt empty and alone. And angry.

The anger never went away.

19

The body was found the next morning, and it was no great mystery who had wanted Abner dead. We learned that David cursed Joab and all his house in a fit of rage. He then summoned Joab and me, as well as all of our friends. We met in the outer garden of David's house. Joab and I withered under their disappointed looks.

"Why didn't you tell us what you were planning?" asked Benaiah.

"Because you would have tried to stop us," said Joab.

Benaiah threw up his hands in exasperation.

"Shouldn't that tell you it's a bad idea in the first place?" said Ittai.

"I never thought it was a *good* idea," said Joab. "I just had to do it."

"And you would have told the king," I said.

"I wouldn't," said Zelek.

We all looked at him with surprise.

He shrugged. "I would have tried to stop you at

first. But if you're going to get in trouble, I would have gone with you."

"Me too," said Uriah.

My friends' loyalty floored me. I suddenly felt guilty for how I had ignored them the past few years. In spite of how we treated them, they were still willing to go through the fire with us.

"I'm sorry we didn't trust you," I said.

Uriah laid a hand on my shoulder.

"How many battles have we been through together?" he said. "You are the brothers I never had."

"Whatever happens, we're with you," said Benaiah.

The others nodded.

Ittai grinned. "Anyway, it must have been nice to pay Abner back for Asahel."

They all looked at us with grim smiles. Joab nodded darkly with a fierce satisfaction in his eyes.

The six of us were called into David's salon, and we knelt in front of him.

"Get up," he said. "I want to look into your eyes."

We rose to our feet.

"Alright, Joab," he said. "Who did you involve with you? How many of you helped him kill Abner?"

"I acted alone, my king," said Joab. "None of them helped me. They had no idea of what I was planning."

His words jolted me. I should have guessed that my brother would lie to protect me, but it came as a surprise.

"That's not true, my king," I said. "I was there with

him."

The thought of being hanged or decapitated made my hands tremble, but I would not let another brother die alone.

David growled. "Did I not order you *not* to chase him down?"

"We didn't chase him down, my king," said Joab. "We remained in He-"

"Do not twist my words, son of Zeruiah," shouted David.

I cringed at the appellation. It was an implication of our fatherlessness, our illegitimacy. He was calling Joab, and by extension me, a bastard.

"You know very well that Abner was not to be harmed. He had just turned the Benjamites to our cause. Now what are they going to think? That I have betrayed Abner and had him assassinated? Now they might return to Ish-bosheth."

He sank back in his throne and covered his face with a weary hand.

"That could mean *another* seven years of war. Seven more years of husbands, sons, fathers, and yes, brothers dying because you two could not see past your own pain."

Joab hung his head like a kicked dog.

"I will do anything to make this right," he said. "Give me a chance, my king, and I will prove myself. I swear it."

"The only thing," said David. "That I want from

you is that all of you rend your clothes and put on sackcloth. I want the whole nation to see all of you mourning for Abner the way he deserves."

We looked at each other awkwardly.

"Didn't you hear me?" said David. "Now. Start tearing."

We obeyed and ripped our clothing. Each of us went to the hearth and rubbed ashes on his face and beard. It was humiliating, but it was better than being executed.

A little better.

"Good," said David. "Now go, put on sackcloth, and I will see you at Abner's bier."

As we filed to the door, a servant scurried in and tried to press some bread and fowl on David with the air of having tried to get him to eat several times already. David wearily refused.

As I was walking out I heard him say, "I feel so low. I may be the anointed king, but I feel as low as *Sheol*. These sons of Zeruiah are too hard for me."

It was like a dart in my chest. No one had called us "sons of Zeruiah" or bastards in years, and David had twice in a minute. I thought we had won renown that would put all that behind us, but one misdeed had sullied our names again.

I turned to look at him. He was glowering at Joab and me. He had said it maliciously, intending for us to hear it. Then he twisted the sword in our guts.

"May Yahweh reward them for their evil deeds."

My bowels turned to ice. I looked at Joab. He was

crushed.

When we were in the garden, I turned to the servant who had escorted us.

"I heard that David cursed Joab this morning," I said under my breath.

He nodded. "I was there."

"What did he say?" I asked.

He shook his head. "You don't want to know."

David did not eat until sundown, and followed the bier personally to Abner's final resting place. We were there as commanded, wearing itchy burlap that left my skin red and irritated when I took it off that night.

If David was putting on a show for the people, it worked. None of the Benjamites who Abner had turned to our cause blamed David for his death and remained more loyal than ever to him. But it was no act. David had loved and admired Abner the way he loved and admired Saul and Jonathan. Before David killed the Giant in Elah, they three had been the nation's heroes.

They had been *David's* heroes.

In the end Abner's death had the effect that Joab had predicted. Ish-Bosheth was so distraught at losing Abner that he grew depressed and took to lying on his couch and sleeping all day. His followers were alarmed and began to suspect the end was near. Two men of Beeroth snuck into his chamber while he was sleeping past noon, killed him, and took his head. They had not learned much from the Amalekite who had brought news of Saul and Jonathan's death. They thought that

David would reward them. He rewarded them by having them executed.

The six of us saw their corpses hanging by the pool. Their hands and feet had been cut off, and birds had plucked their eyes out. Their once fine clothes were crusted with sun-blackened blood. After so many battles, I should have been used to the smell, but it turned my stomach.

"That could have been us," I told Joab.

He nodded, staring at the bodies as they swayed in the breeze.

"We have to do something. After all we've accomplished, I don't want to be remembered as a murdering bastard."

"It's too late for that," I said. "Perhaps we should be content that David did not kill us."

"Maybe Abeeshai ees right," said Uriah. "I don't theenk David forget anytime soon."

"Then whatever we do, it will have to be big," said Joab. "A grand deed that will wash the stink of this killing off of us, and no one will call us 'sons of Zeruiah' again."

20

This city is called Jerusalem, the City of Peace. It is also called Zion after the ancient stronghold, or more often, the City of David. But when I was your age, we called it Jebus, and the Jebusites still inhabited the city and the land around it.

I will tell you the story of how our people finally found the home of our soul. It was not long ago, but already people have forgotten the bloody battle in which we took the City of Peace, and the bloody man who redeemed himself there, if only for a time.

David greatly desired to occupy the city. Our nation was whole again, and David felt Jebus was the missing piece to make the land itself a home for our people.

He was right, of course. It was here that Abraham met Melchizedek, the mysterious king of Jebus, then called Salem. It was here, right on Mount Moriah, they say Abraham nearly sacrificed his son, Isaac, to Yahweh, but the boy was delivered by the angel. Though no Jew had set foot in the city since Joshua, the king sensed something supernatural pulling us back there, and was filled with an inexplicable longing to take the city for his people.

He met with the Jebusites, hoping he could find a way into the city peacefully, either by bribes or threats. He took Uriah as interpreter, for the Jebusites were kin to the Hittites and shared a similar language. We grilled him when they returned, even though it would not be long before David informed the whole army of what had transpired.

"They weell no budge," he said. "They pretty cocky seeting behind their high walls."

"We've taken walled cities before," said Joab.

Uriah shook his head. "These walls are *huge.* I tell you thees, there have no been walls such as thees seence Jericho."

We absorbed Uriah's dour intelligence in silence, after which Ittai spoke.

"We have numbers," he said. "They have to see that we'll take the city eventually."

"They trust een their gods," said Uriah. "The Blind and the Lame."

Benaiah started. "What was that?"

"The Blind and the Lame," said Uriah. "Their idols. I saw them myself. Massive brass statues een their capitol."

"Then it's true," said Benaiah.

"What's true?" asked Zelek.

We leaned forward, all wondering the same thing.

"They say that the Jebusites were once friends to the patriarchs," said Benaiah. "After Father Abraham won the Battle of the Kings and paid tithes to the king of Salem, there was a covenant between our fathers and the Jebusites. Generations later, they built a brass statue in honor of Isaac, the Blind, and another in honor of Jacob, the Lame."

"Because of Isaac's dim sight in his old age," I said. "And Jacob's bad hip after his tussle with the angel."

"Exactly," said Benaiah. "Over time the Jebusites forgot the origin of the statues and worshipped them as idols."

I mused that this was a strange way for a religion to begin.

Uriah said, "However they get them, they no believe they can fail as long as the idols stand."

Later that night the war counsel was called, and we met in a great hall. David's salon was too small to hold all the officers, let alone the sergeants of the great army. Joab and I sat at the back of the room, where only our four friends joined us. The other men sensed that we had fallen out of favor with David and kept their distance. Some of the men who had served with us at Adullum were still polite to us, but not all. David recounted to everyone what Uriah had told us and confirmed there would be a battle.

"Starve them," said one captain. It was one of the Jozabads, the more talkative of the two. "Let's surround the city, keep any food or water from entering. Then they'll beg us to come in and let them go."

"No good," said Eleazar, who had gone with David. "They are well-stocked with food, and the spring of Gihon runs into the city. They could sit behind those walls for a year. Our army might starve before they do."

"Could we dam the spring?" suggested Zadok.

"It's possible," said Shammah. "But it would take time. We have a more expedient plan we want to try."

With that he yielded the floor to the king.

"The Gihon is fed into the city through an underground sluice," said David. "I will set the main body of our army opposite the portal at the main gate. A thousand men will wade through the tunnel and enter the city to let us in. It will be the most dangerous part of the siege, and I only want volunteers."

"I will go!" shouted Joab, shooting to his feet.

The men looked at him in surprise. David regarded him coldly.

"Very well," he said. "I also have an extra task for those going in, with an added incentive. The Blind and the Lame, the brass idols inside, are sacred to the Jebusites. They stand by a temple atop Mount Zion within the city. I want them knocked down and destroyed. This will cripple the morale of the soldiers within. We expect they will be heavily and zealously defended."

Then he delivered his greatest surprise that evening.

"The man who accomplishes this," he said. "Will become the captain of the host, my number one general."

There was a surprised rumbling among the men. David had not needed a general before, but it made sense that he would now that his army had grown and he was taxed with the duties of a king. The man who knocked down those idols would have the most coveted position in the army.

"Who else will go through the sluice?" David asked.

I stood at the same time as Uriah, followed by Benaiah, Ittai, and Zelek. The Jozabads stood, as well as Shammah, Zadok, and dozens of other men. David thanked us and told us to find volunteers from among our soldiers, telling them of David's promise. If even the greenest footman destroyed the statues, he would become our general and the greatest hero in Israel.

About two hundred thousand men marched to Jebus, leaving half that many to defend Hebron. Several score of thousands more were on leave in their tribal homelands, and David saw no reason to call them up yet.

Achish had heard of David's ascension, and I only wish I could have seen Achish's fat face when he realized how badly he had miscalculated in his dealings with us. We had fought a few skirmishes with the Philistines. They were nothing serious, but we did not want to leave Hebron without adequate defense.

Even with a fraction of our forces, the march to

Jebus was the longest military procession I had ever participated in. The men filled every span of road I could see for miles. There was no way to hide the enormous column. When we came near the city, the villages outside were already deserted, the people fled to sanctuary behind the broad walls.

My friends, my brother, and I rode asses the whole way, another first for me. Our wealth and stature afforded us the privilege, and the whole trip was a comparatively leisurely affair. It was not only a status symbol for us to ride, but something of a necessity.

Soldiers who stay in the profession as long as we had tend to have problems with their feet. The arches of mine had begun to flatten, and I would awake with a terrible ache that my squire massaged out before I went to battle. At night I would have him heat water for me to soak them in. It helped, but the toll that walking thousands of miles in full kit, and worse, standing at attention in formation hours before a battle, had taken on my feet and knees was irreversible. I still live with the pain today.

Hundreds of company banners fluttered gaily in the summer breeze, each one a variation of that company's tribal badge. Pipes were lilting some of David's more martial psalms, and the music and panoply gave the procession a festival atmosphere. We chatted among ourselves easily. Few of the soldiers were nervous, most of them blooded veterans from the civil war with Ish-bosheth. As always, David was sure of victory, and that optimism spread to the rest of us.

Even Zelek's face was serene and cheerful. The only note of sobriety was Joab. He scowled thoughtfully the whole trip, speaking only when spoken to. He had taken David's disapproval to heart, and wanted desperately to earn his way back into the king's favor.

For me the need was less urgent. Our uncle was not happy about the part I had played in the murder, but it was Joab that he held most responsible. Perhaps that was fair. While I had been there to assist, it was Joab's sword that had sheared through Abner's heart, and his will that drove us to complete the deed.

We did not attack immediately when we arrived at Jebus. We made a great show of pitching our tents, digging latrines and middens, and felling trees, as if preparing for a long siege. The walls of Jebus were at least fifty feet high and made of stone. The gates were giant, oaken slabs hinged and barred with iron. The Jebusites were justified in their confidence in them. They stood on the walls and watched our preparations in mute sullenness. They held bows and slings at the ready, but we stayed well out of range.

As expected they sent envoys out to treat with David. Nothing was accomplished. The Jebusites were unwilling to budge from the city, and David was unwilling to give up the dream of conquering it. The Jebusites returned to their walled city, and David to his camp.

That night after looking to my men, I couldn't sleep. Wandering aimlessly through the camp, I found Zelek sitting alone, drinking from a skin of wine by a fire. He greeted me with a nod, and I sat down. He passed me the wineskin, and I took a draught.

"Couldn't sleep?" he asked.

I shook my head.

"Me either," he said. "Thinking about the coming battle?"

"Not really," I said.

"Me either," he repeated.

I handed him the wineskin.

"I understand why you had to kill Abner," he said. "The others think they do, but they don't. Until you feel it for yourself, you can't understand."

I leaned forward. "You know, you never told us why you hated Saul so much."

He took a long pull from the skin and peered into the fire. The orange glow reflected as twinkling specks in his pupils.

"It was my father," he said.

"Killed in battle?"

He nodded.

"By Saul?"

Again he nodded.

"I was only a boy," he said. "Eleven years old. After I came of age, maybe a little before, truth be told, I waited and looked for Saul the way you did for Abner."

"Did you feel better when the Philistines killed

him?" I asked.

"Did you feel better when Joab killed Abner?"

The answer was obvious to both of us, for here we were still unable to sleep for the anger that would not go away.

"Maybe if we had done it ourselves," I said. "Then we would feel better. Maybe in letting Joab kill him, I cheated myself out of my own revenge."

I sighed.

"I don't know," I said. "Maybe I'll never feel better."

"Revenge won't give you back your brother or me my father," said Zelek. "So no, that wound will never heal. I've had longer to think about it, and I've realized the reason the anger never went away. Saul wasn't the person I was most angry at. I was angry at him, sure. But I was–I *am* even angrier at someone else."

"Who?" I asked, already knowing the answer.

"Myself," he said. "I never forgave myself for not being with my father and defending him, or at least dying beside him."

"But you were only a boy," I protested. "There was nothing you could have done."

"And you are just a man," he returned. "There was nothing *you* could have done. You can't be everywhere at once, especially on the battlefield."

He took another pull of wine. I looked away so he would not see the tears in my eyes glisten by the firelight.

"Asahel was impetuous. It's a miracle you kept him alive as long as you did. And still you blame yourself."

With every word my eyes became fuller, and the lump in my throat larger. I could not speak, so I nodded agreement. I did indeed blame myself.

"I also blamed God," he said. "Joshua started the war at His command, and Saul was continuing it. My father was not a good man. He beat me and my mother–once broke my arm. But he was the only father I had, and I didn't want God to take him from me."

"David sings about God being his refuge," I said, my voice ragged. "Why didn't He protect my little brother?"

Zelek shook his head and sighed.

"I don't know," he said. "He's a hard God, Yahweh is. But following David, I've seen that He can be good too."

He turned to me.

"I asked Abiathar about it once, and he told me a story about a man who had his guts kicked out of him by God, and all he would say is, 'The Lord gives, and the Lord takes away. Blessed be the name of the Lord.'"

"Job," I supplied.

He nodded. "He said that God knows best. I guess that makes sense. He wouldn't be much of a god if He didn't. But sometimes I can't see it."

He might have been reading my mind. I could not see the goodness of God, not after all the suffering I had witnessed.

"Maybe the trick is to be thankful when He gives, and endure it when He takes away. After all, there's nothing else you can do."

"There is something you can do," I said, and raised my spear. "You can shove this into any man who tries to take away from you."

"I hope that works for you," he said with a sad smile. "It hasn't for me."

21

For three days we made a show of challenging the Jebusites to battle, lining up in array in full armor, careful to keep out of bowshot from the walls. Of course, the Jebusites never left their walls. It would have been madness. They were well stocked, well protected, and well outnumbered. We also began to fashion a battering ram on the third day from a large oak, the men on the wall looking on in consternation.

On the third night, a few hours past midnight, the thousand of us who were to infiltrate through the sluice sneaked around back through the trees. We figured most of the city would be sleeping. There were no torches, and we spoke in whispers. Several men slung their shields on their shoulders and carried axes with broad iron heads. Joab was carrying two, his sword sheathed at his waist.

We found the spring and followed it to where it was diverted by a squarish stone trench. A mile from the walls the trench turned into a tunnel whose portal was blocked by a rusty iron grate. We hacked through the grate with the axes and slipped into the tunnel.

My brother was never the fastest soldier, but I had trouble keeping up with him in the tunnel. He shouldered his way to the front and entered the tunnel first. He had been imbued with a crazed energy.

The tunnel was not intended for human traffic, and we had to hunch over as we walked. The water flowed around our waists; it was like wading in a river. I was used to close places from the caves at Adullum, but some were not. One of the men behind me was breathing in sharp, panicked gasps. His fear mastered him, and he vomited into the water.

"Watch it!" hissed Shammah. "This will be our drinking water when we take the city."

"*If* we take it," said Zelek, ever the optimist.

"Don't worry," whispered Joab. "The way it's flowing, there must be an outlet on the other side."

We scurried through the tunnel until we came to a branch that shot straight up into the city. There were no handholds, so I boosted Joab, and he planted his back on one side of the chimney and his feet on the other. He scooted to the top where a heavy wooden lid covered the opening. Carefully he cracked it open, peeked out, and scooted back down to whisper to us.

"The water is guarded."

"They must have anticipated this," said Shammah. Joab did not hesitate.

"I'm going anyway," he said. "Tell David how I

died."

"They can tell heem," said Uriah, jerking his thumb toward the men who had heard the news and already started heading out of the tunnel. I cursed them under my breath for their cowardice.

Uriah simply said, "I weell die weeth you. I weell help you clear you name."

"Face it, Joab," said Benaiah. "We won't let you go alone. You go, we go."

Joab gripped Benaiah's arm.

"I know it was your dream to become captain of David's host."

Benaiah shook his head.

"You need this," he said. "I will help you restore your honor. If I live, perhaps one day I will be captain of the host. If we die, it won't matter. Whatever happens, I will fight by your side."

Joab nodded gratefully and turned to me.

"There's no need for our mother to lose all of her sons. Go and tell her that she may be proud of me for once."

"I'm not losing another brother," I said. "Let her be proud of both of us."

He opened his mouth as if to argue, then nodded, and began shimmying up again. This time we followed. When we got to the top, Joab signed to me with his hand, and I propped the lid open with my spear.

I could see about twenty men guarding the water, although they were not paying much attention at that late hour. Joab slipped between the rim of the tunnel and the lid and buried both axes in the faces of two of the guards. Another began to call out, but I destroyed his larynx with a thrust of my spear and silenced him forever.

Others cried out as they saw our men popping out of the tunnel like ants. We fended off the guards as about forty of our mates joined us.

"If we can open the gate to let in the others we'll have a chance," said Shammah.

"Good idea," said Joab, his axes cutting those down in front of him. "You take the gate. I'll destroy the statues."

"The plan's changed," said Shammah. "We came with a thousand men, now we have forty. We need to regroup if we're to stay alive."

"You regroup," said Joab over his shoulder, already running toward the hill with me at his heels. "I'm going to Zion!"

"You daft fools!" shouted Shammah after us. "You can't fight the whole city by yourselves."

I heard Benaiah behind us. "No, they can't." And he, Zelek, Ittai, and Uriah ran after us.

Joab ran at a pace that would have made Asahel proud, slashing at every Jebusite he met and not stopping to see if they were dead. He wielded the axes like swords, and the rest of us had little fighting to do on the short trip up the hill.

I could see the brazen statues from the bottom. They

were twenty feet tall and flanked a small temple. I barely had time to notice their bearded faces as we humped up the hill; I was too concerned about the growing mass of soldiers that were flooding to the top at their feet. There were at least a hundred.

Joab did not pause when he reached the top. He plunged into the thick of the mob and was immediately surrounded. For a moment, though it seemed like an hour, I could not see my brother and was filled with terror. I screamed and started killing, fighting frantically toward Joab.

There he was! Axes whirling around him like furious twin vortices. Then Uriah broke through, bracing his back against Joab. Uriah's sword and Joab's axes were like a deadly triangular beast, and none could come near the beast without tasting death.

"Give me some room," shouted Joab.

I thrust myself between my brother and the enemy. Benaiah, Ittai, and Zelek fought toward us, and we formed a ring around the massive idols. Joab stood upon the porch of the temple, heaved, and toppled the statue on the right. Laying one axe aside, he began to hack away at the wide neck of the god of the Jebusites. The hill rang with the sound of iron on brass.

The Jebusites howled at the blasphemous outrage. Infuriated, they threw themselves at us and died upon our bronze. I was the only man to bring a long spear in the confines of the tunnel, so I protected the center. The swords of Uriah and Zelek held back the men on my right, while Benaiah and Ittai fought on the left.

Filled with religious zeal, those Jebusites died bravely. They broke upon us like waves upon a rock. More than once a man slipped past my spear, and I was obliged to bowl him over with my shield and finish him with its edge.

But even a cliff can be worn away by the pounding of the water, and our circle began to slowly shrink backward. Joab finished decapitating the Blind, threw away the blunted axe, picked up the fresh one, and chopped away at the neck of the Lame.

"Joab," shouted Ittai as his sword slashed the neck of a Jebusite, whose flesh tore more easily than the brass of the statues. "Hurry!"

More soldiers had gathered at the sound of the axe, and they completely covered the hill. Our circle shrunk just enough to let Joab work. Ittai stood behind the headless corpse of the idol, while I straddled the corpse of one of its worshippers. If I had but taken a step back, Joab might have struck me with the axe. I could hear by the sound that the last stroke had cut through the neck. Reaching over his shoulder for his shield and drawing his sword, Joab flung himself back into the melee.

"Joab!" I screamed.

I beat my way to his side, but Benaiah was already there. I buried my spear in the chest of a Jebusite whose sword was poised to cleave Benaiah's skull, just as Benaiah's sword sliced a man behind me who was about to crush me with a mace. He was so close he actually fell against me as he died.

Joab caught a man with a downward cut that split his nose and lips, then cut deeper through the cartilage between his ribs and breastbone, then his belly and groin. The man's intestines slithered out and he fell to his knees.

Joab's sword never paused as he spoke. "I'm sorry, brothers. I fear I've led you to death this time."

Benaiah's grin was feral. "But what a death!"

Uriah called out. "There ees no place I would rather be."

"To the death!" called Zelek.

And we lustily answered, "To the death!"

At that moment our enemy actually shied away from us, but recovered and pressed us together. Acknowledging our doom lent me a sense of calm. In a relaxed state of mind, my fighting became sublime.

As a sword lunged toward me, I spun upon it. The flat of the sword slid along my side, it's edge nicked the inside of my arm. I raised my spear and stabbed the man behind my attacker while I simultaneously hooked my arm around his neck. Pivoting I caught him under the chin with the shaft and yanked him off his feet. He would have choked if I gave him time, but I twisted viciously, snapping his neck.

I slashed several men across the face, smashed one in the face with my shield, and stabbed clean through another. I went to pull it out, but the butt of my spear jammed against Joab's shield behind me. As another

Jebusite rushed in, I turned my spear, with the dead man still on it, into his rushing body.

I tried to pull it free again, but we were pressed too close. I had to let go, move forward, and grab the spear just under the warhead to pull it out the other side.

While I was freeing my weapon, a man grazed my ribs with a thrust of his sword and, with a downward stroke, carved a small chunk from my thigh. Still choked up on the spear haft, I stabbed him in the eye as if with a dagger.

I saw Uriah slice from the ground up, catching a man in the groin with a cut that stopped at his chin. He whirled and split a man from shoulder to hip, then turned the blade and cut across the opposite shoulder making a ghastly cross-shaped furrow in the man's torso. A gash in his forehead was bleeding, obscuring the vision in his left eye, but still he outfought the foe.

Zelek was actually chasing the Jebusites down the hill, heedless of the spear still stuck in the back of his shoulder, it's broken haft shaking as he ran. He was slashing them across the back and spewing a stream of filthy oaths. He was headed toward a mass of men who did not look like they were in a mood to retreat at the foot of the hill.

Seeing him head toward a trap, Uriah grabbed him by the back of his armored jerkin and was nearly cut by Zelek's blade when he turned in anger. Zelek came to himself, and the two stood back to back to prevent any further nasty surprises. I do not know what terrified the

Jebusites more, Zelek's snarl and curses or Uriah's calm smile.

Ittai's iron sword smashed through armor, bone, flesh, organs, and brains. He moved deliberately through the enemy and looked slow compared to the rest of us. But the methodical chopping of his sword was just as effective. The sword was sharp, but heavy, and I could hear the crunching of bones beneath the armor that tore under its edge.

I do not know how anyone could keep attacking hearing that awful crunching, but they did. A sideward slash took a man in the face, and I saw his teeth fly several feet away to rattle against his comrades' shields. Another cut smashed a man's arm, and he helplessly watched Ittai's sword rise and descend to destroy his collarbone and the artery beneath.

Every swing of Benaiah's sword seemed to bring down two men. He cut in long graceful arcs as his feet danced through pivots away from attackers and toward his prey. Defense and offense were one to him. He could turn a block into a cut, a swing into a parry, and a weakness into an opportunity.

A Jebusite came at him overhead, and Benaiah parried the blow, guiding it to cut into the Jebusites own fellow. Another caught his sword arm, and Benaiah broke his jaw with his elbow, then finished him off with a savage backhanded slash.

Another overhanded strike came at him, and he covered his face with his shield, stepping into the blow and stabbing under the shield into the man's abdomen. Seeing his chance, a Jebusite rushed him from behind. Benaiah pulled the sword free of the first man's belly, using the extra momentum to cut the man down faster than should have been possible.

Then Benaiah went down. A lucky swipe of a sword had caught his hamstring. Benaiah returned the favor by splitting his skull as he fell to the ground. The enemy, smelling blood, howled and rushed to finish him. Benaiah lifted his sword toward them from his prone position, but he was nearly helpless. Just as the Jebusites closed on him, Joab lunged in between them and Benaiah, and began cutting down the surprised foe.

His shield was missing, but he had picked up an extra sword. Men fell at his feet a half dozen at a time. One sword cut across a man's throat and another's face while the other cut through a chest and his neighbor's abdomen. Sometimes he used the swords like giant shears, crossing his arms and cutting inward and outward.

He flung the borrowed sword end-over-end into a man's chest and pulled Benaiah to his feet. Benaiah leaned on Joab's shoulder and fought left-handed.

Suddenly the foot of the hill was surrounded by our own soldiers. Shammah had opened the gate. Our men were inside the city! Filled with new hope, we fought with renewed vigor.

The Jebusites fought on for a while, but when they saw their countrymen being attacked from behind, they threw down their weapons, fell to their knees, and raised their hands for mercy. We were inclined to be merciful, all but Zelek. Uriah had to restrain him before he mowed down the unarmed men. Finally his fury abated, and he calmed.

As our men led the captives away, we stared at each other with wide, unbelieving eyes. Joab began to laugh, and we all started laughing. We expected to give our lives to fulfill David's mission and restore Joab's name, and here we stood, all six of us, *alive!*

Water was brought to us, and we drank it greedily. My tongue cleaved to the roof of my mouth like a slug against a hot rock, and the water tasted better than honeyed wine. I was not weary yet, but still filled with the exhilaration of battle.

At that moment, David walked up the hill. He wore his crown, and his clothes were spattered in blood. Between his shoulder blades hung that impossibly large sword. Later when we heard of his valor during the battle, I almost wished I had been with him. *Almost.* There was nowhere I would have rather been than fighting by my brother on Zion.

David looked at hundreds of dead Jebusites on the hill and the two headless idols. My friends and I stepped back and pushed Joab to the fore. David did not have to ask who had toppled the statues. Smiling, he laid a hand on Joab's shoulders and looked into his eyes.

"Well done, Joab," he said.

Joab smiled, his teeth beaming white through his black beard and filthy, blood-splattered face. The tears welled in his eyes but did not trickle down his cheek. My uncle pulled my brother into a hug, slapping his shoulder blades. Joab's fingers pressed into David's back.

When they pulled away from their embrace, I saw that my brother had been restored. The cloud had passed from his face, and his body looked relaxed. Joab was the shortest of us, but at that moment he stood like a giant. Joy and relief swept over me as David raised Joab's hand into the air.

My voice mingled with the cheers rising from the throats of thousands of soldiers. If Joab heard us, he gave no sign. He did not take his eyes off of David, our uncle, our king, our *hero*; to whom he had finally reconciled.

"Behold! The captain of my hosts," cried the king. "Joab!"

This time he did not add *son of Zeruiah*.

Epilogue

Abishai smiled at the memories his tale had evoked.

"As you know," he said. "The Temple where you and I met was later built on that hill. Today when any Jew prays, he orients himself to the spot where my brother won his greatest victory, bathing himself in glory, and for the moment washing away the memory of his sins."

I thought of how flippant I had become in my duties at the Temple. Somehow Abishai's recounting of the battle had sanctified the landmark for me in a way that the very seat of God's shekhina *presence had not.*

"Jerusalem means 'city of peace.' But that word for peace, shalem, *which is even the root of our Good King Solomon's name, can also mean wholeness or completeness. That is how I think of this city. This is where my brother became whole again. This is where he found peace."*

I imagined him as he must have been on that day, with no grey in his beard which must have been shorter then, and no stoop in his back. What I would give to have been his companion in those days!

"It's a pity," I said.

His eyes, which had been gazing deep into the past,

turned to regard me.

"What's that?"

"That those days of adventure are over."

He chuckled. "Days of war, you mean."

I nodded. It sounded so grand, overcoming these heathen bands and witnessing such mighty exploits. Abishai's hand fell on my shoulder.

"These days of peace are a blessing," he said. "Never take them for granted. They won't last forever."

I smiled back at him but did not really believe what he said. Abishai had obviously forgotten what it was like to be young and hot-blooded. Of course, a life of adventure is better for a young man. I did not say this to the old warrior.

"I think I understand why you told me that story."

"Really?"

"You wanted to show that if I kill Mishael, I must accomplish something great, the way you and Joab did, to make up for it."

Abishai's face darkened. He looked angry, and I began to feel fear toward him. But when he spoke, his voice was gentle.

"Is that what you think? That Joab and I washed away the stink of that bloodshed with more bloodshed?"

"Why else would you tell me that story?"

His smile was serene. He leaned forward.

"Perhaps you will understand," he said. "When I finish the story."

My eyes darted to the window. The sun had long set. The sky was black as pitch.

"Your story isn't finished?"

"Not by half."

It had taken him hours to recite his tale so far. He must have seen the surprise on my face and interpreted it as reluctance to take up the tale. His shoulders drooped and his eyes lowered.

"Of course, it is getting late," he said. "Perhaps I have troubled you enough for tonight."

But I was eager to hear the rest of the story. I leaned forward and took his hand.

"No, please," I said. "I want to hear the rest."

He looked up at me, saw that I was indeed unwilling to break off from the tale's telling, and smiled.

"Besides," I said. "How can I stop now that everything is well between David and Joab?"

His smile faded, then it died.

"It was well between them. For a while."

His shoulders rose and fell in a heavy sigh.

"But it would not last. You see-"

A pounding at the door interrupted Abishai.

"Who could be calling at this time of night?" he wondered.

He rose and hobbled over to the door. He opened it the barest crack and peered out with one eye. Evidently it was someone he recognized, for he relaxed and opened the door wider. I could not make out what they said, nor did I recognize the voice whispering on the other side.

Abishai gasped, and I leaped to my feet in alarm. He shut the door and leaned against the wall. His bony hands went to his face, covering it like a mask.

"God be merciful," he said, his voice ragged with horror. "But your mistakes always come back to haunt you."

"Abishai," I said. "What is it?"

"I should have killed him when I had the chance," he said. "It should have ended then. But it's too late now. Too late."

My voice became shrill. "Who? For the love of God, Abishai, what's wrong?"

He slid down to the floor. I rushed to his side and held his shoulders. There was an apology in his eyes as they looked up into my face.

"It's Hadad," he said. "The last of the Edomites."

I had no idea who he was talking about. He clutched my arm and whispered.

"He's coming. And when he does, he will destroy Jerusalem."

Acknowledgements

Many thanks to my precious wife and first fan, Audrey Meyer. Without your support and encouragement, which was vital to this work, I could never complete it. I love you. Thank you for loving me back in spite of the typos.

To Patrick, Adelaide, and Charlotte, thank you for putting up with all the hours Dad was shut away in his office. I hope that when you are all old enough to read this, it will be a part of me that will last beyond my lifetime, so I will always be with you.

Thank you to my editor, Gary Smailes of Bubble Cow. It was an honor and pleasure to work with you. A special thank you to my friend, editor, and beta reader, Tyler "Gandalf" Randolph. You told me not what I wanted to hear, but the truth. For that you are priceless. To Jonathan Keen, thank you for your enthusiasm, which greatly encouraged me. This book owes much to Jordan Geeting for his honesty and attention to detail. Luke Engstrom, like me, has been waiting a long time for this book, and I doubt he understands how helpful he was during the editing stage. I would like to extend my gratitude to Brice Greer for her insight and perpetual example. She is a balm to my spirit and the "iron that sharpeneth iron." Thank you all for your feedback and, more importantly, your friendship.

Thanks to my family Don and Sue Meyer, Kailley

Sells, Karissa Gibson, and Ashley Squires, who encouraged me, not only as I wrote this novel, but throughout their lives. To my father, writing this novel has made me appreciate you even more. I know who my father is, and he is a great, good man. A special thank you goes to my webmaster and the best brother in the world, Brad Meyer. Thank you for using your gifts to help me.

I would like to thank my grandmother, Barbara Stanton, "Nanny," for giving me the books that I first fell in love with. She did not live long enough to see my book in print, but without her, it would not exist. Thank you to my two dogs, Penny and Sophie II, who hitchhiked to Savannah and inadvertently changed my life.

I humbly thank the Author of all things, who preserved the history behind this fiction and is working to make my life a story that will bring him honor. You alone, Lord, create that which has never existed before. I stand in awe of your work, commit my own to you, and cast all glory at your feet.

Lastly, thank you, dear reader, for letting this story live in your heart and imagination. Take pride especially in my esteem of your unique self. You are above all the casual readers of fiction, for you, in your wisdom and curiosity, take the time to read *acknowledgements.*

May inspiration find you with a pen in your hand!

CPSIA information can be obtained
at www.ICGtesting.com
Printed in the USA
FFHW021418261018
48959348-53200FF